Bullets, Biscuits, and Bloodshed

LOOK FOR THESE EXCITING WESTERN SERIES FROM BESTSELLING AUTHORS WILLIAM W. JOHNSTONE AND J.A. JOHNSTONE

The Mountain Man
Luke Jensen: Bounty Hunter
Brannigan's Land
The Jensen Brand
Smoke Jensen: The Early Years
Preacher and MacCallister
Fort Misery
The Fighting O'Neils
Perley Gates
MacCoole and Boone
Guns of the Vigilantes
Shotgun Johnny
The Chuckwagon Trail
The Jackals
The Slash and Pecos Westerns
The Texas Moonshiners
Stoneface Finnegan Westerns
Ben Savage: Saloon Ranger
The Buck Trammel Westerns
The Death and Texas Westerns
The Hunter Buchanon Westerns
Will Tanner: U.S. Deputy Marshal
Old Cowboys Never Die
Go West, Young Man

Published by Kensington Publishing Corp.

BULLETS, BISCUITS, and BLOODSHED

WILLIAM W. JOHNSTONE
AND J. A. JOHNSTONE

PINNACLE BOOKS
Kensington Publishing Corp.
kensingtonbooks.com

PINNACLE BOOKS are published by

Kensington Publishing Corp.
900 Third Avenue
New York, NY 10022

PUBLISHER'S NOTE: Following the death of William W. Johnstone, the Johnstone family is working with a carefully selected writer to organize and complete Mr. Johnstone's outlines and many unfinished manuscripts to create additional novels in all of his series, like The Last Gunfighter, Mountain Man, and Eagles, among others. This novel was inspired by Mr. Johnstone's superb storytelling.

All Kensington titles, imprints, and distributed lines are available at special quantity discounts for bulk purchases for sales promotion, premiums, fundraising, and educational or institutional use.

Special book excerpts or customized printings can also be created to fit specific needs. For details, write or phone the office of the Kensington Sales Manager: Kensington Publishing Corp., 900 Third Avenue, New York, NY 10022. Attn. Sales Department. Phone: 1-800-221-2647.

First Trade Paperback Printing: May 2026

ISBN-13: 978-0-7860-5220-2

ISBN-13: 978-0-7860-5221-9 (ebook)

10 9 8 7 6 5 4 3 2 1

Printed in the United States of America

The authorized representative in the EU for product safety and compliance
is eucomply OU, Parnu mnt 139b-14, Apt 123
Tallinn, Berlin 11317, hello@eucompliancepartner.com.

Bullets, Biscuits, and Bloodshed

Chapter 1

Dewey McKenzie tightened his grip on the gun he held, a Smith & Wesson Model 3 .44 caliber revolver.

He said in a quiet voice, "I'm not so sure about this."

From where Luke Jensen stood, with his back pressed against the cabin wall on the other side of the door, he said, "You can't mean you're nervous, Mac. You're as cold-nerved a fellow as I've ever met."

Mac shook his head. "It's not that. I'm not scared of this bunch. But I'm just not sure I ought to be hunting fugitives this way. For years, I had bounty hunters chasing me for the price on my head, and it wasn't a nice feeling."

Luke grunted, shook his head, and said, "There's a big difference. *You* weren't guilty of the crime that put that price on your head. Having lawmen and bounty hunters coming after you wasn't right."

Luke paused for a second and then went on, "I promise you, the Bishop brothers deserve everything that's coming to them. They've got plenty of blood on their hands. You don't need to lose a minute of sleep worrying over what happens to them."

"That's true, I suppose," Mac said, remembering all the charges on the wanted posters Luke had shown him: murder, armed robbery, rape, assault, arson. . . . The list of atrocities went on. Dave, Warren, Brad, and Mingo Bishop were bad hombres, no doubt about that.

And Luke was right. This situation was totally different from the dangerous time Mac had spent on the run from the law some ten years earlier. That had been what they sometimes call a miscarriage of justice.

What he and Luke Jensen delivered? That was actual justice.

"All right," he said to Luke with a nod that was barely visible in the predawn gloom. "Let's do this."

Luke returned the nod, wheeled away from the wall, raised his right leg, and kicked the cabin door open. He went through it in a rush, his hands filled with a pair of long-barreled Remington revolvers.

Mac followed close behind him, the Smith & Wesson up and ready.

The Bishop brothers had been asleep; Luke and Mac knew that from the raucous snores that filled this isolated hideout cabin.

But the crash of Luke kicking the door open jolted them awake. They tried to leap out of their bunks as they grabbed for holstered guns that hung within reach.

Luke and Mac could have started blasting as soon as they cleared the entrance. Even better, maybe, Luke could have stood in the door and blazed away from there while Mac fired through the cabin's one window.

The Bishops wouldn't have had a chance.

But that wasn't the way Luke had carried out his business during the years he'd been a bounty hunter, and since Mac was pretty new at this game, he followed Luke's lead.

Luke leveled the Remingtons and shouted, "Hands up! Don't touch those guns!"

The outlaw brothers ignored the warning, just as Mac had a hunch they would. A lantern with its wick turned low hung from a hook on the wall, and the faint glow from its flame reflected from gun barrels as steel slid out of leather.

Luke dropped the hammer on both Remingtons as those menacing gun barrels started to tip up.

Foot-long tongues of flame gouted from the muzzles of the .44s in Luke's strong, capable hands. One of the bullets launched from those weapons crashed into the chest of a wild-eyed owlhoot struggling to get clear of his blankets even as he tried to line up a shot at Luke.

The other round smashed the left shoulder of another Bishop brother. Luke had aimed at his chest, too, but the man had darted aside just in time to avoid a fatal impact. The hammer-blow of lead against flesh twisted him halfway around, but the gun in his right hand flashed up anyway.

The Smith & Wesson in Mac's hand barked. The wounded man's head snapped back as a red-rimmed hole appeared just above his right eye. Mac's bullet bored into his brain and dumped him on the hard-packed dirt floor.

Two bunks were built against the back wall, with another bunk on each side wall. The men Luke and Mac had shot had been sleeping in those back bunks. As those two outlaws went down under the onslaught of lead, Luke swung right and Mac pivoted left to deal with the remaining Bishop brothers.

Luke triggered both revolvers again. Neither shot missed as the wanted man on that side of the room surged to his feet and tried to fight back. The bullets threw him back against the wall above the bunk. He slid down onto the thin mattress and rolled limply to the floor.

Mac, turning the other way, caught his breath sharply. The bunk on the left side of the room was empty. Where was the fourth and last Bishop brother?

He got the answer to that question even as it flashed through his brain.

A bellowed curse behind him made Mac jerk his head around to look over his shoulder. A man carrying a double-barreled shotgun loomed in the doorway. Each barrel looked like the mouth of a cannon as the Greener swung toward Mac.

He threw himself backward into a diving roll that carried him underneath the rough-hewn table in the center of the room. The outlaw fired one barrel, the sound of its report a deafening boom that pounded the ears painfully in the cabin's close confines.

The range was too close for the load to spread out much. The buckshot peppered the tabletop, for the most part.

Mac experienced what felt like a bee sting in his left calf as he hit the floor. He twisted and tried to bring the Smith & Wesson to bear, thinking he might be able to shoot one of the legs out from under the outlaw.

Before he had a chance to do that, Luke's Remingtons blasted again, and the shotgun hit the floor with the second barrel unfired. The fourth Bishop brother followed it down, landing hard and grunting as he pawed at the blood-spouting holes in his chest. A shudder went through him and then smoothed out, leaving him motionless in death.

There had been so much racket that the silence following it seemed to echo, too. Into that hollowness, Luke asked urgently, "Mac, are you all right?"

Mac crawled out from under the table and sat on the floor to check his injury. A single piece of buckshot had torn the leg of his denim trousers and left a red welt on the flesh underneath, but he didn't see any blood.

"Just a little graze, and about as close to a clean miss as you can get and still hit something," he reported to his partner. "I'll be fine."

"That's too close to suit me."

"Anywhere around a scattergun is too close when it's going off," Mac said.

He climbed to his feet while Luke checked the outlaws.

"All four dead," he said. "Well, as usual, we collect on 'em either way, and this makes things simpler, so I guess I can't complain."

"One of them was outside the cabin somewhere." Mac made that comment as he began to replace the rounds he had fired.

"Probably went out to answer the call of nature before we got here and didn't hear us ride up, didn't know we were here until the shooting started. Him showing up like that could have been a mighty unlucky break for us."

"Why did he have a shotgun with him?"

Luke shrugged. "Bears like to roam around in the early morning like this. I suspect he didn't want one of them coming along and interrupting important business."

Mac chuckled and holstered his reloaded revolver. "I can't really blame him for that, either—although I would have been mighty unhappy if more of that buckshot had wound up in my hide."

Luke looked around the room and said, "We might as well load up the supplies they have here, too. They sure don't need them anymore."

"Where do you figure on heading next?"

Luke holstered the left-hand Remington and began reloading the other revolver. "We're in Oregon now," he said. "We crossed the border from Idaho late yesterday afternoon."

That didn't answer Mac's question, but it piqued his curiosity. "How do you know that? I don't recall seeing any signs."

"I've been through these parts before. It's been a while, but once I've traveled somewhere, I usually remember it pretty well." Luke pouched the iron he had just reloaded and then tugged at an earlobe as he frowned in thought. "The closest good-sized town is Pine Knob, west of here. We ought to be able to collect on these carcasses there. And that reminds me of something . . ."

His voice trailed off. Mac waited a moment before saying, "What does it remind you of?"

"I need to look through my collection of reward dodgers. I'll do that once we've loaded everything up and gotten started."

"You mean you have an idea which wanted man we're going after next?"

"An idea," Luke agreed. "But just because we have a place to start looking, that doesn't mean it'll be easy to find him."

CHAPTER 2

It was midmorning when Luke rode into the settlement of Pine Knob, a good-sized town nestled in a range of beautiful, pine-forested hills. The snowy peaks of the Blue Mountains rose not far to the west.

He drew a great deal of startled attention from the town's occupants, which came as no surprise to him. Trailing a string of horses with dead hombres lashed face down over the saddles tended to do that.

Luke was alone now, Mac having stopped a couple of miles back because his horse had gone lame. He was going to walk on into town, leading the animal. Luke had offered to stay with him, but Mac had said for him to go on ahead.

"Maybe you can settle up with the sheriff before I get there," Mac had said with a rueful smile. Even though the bogus charges against him had been quashed long ago, he had been leery of lawmen for so long that it was hard for him to break the habit of avoiding star packers.

Luke had ridden on ahead, taking the dead Bishop brothers with him. The railroad and the telegraph hadn't reached the settlement yet, but there would be a stagecoach traveling to the bigger settlements to the west. The local lawman could send word that way about Luke's claim and arrange for the rewards to be paid.

When the citizens stopped staring at the outlaw corpses and looked at the bounty hunter instead, they saw a man who looked as if he had followed plenty of hard trails in his life—and that was the truth.

Luke Jensen was in his forties, a weathered, craggy-faced man with crisp dark hair under his black hat and a thin mustache under his slightly prominent nose. His face was much too rugged to be considered handsome, but it possessed a powerful strength that men admired and to which women were attracted.

His shirt and trousers were black, like his hat. He wore a brown, sheepskin-lined coat, and the ivory handles of his Remingtons somewhat relieved the darkness of his aspect as well. He wore the guns butt-forward on each hip in cross-draw rigs.

While a young man, Luke had endured the bloody ordeal of the Civil War as a Confederate soldier, having enlisted back in the Missouri Ozarks at the beginning of the conflict. In the last days of the war, he had been betrayed by men he believed were friends and comrades, men whose greed for a shipment of gold had drawn them to commit evil treachery.

Left for dead, Luke had recovered, but guilt at his failure to carry out his mission had plagued him. Calling himself Luke Smith, because he didn't want to bring that shame on his family, he had let them believe he was dead. Instead of going home, he wandered the West as a bounty hunter, putting the violent skills he had gained to good use.

Then the day had come when he was reunited with his younger brother Kirby—who by then was famous as the gunfighter Smoke Jensen—and Luke had rejoined the Jensen family, meeting his adopted brother Matt and eventually discovering that he had two fine, strapping sons he hadn't known about, the Jensen boys who went by the nicknames Ace and Chance.

But even though he now used his real name, and it would have been easy to settle down into a comfortable middle age on Smoke's Colorado ranch, the Sugarloaf, the years spent wandering had left Luke too fiddle-footed for a life like that. He had to be on the move, and bounty hunting was what he knew, so he continued doing it.

Some months earlier, while delivering a prisoner over in Wyoming, Luke had met Dewey McKenzie. A former chuckwagon cook with a troubled past of his own, Mac actually had settled down for a while, using his knack for cooking to start a café.

But Luke had a knack, too—for finding trouble. A shooting war had erupted in that Wyoming town, and when it was over, Mac had given in to his own restless nature and ridden out with Luke, since the two of them had hit it off and become friends.

Since then, they had corralled several wanted fugitives and collected rewards on them. Neither man worried about how long this partnership was going to last; they were content to ride together and watch each other's back, for now.

Luke spotted a squarish, sturdy-looking stone building ahead on his left. A sign reading MARSHAL'S OFFICE hung from the awning over its porch. It was the only stone structure he had seen so far; lumber was easy to come by here since Pine Knob was located in timber country.

There were ranches in the area, too, mostly north and east of town. Being a supply center for both logging and cattle interests meant that Pine Knob was a bustling, growing settlement.

Luke angled his mount toward the marshal's office and led the other horses with their grisly burdens. One of the townspeople hurried along the boardwalk on that side of the street and ducked into the office.

Probably alerting the lawman to the fact that some stranger had just ridden into town bringing a bunch of dead bodies with him, Luke mused.

Sure enough, the office door opened again and a man stepped

out to regard Luke with a suspicious stare. The man was of medium height, thick-bodied but not flabby, mostly bald with a fringe of dark hair around his ears and the back of his head. A dark mustache curved above his mouth. He wore an open black vest over a white shirt, and a badge was pinned to that shirt.

Luke reined in and nodded to the lawman. "Hello, Marshal," he said in his deep, cultured voice, which was somewhat at odds with his rough-hewn appearance.

"What in blue blazes do you have there?" Before Luke could answer the man's question, the marshal held up a hand to stop him. "Never mind, I can see for myself." He squinted in thought. "Did you just happen to find those carcasses, or are you responsible for making them that way?"

"I think they bear the actual responsibility for their ultimate fate," Luke said, "since they're the ones who lived a reprehensible existence as murderers and owlhoots."

The marshal sighed. "I had a hunch you were going to say something like that. Maybe not quite so long-winded and highfalutin."

Luke leaned his head toward the bodies and went on, "Marshal, meet Dave, Warren, Brad, and Mingo Bishop."

"The Bishop boys!" The marshal's startled exclamation was mirrored on his face as his bushy eyebrows crawled upward.

"I take it you've seen reward posters on them?"

"Sure I have. Every lawman in this part of the country has. I thought they were still holed up somewhere over in Idaho, though."

"If it's all right, I'll come in your office and tell you about it."

"Sure, sure, come ahead."

"And I suppose someone should summon your local undertaker . . ."

The marshal turned his head and opened his mouth to say something to the wide-eyed townie who had brought word of Luke's arrival to him. The man had been goggling over the marshal's shoulder as the lawman talked to Luke.

"Randolph, go fetch—"

"No need, Marshal," the townie interrupted. He pointed and went on, "Here comes Mr. Endicott now. Somebody must've told him he had some business pendin'."

Luke turned his head to look where the townsman was pointing. He saw a tall, slender man in a black frock coat and top hat walking along the street, rubbing his hands together in an anticipatory manner. Behind him, a burly man in work clothes drove a wagon pulled by a couple of mules.

Luke had thought more than once that there must be a school somewhere that taught potential undertakers how to dress and act. Most of the ones he had encountered during his long career possessed definite similarities. This one managed to look solemn and gleeful at the same time as he came up to the marshal's office.

"What have we here, Abner?" he asked.

The marshal waved a hand at the bodies and said, "You can see them just as well as I can, John. You won't need the wagon. Just leave them on the horses and take them back down to your place."

He added, "Just lay them out for now. I'll be down in a little while to take a look at them and confirm who they are."

The undertaker had stopped rubbing his hands together but looked like he wanted to start again. He nodded and said, "Of course." He held out his hand to Luke, who passed the lead rope to him.

Luke swung down from the saddle as Endicott headed back toward the undertaking parlor. He looped his own mount's reins around the hitch rail in front of the marshal's office and stepped up onto the porch.

A glance back along the street told Luke that Mac was nowhere in sight. That wasn't surprising. Mac would take his time walking into town with his lame horse.

The marshal waved Luke into the office and followed him, closing the door behind him even though several curious bystanders were just outside and might have come in, too, if the lawman had allowed it. He went behind his desk, sighing and shaking his head as he did so.

"You and your, ah, friends are the biggest thing to hit this town in quite some time," the marshal commented as he went behind the paper-littered desk.

"The Bishop boys were no friends of mine," Luke said. "They were a blight on the face of the earth and needed to be removed. And the rewards for them add up to a nice sum, as well."

"If you're going to do something good, you might as well get paid for it, eh? I figured you for a bounty hunter as soon as I laid eyes on you. My name's Abner Sundell, by the way."

He didn't offer to shake hands, just waved Luke into the worn leather chair in front of the desk.

"Sit down and tell me about it. I want to hear how one man took down four vicious outlaws like the Bishop brothers."

As Sundell sat down, he added, "I noticed they didn't have any bullet holes in their backs."

Luke had started to relax after settling into the chair, but he stiffened at the lawman's words and said, "I'm not a backshooter, Marshal. And I didn't take the Bishops down by myself. I had help from my partner."

"You have a partner? Where's he?"

"He'll be here soon, I expect," Luke said, but in truth, he didn't know exactly where Mac was, right this minute.

Chapter 3

The roof on top of the building was painted a bright, eye-catching blue. It sure caught Mac's eye as he walked into Pine Knob leading his horse.

He also noticed and recognized the four horses being led up an alley beside a building across the street. They were the mounts that had belonged to the Bishop brothers and, in fact, those grim, blanket-wrapped bundles he and Luke had tied over the saddles early this morning were still there.

The frock-coated man leading the horses disappeared with them around the building's rear corner. Mac didn't need a sign to tell him that was the undertaking parlor over yonder, and the man who had taken charge of the horses and the bodies was no doubt the proprietor.

In all likelihood, that meant Luke had spoken already to the local law and might still be talking to the star packer. Mac turned his gaze back the other way toward the building with the cheerful blue roof.

Curtains hung in the front windows, and gilt letters on the left-hand window announced BLUE TOP CAFÉ. On the right-hand window, on the other side of the door, the words GOOD EATS were painted.

A simple message was often the most effective, Mac thought. The sign on the awning in front of his café back in Wyoming had had GOOD EATS on it, along with MAC'S PLACE.

He told himself he would pay a visit to the café later. He took a professional interest in such places, having operated one himself, and besides, it was the middle of the day and he was getting hungry.

First, though, he needed to tend to his horse. He raised a hand to stop a man passing by on the boardwalk and said, "My horse has gone lame, friend. Is there a livery stable in town where somebody could take a look at it?"

The man nodded and pointed. "Patterson's Livery, on the right there, two blocks down." He brightened. "Say, were you here a while ago when that fella brought in all those dead outlaws?"

"No, I missed that," Mac replied, not adding that he had, in fact, been responsible for sending one of those owlhoots across the divide.

"Biggest thing to happen in Pine Knob in a month of Sundays." The man sobered and added, "Well, if you don't count all the trouble between the Triangle 7 and those lumberjacks. That brawl a couple of weeks ago in the Lonesome Pine was quite a ruckus!"

"Missed that, too," Mac said. He wasn't interested in local gossip, and he wanted to get his horse's problem taken care of as quickly as possible. He nodded his thanks to the man and moved on.

He found Patterson's Livery without any trouble, and after examining the horse's injured leg, the red-bearded liveryman declared he had some liniment that ought to fix it right up, along with a few days of rest. That sounded good to Mac, who paid him for four days and nights in advance.

More than likely, he and Luke would have to wait in Pine Knob at least that long before they could collect the rewards on the Bishop brothers.

As he strolled out of the stable, Mac spotted Luke's horse tied at a hitch rail in the next block on the other side of the street. The horse was in front of the marshal's office, which confirmed Mac's hunch that Luke might still be talking to the lawman.

Once again, Mac told himself that Luke could handle all the details concerning the rewards just fine by himself. He turned to the left and headed his steps back toward the café.

The place was as cheery and welcoming inside as outside. Round tables covered with blue-checked cloths filled most of the room. A counter with stools in front of it was to the right, with a door behind it leading into a kitchen.

The young woman working behind the counter glanced in Mac's direction as he closed the door behind him and made the little bell mounted above it jingle a second time.

He liked what he saw.

She was past the first flush of youth but was no more than twenty-three or twenty-four. Blond hair fell in waves around her pretty face and brushed her shoulders. She wore a light-blue dress with white lace at the sleeves and collar. She looked about as wholesome as could be, but even across the room, Mac saw some fire flashing in her eyes.

He got the distinct impression that, for some reason, she didn't approve of him.

Well, he supposed he looked sort of like a saddle tramp. He wore a brown duster that had seen better days over canvas trousers, with suspenders that went up and over the shoulders of a faded blue shirt. His slouch-brimmed black hat and his high-topped boots looked as well-worn as the rest of him. Long dark hair touched here and there with streaks of premature gray hung from under the hat.

He didn't wear a gun belt, but the walnut grips of the Smith & Wesson were visible where the revolver was stuck into the waistband of his trousers.

Mac put a smile on his face as he headed for one of the empty stools at the counter. There were only a few of them, and all the tables had customers sitting at them. The Blue Top Café was doing good business.

He sat down and took his hat off, ran his fingers through his long hair to straighten it as the young woman came along the counter toward him.

"What can I do for you?" she asked in a cool, professionally polite voice.

Tell me why the sight of me put a burr under your saddle, Mac thought, but he said, "I'll have a cup of coffee to start." He glanced at the menu chalked on a board on the wall between the main room and the kitchen. "What do you recommend, the stew or the steak?"

"That's up to you. They're both good."

"I'll have the steak, then. It's been a while."

"All the trimmings?"

"Sure."

She pushed the swinging door open and called the order in to the kitchen where, obviously, someone else handled the cooking. Then she got a cup and saucer from a shelf and filled the cup from a pot simmering on a small, wood-burning stove.

"That's mighty good," Mac said when he'd taken a sip of the coffee. It was good, but maybe not quite as tasty as he made it sound.

"Your food will be along in a few minutes," the young woman said.

"I'm mighty obliged to you." Mac went on, "My name's Dewey McKenzie. My friends call me Mac."

"Hello, Mr. McKenzie," she said. He couldn't tell if she meant the formal use of his name to be insulting, considering what he had just said, or if that was just her customary greeting when she first met someone.

No reason not to give her the benefit of the doubt, he told himself.

"You know, I used to own a café a lot like this," he went on. "Over in Wyoming."

"Is that so?" She didn't really sound interested, but she didn't move away.

He grinned. "I had GOOD EATS painted on my sign, too. It sort of says it all, doesn't it?"

Her tone didn't thaw out much, but it sounded a tiny bit warmer as she said, "My father had that put on the window. He started this place."

"He had the right idea. Folks like a nice, clean place to eat, but it doesn't matter if it's fancy as long as the food is good."

The blonde cocked an eyebrow. "Oh? You don't think the Blue Top is fancy?"

"I didn't mean it like that," Mac said hastily. "It's a really nice place. Homey, you know? And I love the roof. Folks can see that bright blue for a long way. I spotted it right off as I was walking into town."

Now she looked puzzled. "You walked into town? All the cowboys around here ride."

"My horse went lame a ways out of town," he explained. "And I'm not a cowboy."

He hoped she wouldn't ask what he did for a living if he didn't punch cows, because for some reason he didn't want to tell her he was a bounty hunter.

"I thought from the look of you that you rode for the Triangle 7 or one of the other spreads around here."

"No, ma'am," he said with a shake of his head. "Although to tell you the truth, I've been part of quite a few cattle drives, and I can help push along a herd if I need to. My main job, though, was always as the cook."

"Really?"

"Yes, ma'am. Fact of the matter is, I hate to think about how many hundreds of miles I've driven a chuck wagon. All over the West, from the Rio Grande to the Milk River, and out west almost to the Pacific Ocean."

"You really have been around." She definitely seemed friendlier now. He had figured his charm would win her over. "And you used to own a café in Wyoming?"

"That's right."

"But you don't anymore?"

"No, I gave it up after a while. I guess I've got what you'd call a restless streak in me. I wanted to move on."

A small wooden door that closed off an aperture in the wall slid up, and a rough voice called, "Steak's ready, Violet."

The blonde turned to the opening, where a plate piled high with steaming food slid through on a shelf. Mac glanced through the opening and saw a burly old-timer with a grizzled white beard back there. The apron he wore marked him as the cook.

Violet took the plate and turned to set it in front of Mac. The smell rising from it was tantalizing and reminded Mac that he was hungry.

"When you're finished with that," Violet said, "we have some deep-dish apple pie."

Mac smiled and said, "I can't think of anything that sounds better right now, ma'am."

CHAPTER 4

Luke introduced himself and told Marshal Abner Sundell about how he and Mac had been on the trail of the Bishop brothers for a while. He went on to explain how, early that morning, they had caught up to the outlaw siblings at the cabin several miles east of the settlement.

Sundell listened to the story with a slight frown on his face. When Luke was finished, he said, "I'll be honest with you, Jensen. I'm not fond of bounty hunters. Most lawmen aren't."

"I'm aware of that, Marshal," Luke replied with a nod. "I'm used to being tolerated rather than accepted. But I honestly believe that men such as my partner and myself provide a valuable service out here on the frontier."

Sundell grunted. "Oh, I'm not saying it bothers me knowing those no-good Bishops won't cause any more suffering to innocent people. The world's better off with them not wasting perfectly good air. But the way you go about it . . ."

"Sometimes that's the only way," Luke said.

"Well, I'm not going to argue with you. That'd be a waste of air, too. I'll go through my wanted posters, find the ones on the

Bishops, and then check those carcasses down at Endicott's undertaking parlor." The lawman waved a hand to forestall any protests from Luke. "It's just a formality. I'm sure they're who you say they are. Once I've confirmed that, I'll write to the U.S. Marshal's office in Salem and let them know. There'll be both state and federal rewards to process, I expect. The marshal's office will handle all of that."

Luke sat forward and said, "You have to send word all the way to Salem? That's on the other side of the state."

Sundell shrugged. "It's the capital, and that's where the U.S. Marshal's office is located."

"You don't have a telegraph here."

"Nope, we sure don't."

"Sending letters back and forth by stagecoach, it'll take a couple of weeks to get everything squared away."

Sundell smiled faintly. "At least. I reckon if you want to give me a forwarding address, I can have the bank send your money on to you somewhere else. Otherwise, you're welcome to wait here for it. Pine Knob is a pretty pleasant place, if I do say so myself."

Sometimes Luke had bounty money sent to Smoke, who had established an account for him at the bank in Big Rock, the town nearest the Sugarloaf. He felt confident that Mac would probably agree to have his share of the reward handled in that manner, as well.

However, they were running a little low on funds for supplies and other necessities, and anyway, Luke had another reason—maybe—for staying around Pine Knob for a while.

"Before I decide, let me ask you something, Marshal."

Sundell spread his hands. "Sure, go ahead."

Luke reached inside his jacket and took a piece of paper from a pocket. He unfolded it, placed it on the desk, and slid it across so the marshal could get a good look at it.

"Do you recognize the fellow whose description is on this dodger?" Luke asked.

Sundell leaned forward to study the wanted poster. A look of concentration came over his bulldog face.

"'Asa Dunnigan,'" he read aloud. "'Wanted for murder, attempted murder, kidnapping, train robbery, stagecoach robbery, bank robbery'—" He glanced up at Luke. "Is there anything this hombre *hasn't* robbed?"

"Officially, he's never raided the poor box in a church, but I sure as blazes wouldn't put it past him."

"'Rape, assault, arson . . .'" Sundell went on. "This Dunnigan fella is a genuine bad article, isn't he?"

"Do you recognize the name?"

Sundell shook his head. "There's nobody in these parts by that name, I can tell you that."

"Or at least nobody who goes by that name," Luke said.

"Well, that's true," the marshal said, nodding. "He could be using a false monicker and I wouldn't have any way of knowing the difference."

Luke pointed at the reward poster and asked, "How about the description? That sound familiar?"

"Let's see here. Brown hair, brown eyes, clean-shaven, medium height. Is that it?" Sundell leaned back, rested his hands on the desk, and shook his head. "Shoot, there's probably at least a hundred men around here who could fit that description, Jensen. Maybe more."

"That's what I was afraid you'd say, Marshal."

"You and your partner are hunting Dunnigan?"

"We're usually on the trail of several different fugitives at the same time," Luke said. "Dunnigan is one we're looking for currently. I picked up a rumor back down the trail that he might be headed in this direction. There was a time when he worked as a lumberjack, so I thought he might have signed on with one of the logging crews in this area. That would give him the chance to lay low for a while, in the hope that anyone looking for him might give up."

Sundell scratched his jaw for a moment, then sat back and laced his fingers together over his belly.

"That makes sense, I suppose. You probably know as much or more than I do about how lawbreakers think. But there's only one big timber outfit around here. A few smaller companies operate in these parts, but I know everybody who works for them and they've all been around for a while. The Empire bunch, though, that's a big crew and there are always men coming and going. If that Dunnigan owlhoot knows anything about working timber, he could probably get a job with them and blend in, as long as he didn't do anything to call attention to himself."

That sounded intriguing to Luke. "Empire you say?"

"Yeah. The Empire Logging Company is the outfit's official name. There's an office here in town."

Marshal Sundell chuckled. Luke didn't see where there was anything funny about what the lawman had just said. He was on the verge of asking Sundell to explain when the man suddenly leaned over and opened a drawer in the desk.

"Endicott's had time to get those corpses laid out where I can take a good look at them," he said. "As soon as I've dug out the dodgers on them, I think I'll go on down there and do that. Where can I find you, Jensen?"

"Why don't I just go to the undertaker's with you?" Luke suggested. "Even if we have to wait around for a while, I'd like to see to it that the details are taken care of as efficiently as possible."

"Suit yourself."

The marshal took a sizable stack of wanted posters from the drawer and set them on the desk. He began to flip through them, humming softly to himself as he did so. He didn't get in any hurry, but patience had always been one of Luke's strong suits.

Eventually, Sundell had set aside four wanted posters. He gathered them together, tapped them on the desk to square them up, and put the rest away before coming to his feet.

He snagged a black hat from where it hung on a nail on the

wall and said, "I imagine you're plenty used to the sight of dead bodies."

"More than I'd like to be," Luke said.

He picked up Asa Dunnigan's wanted poster from the desk, folded it again, and stowed it away inside his jacket. He hadn't taken his hat off, only thumbed it back, so he didn't have to put it on again as he followed Sundell out of the office.

Still no sign of Mac, Luke saw, as he looked up and down the street. He wasn't worried about his partner's nonappearance . . . yet.

During the ride into Pine Knob, he had told Mac about Dunnigan, and the rumor that the outlaw might be in this area. That lead was something Luke had come across when the two of them weren't together, and he hadn't thought to mention it to Mac at the time. Mac knew now, though, the other reason they were here besides collecting the bounties on the Bishop brothers. He'd be around, Luke assured himself.

Marshal Sundell's pace increased a little as he noticed a crowd gathered down the street. Luke, who was several inches taller than the lawman, kept up easily as they approached.

"What in blazes?" the lawman muttered. "That commotion is in front of John Endicott's place."

"The undertaking parlor?" Luke said.

"That's right."

"Then I have a pretty good idea what we'll find. There's one thing that always draws a lot of attention."

Sundell called for the crowd to part when they reached the outer edge of it. The townspeople moved aside, some of them reluctantly, until they realized it was the marshal who was demanding a path.

The crowd pulled back to reveal exactly what Luke thought they would see: the corpses of the four Bishop brothers, each lashed to wide planks propped up with one end on the boardwalk and the other leaned against the building's front wall. The dead outlaws still wore the same bloodstained clothing.

The undertaker stood to one side of the bodies, his hands pressed together in front of him almost like he was praying. He looked pleased with himself without actually smiling.

"Blast it, Endicott," Marshal Sundell burst out, "I told you to lay them out where I could take a good look at them, not put them on display so the whole town can gawk at them."

The undertaker gestured solemnly toward the corpses. "I'm sorry, Marshal," he said, "but these men are famous figures, or perhaps I should say *infamous.* The level of interest in such notorious outlaws is so great that I believed it was my duty to arrange this public viewing."

"Well, check with me next time before you do anything like this," Sundell grumbled. He waved an arm at the crowd and ordered, "You folks clear out! You've had your look-see. Now, go on about your business."

Slowly, and with obvious reluctance, the crowd broke up and dispersed. While Luke and Endicott watched, the marshal went from corpse to corpse, studying their faces and comparing them to the drawings and descriptions on the wanted posters he had brought with him from the office.

Finally, he said, "All right, I'm satisfied it's them, just like you claimed, Jensen." He turned to Endicott. "Get them off the boardwalk and inside."

"Is it all right to prepare them for burial, Abner?"

Sundell nodded. "Sure, I don't see why not. Unless you have more urgent chores to take care of."

"Not at the moment." Endicott cleared his throat. "Should I bill the county for the expense of laying them to rest?"

Sundell looked at Luke, who said, "They had some money among their things, enough to cover the basic expenses. Let me know what the total comes to, and I'll see to it you get paid, Mr. Endicott."

"I appreciate that, sir."

"Nothing fancy, though. Like I said, just the basics."

"The cost of four pine boxes and a little labor for the grave-digging, then."

Luke nodded, thinking it was a shame that, in the end, that was what most men's lives boiled down to. More than likely, that was his own destiny, he reflected, although expecting a pine box might be asking a little too much.

The sort of life he led, he'd probably wind up being left in some lonely canyon for the coyotes and the buzzards—and they didn't charge for their services.

They took it out in trade.

CHAPTER 5

The steak that the blonde put in front of Mac turned out to be good. Like the coffee, not the best he'd ever had, but perfectly acceptable. The fried potatoes and beans keeping it company on the plate were tasty, too.

The blonde's name was Violet Channing. He was able to draw that much information out of her before she moved off to help some of the other customers at the counter.

Every few minutes, the old-timer in the kitchen opened the little window again and called to her that another order was ready. She delivered the plates to the tables where folks were waiting for their food.

When she paused across the counter from Mac again, he said, "This food is mighty good. And that's coming from somebody who's cooked up and down all the cattle trails and in a café of his own for a while. I'd appreciate it if you'd pass along my compliments to the fella in the kitchen."

"Oh, I'm not going to do that," Violet replied with a shake of her head.

That response surprised Mac. "Why not?"

"Because his head's already swelled up enough from thinking he's a great cook."

As Violet spoke, she turned her head a little. The pass-through into the kitchen was still open, so her words could be heard back there, Mac thought.

A moment later, he knew the cook had overheard Violet's comment, just as she'd intended, because the man's scowling face appeared in the opening.

"My head ain't swelled up, and I never claimed to be a great cook!" he said. "But I'm a durned sight better than you. I swear, girl, you couldn't boil water without burnin' it."

She laughed. Mac thought it was a nice sound. When he'd first come in here, he would have bet a hat he wouldn't see the girl smile, let alone hear her laugh, so he was making more progress than he expected.

"You're right, Pop," she told the cook. "The ability to cook just passed right by me."

The old man jerked his head in a nod. "Lucky for you, you've got me around to take care o' that chore. If you had to do the cookin', this place'd be out of business in a week!"

He slid the window closed with a thump.

"That's your father?" Mac asked. "The one you said started the café?"

Violet's smile faded. "No, he's my grandfather, but everybody calls him Pop. They always have, even before I was born. My father . . . Pop's son . . . passed away a few years ago."

"I'm sorry," Mac said.

"It's all right. We've honored his memory by keeping the café open." She lowered her voice and added, "And Pop really is a very good cook."

That was stretching things a mite, Mac thought, but he wasn't going to say that to her. Anyway, it was entirely possible that Pop Channing actually was the best cook in these parts.

Or at least he had been until Mac walked into town.

When he had used a biscuit to sop up the last bit of gravy on his plate, Violet sat a dish of apple pie in front of him and refilled his coffee cup. Mac lingered over this part of the meal, luxuriating in the satisfaction of being full.

Violet seemed to be spending more time in his vicinity, so he kept the conversation going by saying, "You mentioned the Triangle 7 when I came in. Is that the biggest ranch around here?"

"That's right. It's owned by a man named Ben Harmon." She frowned. "Are you thinking about trying to get a job there? I thought you said you aren't a cowboy."

"I'm not," Mac said. "Just curious, that's all. I like to get to know the places where I am." He paused. "A fella on the street said there was a big brawl recently between the Triangle 7 crew and some loggers."

Violet rolled her eyes and said, "There's always some sort of fight going on between Mr. Harmon's men and the Empire crew. I'm not sure I'd say what happened in the Lonesome Pine last week was any worse than the other times."

Mac washed down the bite of pie he'd been chewing—which really was good; probably the best thing he'd eaten here so far—with a swallow of coffee and then said, "Bad blood between the two outfits, is there?"

"You could certainly say that."

"I reckon they don't get along because they're in different lines of work."

"I suppose that's part of the reason," Violet said.

Her comment implied there was more than that to the conflict, but before he could ask her to elaborate, the bell over the door jingled a couple of times as a man hurried into the café. He seemed excited.

"Rich Coburn and some of his crew just rode in and stopped at the Lonesome Pine," the newcomer announced to the room at large. "And George Stanton and half a dozen of his boys are already in there."

Mac glanced from that man back to Violet, who was frowning

now, apparently at what the townie had reported. He said, "Let me guess. Coburn rides for the Triangle 7 and Stanton and his friends are loggers. Or is it the other way around?"

"No, you got it right the first time," she said. "Rich Coburn is Ben Harmon's foreman and runs the ranch crew. George Stanton is the bull of the woods of Empire Logging."

She paused and then added, "It's safe to say that they hate each other."

"So, with both bunches being in the saloon at the same time . . ."

"It's a recipe for trouble, as they say," Violet confirmed.

The townsman who had brought the news came to the counter and sat down on the empty stool next to Mac. During the time Mac had been in here, the crowd had thinned out a bit as folks finished their midday meals. The man glanced at the dish of pie in front of Mac and said, "That looks mighty good. I'll have me some, Violet. Can you put a little cream with it?"

"Of course," she said, and then added with a slightly skeptical tone in her voice, "Can you pay for it, Jonah?"

"Sure I can." The man dug a coin out of his pocket, slapped it on the counter, and said, "Rich Coburn give me that nickel and told me to spread the word that him and his boys were gonna teach Stanton and them tree-loppers that they hadn't ought to be comin' into a real man's town."

Violet's eyes widened in alarm. "They're going in there looking for a fight?"

"Lookin' to settle the trouble once and for all, is how I figure they'd put it."

"That's not going to settle anything," Violet said as she shook her head. "It'll just make things worse." She thought for a moment, then went on, "Jonah, go find Marshal Sundell and tell him there's going to be another fight in the Lonesome Pine. Maybe he can get there in time to head it off."

Jonah looked devastated. "But I was fixin' to eat some pie!"

"Do what I told you and then come back here. I'll let you have the pie then. And if you do, I'll give you another dish of pie tomorrow, on the house."

The townie looked like he had just been promised a fortune. "Really?" he asked in amazement. "You promise?"

"I swear," Violet said. "You know you can trust me."

"Well, sure!" Jonah bolted to his feet. "I'll be back!"

He left the café almost running.

Violet sighed as she watched him go. Mac said, "Not meaning any offense, but it seemed like that fella might be a little, um . . ."

"He's a little simple," Violet said plainly. "Everybody knows it, and we all sort of look out for him, or try to, anyway. He helps out at the general store and does other odd jobs."

"I get the feeling that you sort of look out for the whole town, too."

"Why? Because I sent Jonah to warn the marshal that trouble was brewing?" Violet picked up a rag from under the counter and rubbed the surface vigorously. "I suppose I do. My father was the mayor at one time. I still feel a sort of responsibility to the town. But the hard feelings run so deep between the cattlemen and the loggers that I'm not sure anybody can keep the situation under control. Abner Sundell does his best, but he's only one man."

Mac spooned up the last of the pie in the dish. He drank the rest of the coffee in his cup. As he stood up, he slid a silver dollar across the counter.

"You'll have some change coming," Violet began.

"Never mind about that," he told her. "Put it on account for me, if you want to, or just don't worry about it. Seems to me the meal was worth at least that much." He smiled. "Not to mention the company."

She surprised him by reddening slightly. Violet seemed like a very practical, levelheaded young woman, but he supposed any woman might blush a little at a compliment now and then.

"And I'm obliged for the information, too," he went on, not

wanting her to feel awkward. "I like to know some about a place if I'm going to be around for a while."

"You're not just passing through Pine Knob?"

"At this point, I don't really know," he answered honestly. That would depend almost totally on whatever arrangements Luke made with the local law regarding the reward money—but he didn't want to explain that to Violet right now. "I'm going to be here for a while longer, at least."

"What are you going to do now?"

"Thought I'd take a walk down to the Lonesome Pine," Mac said.

"Oh." Violet frowned in disapproval. "You mean you don't want to miss the excitement."

"It's not that so much. But I've got a friend here in town somewhere, and if there's one thing I've learned about him, it's that anywhere trouble is, he's likely to show up right on its heels."

CHAPTER 6

Luke went back to the marshal's office with Sundell. The lawman replaced the wanted posters in the drawer and then drew a turnip watch out of his pocket and flipped it open.

"It's still an hour until the stagecoach gets here. I should have time to write that letter to the U.S. Marshal in Salem."

"Does the stage run every day?" Luke asked.

Sundell shook his head. "Every other day. So you're lucky, I guess. If you'd ridden into town with those corpses tomorrow, you'd have had to wait twenty-four hours for the process to even get started."

"I'll take any lucky breaks I can get."

"Speaking of luck," Sundell said, "are you going to try yours at finding that fella Dunnigan?"

"As long as I'm here in the area, that seems like a reasonable thing to do." Luke propped a hip on the corner of the desk. "If I could ask a favor of you, Marshal, I'd appreciate it if you'd keep our conversation about him to yourself. If Dunnigan actually is in these parts, I don't want word getting back to him that somebody is looking for him."

Sundell's tone was crisp as he said, "I know how to keep my mouth shut, especially when it comes to legal matters."

"I meant no offense, Marshal."

Sundell waved away the apology as he sat down. "Don't worry about it," he said. "And I won't mention it to anybody. If Dunnigan's anywhere around here, though, he's liable to hear about you bringing in the Bishop boys. He'll know there's a bounty hunter in the area."

"Yes, but he won't know that I have my sights set on him. He'll probably try to lie low until I've moved on. But that will give me a chance to poke around and see what I can find."

"Well, if I'm doing a favor for you, then you can do one for me."

"Of course, Marshal. What is it?"

"Try not to get yourself killed while you're in my town," Sundell said. "I don't want to have to tell Endicott not to put your carcass on display."

Luke tipped back his head and let out a hearty laugh.

"I'll do my best, Marshal," he said. "I'll do my best."

Luke left the marshal's office a few minutes later with a recommendation for the best livery stable in town. If he was going to be here for a while, he wanted to leave his horse somewhere it would be well cared for.

As he spoke to the red-bearded liveryman and made arrangements for his mount, he tried to check out the animals in the other stalls without being too obvious about it. A feeling of relief went through him when he recognized Mac's horse. The animal's presence was confirmation his partner had reached the settlement, hopefully without any trouble.

Luke started to ask the liveryman if he knew where Mac had gone when a thought occurred to him. An idea was beginning to form in the back of his mind. Since he and Mac had entered Pine Knob separately, it wouldn't be obvious to anyone in town that they knew each other, let alone worked together.

If they could keep that relationship from becoming common

knowledge, it might come in handy later on. Unless Mac himself told them, people around here wouldn't have any idea that he was a bounty hunter—and that would include their quarry, Asa Dunnigan.

He needed to find Mac and look for an opportunity to have a private conversation with him to work out the details of the plan, Luke decided.

Just as he stepped out of the livery barn, a townsman hurrying past nearly ran into him. Luke stopped short to avoid the collision. He was annoyed and started to call after the man to tell him to watch where he was going, but then he figured it wasn't worth the trouble.

Just out of idle curiosity, wondering why someone was in such a rush, Luke watched him go on up the street—and into the marshal's office.

Now, that's interesting, Luke thought as a frown creased his forehead. Usually, when somebody ran into a lawman's office like that, it was to report that some sort of trouble was about to bust wide open.

Was that about to happen here in Pine Knob?

Of course, even if that turned out to be the case, it was none of his business, he reminded himself. Abner Sundell seemed perfectly capable of keeping the peace. In fact, the marshal probably wouldn't look kindly on Luke, or anyone else, interfering with him.

With that thought in his head, Luke's gaze fell on a substantial-looking building across the street. It had an actual second story instead of a false front, and it took up a full half of the block. The entrance was on the corner where a smaller road crossed Pine Knob's main street. Swinging batwing doors at that entrance identified the place as a saloon, and so did the long sign attached to the awning over the boardwalk.

LONESOME PINE SALOON
—DRINKS—FOOD—ENTERTAINMENT—
COLDEST BEER IN OREGON

That was a bold promise. Luke decided he would have to see if there was any truth to it. A quick stop in the saloon and then he would find something to eat, he told himself. In his experience, the food a fellow could get in a saloon was good enough for its intended purpose—to get customers to buy more drinks—but it didn't serve very well as a meal.

He'd noticed a café with a bright blue roof down the street as he rode into town, he recalled. He would check it out after he'd washed the trail dust from his throat. After eating, he could see about getting a hotel room, since it looked like he was going to be in Pine Knob for a while.

Luke crossed the street, neatly avoiding the piles of dung left here and there by passing horses and mules, and stepped up onto the boardwalk in front of the saloon.

As he did so, he glanced at the horses tied up at the hitch rack and noted the brand on each of them—Triangle 7. He had long since made a habit of observing such details, because a man never knew when they might turn out to be important.

Then he shouldered through the batwings into the saloon.

The Lonesome Pine wasn't the fanciest such establishment Luke had ever visited, but it was far from the most squalid. The long bar was to his left, its surface polished and the brass rail along the bottom front gleaming.

Tables filled most of the room, some of them being used for drinking, others baize-covered for card games. Luke saw a roulette wheel and a faro layout in the back.

A raised stage took up most of the right-hand wall, with several rows of chairs in front of it. That would be where the entertainment took place. Probably dancing girls most of the time. A piano sat on one side of the stage to provide music for their cavorting. Singers likely performed now and then, as well. At the moment, though, the stage was empty.

Oil lamps attached to wagon-wheel chandeliers hung from the ceiling. More light spilled in through the big windows along the front of the building. Although hazed somewhat by tobacco smoke, the atmosphere in here wasn't as murky as it often was in frontier saloons.

Nor was the smell as bad, although the usual odors of beer, whiskey, and human flesh were present. No, it wasn't a bad place at all, and the man standing behind the bar in a brown tweed suit regarded it with a smile on his lips under a sweeping mustache. An expression of possessive pride rested on his beefy face.

That would be the proprietor of the Lonesome Pine, Luke guessed.

Luke paused just inside the batwings to take in all those details. His keen eyes and equally keen brain cataloged all of them in a couple of heartbeats. As he looked at the owner, standing behind the hardwood flanked by a couple of slick-haired bartenders, he saw the man's smile disappear. A worried frown replaced it.

Luke's gaze followed the direction of that frown.

In a rear corner, not far from the stage, eight men sat around a large, round table. They had a pitcher of beer they were passing around as they filled mugs from it, and the presence of a couple of empty pitchers testified that they had been drinking for a while already. A jar half full of pickled eggs sat in the middle of the table as well.

As Luke watched, one of the men reached into the jar, pulled out an egg, and popped it whole into his mouth.

Luke, looking askance at the jar, hoped it hadn't been full when the men sat down there. If it had, it meant they had put away an awful lot of pickled eggs recently.

Some of the men were taller than others, but each sported broad, muscular shoulders, and their arms bulged the sleeves of the flannel shirts they wore. Canvas trousers and lace-up work boots completed their outfits.

Luke had been around enough loggers to recognize the breed. Without being too obvious about what he was doing, he studied the men, trying to determine if any of them matched the description he had of the fugitive, Asa Dunnigan.

Deciding that none of them did, Luke headed for the bar at a deliberate pace.

He wasn't sure why the saloonkeeper seemed concerned. The loggers were a little loud and boisterous as they talked, drank beer, and ate eggs, true, but they weren't really causing much of a commotion.

Then Luke noted that he and the proprietor weren't the only ones looking at the timbermen. So was a man in range clothes as he stood with his back to the bar, his elbows resting on the hardwood, while the heel of his right boot was hooked over the brass rail. He was a cowboy, no doubt about that, as were the men lined up at the bar on either side of him.

Pure hatred burned in the eyes of the man staring at the loggers.

Luke took a closer look at him. The man's battered Stetson was pushed back on a thatch of sandy hair. A Colt with walnut grips rode in a well-worn holster on his right hip. The sleeves of his butternut shirt were rolled up over brawny forearms despite the chill in the air today. The saloon's entrance doors were open other than the batwings, but it was comfortably warm in the Lonesome Pine because of the crowd and the potbellied stove in the corner.

One of the other cowboys nudged the man's arm with an elbow. When the man looked around, the one who'd nudged him slid a full glass over to him.

"We came into town for a drink, Rich," he said. "Better go ahead and have one. The boss'll expect us back on the spread before nightfall."

"There's plenty of time for us to get back," the man called Rich said. But he picked up the glass anyway and threw down the drink. He turned to the bar, thumped the empty on the hardwood, and dragged the back of his hand across his mouth.

The man beside him picked up a whiskey bottle and started to refill the glass. Rich shook his head and put his hand over the top to stop him.

"I want a clear head for what I'm about to do," he said.

The saloonkeeper had drifted along the bar until he was directly across it from Rich and could hear what the man said. He asked in a flat voice, "What's that going to be, Coburn?"

The cowboy's chin jutted out defiantly. "I reckon you know, Butler."

The saloonkeeper shook his head.

"Not in here," he declared. "If you're looking for a fight with Stanton and his boys, you can take it outside. I'm not going to have things busted up again just because you cowboys are on the prod."

"Those stinkin' loggers don't have any right to be drinkin' in a cowboy saloon." Coburn raised his voice as he spoke so that it carried throughout the room, especially when most of the other conversation in the Lonesome Pine died abruptly. "A real man's saloon is no place for the likes o' them."

The proprietor, Butler, placed his hands flat on the bar and leaned forward slightly.

"This isn't a cowboy saloon, as you put it," he said. "It's a saloon for anybody who wants good liquor and fair games of chance. Everybody's welcome in my establishment, and that's the way it's always been."

Coburn sneered across the hardwood. "It was different before that bunch took up loggin' in these parts. They're ruinin' the whole basin, and you know it! When the rains come later this fall, mudslides are gonna swamp all the good grazin' land. Mr. Harmon and the other ranchers will be wiped out."

"We don't know that—" Butler began.

"It's happened in plenty of other places. We've all heard about it. It'll happen right here, too, and you know it."

Luke had sauntered up to the bar a short distance away from Coburn and the other cowboys. He had a hunch those Triangle 7 horses outside belonged to them.

Evidently, the men at the table in the corner worked for the Empire Logging Company. Marshal Sundell had told Luke a little about the operation. It was the biggest timber company in these parts, although it had been operating for less than a year. Luke didn't know anything about the Triangle 7 ranch, but clearly, bad blood existed between the two outfits.

Luke intended to steer clear of that conflict, so when one of the bartenders sidled up to him and asked, "What'll it be, mister?" he replied quietly, "Beer."

Then he added, "Is there about to be trouble in here?"

"I don't know, mister," the bartender replied with a nervous glance toward the two groups glaring at each other. "I sure hope not, though. The last time those two bunches got into it, we had to replace a window, two tables, and half a dozen chairs that got busted all to pieces."

Luke raised an eyebrow. "Sounds like quite a ruckus."

The bartender drew the beer and set the mug of foamy amber liquid in front of him.

"It was," he agreed, "and ever since, both sides have been itching for all Hades to break loose again."

Luke might have tried to elicit more information from the man, just out of idle curiosity, but at that moment the batwings swung open again, and he glanced in that direction as he picked up his mug of beer.

Dewey McKenzie stepped into the Lonesome Pine and paused with his hands resting on the tops of the batwings as he looked around.

CHAPTER 7

Mac had noticed the brand on the horses outside—Triangle 7. That was the ranch Jonah had mentioned in the café. Mac needed only a second to pick out the cowboys standing at the bar and figure they went with those horses.

The hostile glares going back and forth between those punchers and a group of men sitting at a large, round table located catty-cornered on the other side of the room were so intense they might as well have been visible streaks in the air.

The fellas at the table would be the lumberjacks who worked for the Empire Logging Company. Mac was confident he had sized up the situation in the blink of an eye.

He had also spotted Luke Jensen standing at the end of the bar closest to the entrance. Luke glanced toward him, then looked away and took a long swallow of beer from the mug in his hand, as if he found the newcomer of no interest whatsoever.

Instantly, Mac knew the message that Luke was trying to get across to him.

They were to act as if they didn't know each other.

That was easy enough to do, Mac thought as he stepped on

into the saloon and let the batwings swing closed behind him. He hadn't entered Pine Knob until quite a while after Luke arrived with the bodies of the Bishop brothers. They hadn't laid eyes on each other until just now. As long as they didn't speak and steered clear of each other, no one in the settlement would have any reason to believe they were even acquainted, let alone trail partners.

Mac didn't look at Luke as he ambled toward the far end of the bar.

That took him closer to the table where the loggers sat. George Stanton was the name of the crew's foreman, Mac recalled from Jonah's excited babbling. A man who appeared to be somewhat older than the others sat on the far side of the table, leaning back in his chair with his muscular arms crossed over his chest. His graying hair was cropped short. A short, salt-and-pepper mustache bristled on his upper lip. He had an air of command about him that made Mac have a hunch he was looking at George Stanton.

The other men were equally burly in their flannel shirts, canvas trousers held up by suspenders, and work boots. All of them looked like they would be right at home swinging a double-bitted axe or wielding a crosscut saw.

On the other hand, the men at the bar were dressed for range work. They would be more comfortable on horseback than in the woods.

Mac had worked on many trail drives and spent much time on ranches, so he supposed if he was going to pick a side in this clash, it ought to be the cattlemen's.

But for some reason, he liked the look of those timbermen. They appeared to be rugged, hardworking hombres. Mac respected that.

He also remembered that Luke thought Asa Dunnigan might have gone to work for a logging outfit around here, so he looked them over carefully to see if any of them matched the description on Dunnigan's wanted poster.

A couple were medium-sized, like Dunnigan was supposed to be, but neither had brown hair and both sported beards. The men who did have brown hair were too big to be Dunnigan, and they weren't clean-shaven, either.

A man could always grow a beard, though, Mac reminded himself. The presence or lack of one didn't have to mean anything. But a man couldn't shrink himself by several inches or lose twenty or thirty pounds in a hurry, either. It was still possible Asa Dunnigan might work for the Empire Logging Company, but it didn't appear he was one of the bunch in the Lonesome Pine today.

Two bartenders were on duty behind the hardwood. Mac wound up at the end of the bar farthest away from Luke, and the man working that end came up and asked, "What are you drinking, friend?"

"Beer, I think." Having just eaten lunch, Mac didn't really want anything, but fellows who worked in saloons tended not to take it kindly if a man didn't drink. Even as satisfied as he was from the meal, he could nurse a beer along for a good while.

He was actually here just out of curiosity about the trouble brewing between the cowboys and the loggers. He supposed that deep down, he was just as nosy as anybody else.

Besides, hadn't he looked over the loggers to see if any of them might be Asa Dunnigan? That meant he was working, he told himself with a faint, wry smile.

The bartender set a mug of beer in front of him. Mac dropped a nickel on the hardwood. The bartender scooped up the coin with practiced deftness.

"New in town, aren't you, friend?" the man asked.

"Just got in a while ago," Mac said. "My horse went lame, so I'm having him seen to. Stopped at the Blue Top Café for a meal while I was at it."

The bartender let out a low whistle. "That Violet Channing is a looker, isn't she? I don't mean to be disrespectful by saying that, but it's just a plain and simple fact, ain't it?"

"It is," Mac agreed solemnly.

"And old Pop can whip up a good meal."

"He sure can."

"If I wasn't married, I'd stop in there more often. For the food, you know. Good eats, just like the sign says."

Mac took a sip of the beer, which was cool and reasonably good. Then, keeping his voice low, he said, "When I walked in here, it seemed like there might be a little tension in the air."

The bartender rolled his eyes. Leaning forward, he said in not much more than a whisper, "It's the cowboys and those lumberjacks. They can't stand one another. Seems like they're always on the verge of a ruckus. If you ask me, Marshal Sundell needs to lay down the law to them. Set up some sort of schedule so that neither bunch is ever in town at the same time as the other."

"The problem with that is that it's a free country," Mac said with a shrug. "It'd be up to their bosses to work out something like that, not the law."

The bartender shook his head. "That would mean cooperating, and trust me, friend, those two aren't going to do that."

That comment piqued Mac's curiosity even more, but before he could ask the bartender to elaborate, one of the cowhands pushed away from the bar and sauntered between tables toward the one where the loggers sat. He carried a half-full bottle of whiskey.

Behind him, the beefy gent in the brown tweed suit behind the bar exclaimed, "Blast it, Coburn, don't go starting anything."

"I'm not starting anything," the lean range rider said over his shoulder. "You're so worried about trouble, Butler, that I thought I'd head it off and make a peaceful gesture."

Butler, who Mac figured was the owner of the Lonesome Pine, didn't look convinced of Coburn's diplomatic intentions. He stood behind the bar and watched fretfully.

Mac watched, too, half-turning from the bar to do so.

The loggers saw Coburn approaching and grew even more

tense. The middle-aged man Mac had pegged as the foreman rose to his feet and said, "What do you want, Coburn?"

"Now, is that any way to be?" Coburn asked as he came to a stop. A smirk tugged at his lips. "You sound all suspicious, Stanton, and here I am tryin' to be friendly."

"I don't recall ever saying I wanted to be friends with you."

"Well, maybe we don't have to be friends, but we don't have to fight, either." Coburn held out the bottle, which didn't have a cork in the neck. "The boys and me drank half this hooch. We figured it'd be a nice gesture to offer the rest of it to you fellas. Share and share alike, you know?"

"What'd you do, doctor it up with something foul that'll make us sick?"

"You think we'd do a thing like that?" Coburn lifted the bottle and took a swig from it. "If there was anything wrong with this Who-Hit-John, I wouldn't have done that, would I?"

One of the loggers said, "Maybe he's tellin' the truth, George. You know how the boss says we ought to try to get along with that bunch from the Triangle 7."

"I know it," Stanton said with a scowl, "but that doesn't mean I have to agree with that sentiment."

Coburn shrugged and said, "It's up to you. I'm extending this here, what do you call it, olive branch. You can decide whether or not you want to take it."

Several long seconds ticked past before Stanton jerked his head in an abrupt nod and said, "All right. I suppose it won't hurt anything to believe you—for now."

"You mean you'll take the whiskey?"

"Sure."

Coburn smiled. "I was hoping you'd say that."

Without giving anybody time to react, he upended the open bottle and poured the whiskey in it over the head of the logger who was nearest to him at the table.

For a moment, everybody in the place was too stunned to move.

Then the man who'd had the whiskey poured on him exploded

up out of his chair, howling curses as he swung a fist at Coburn's head.

The cowboy was too quick for him. Coburn swayed backward so the looping punch missed, and while the logger was off-balance, he slammed the empty bottle against the man's head. The logger went down instantly.

The other timbermen were leaping to their feet by now, so violently that their chairs overturned. They were ready to swarm the Triangle 7 foreman, pull him down, and stomp him into the floorboards.

But the other members of the ranch crew were moving, too, charging across the room, knocking tables and chairs aside as they whooped with anticipation.

The two sides came together in a welter of curses, grunts, and flying fists.

Behind the bar, the saloonkeeper, Butler, waved his arms in agitation and yelled for the combatants to stop. None of the battlers paid the least bit of attention to him. They just continued slugging away at one another, surging back and forth, knocking over chairs and pushing tables aside, spilling drinks and scattering cards and the pots that had accumulated in several poker games.

The saloon's other customers, who had just been trying to drink or gamble in peace, scrambled to get out of the way. Some slapped the batwings aside and fled out into the street.

No real damage to the premises had been done so far, but that couldn't last. Men were fighting perilously close to the front windows. Mac expected somebody to go crashing through one of the panes at any moment, shattering the glass into a million pieces.

Like all brawls, this one was chaotic and out of control. No longer were there "sides" in the barroom. The men fighting each other were all jumbled up, cowboys and loggers going every which way as they hammered punches at one another, tackled their enemies, and rolled around on the sawdust-littered floor.

But so far, this was just a typical free-for-all. No guns or knives had put in an appearance. The empty bottle that Coburn had used to clout one of the loggers was the only weapon that had been used. Otherwise, it was strictly a matter of fists and feet and wrestling holds.

Then one of the loggers staggered back and crashed against the bar next to Mac. The cowboy who had knocked him there rushed in, slammed his left forearm across the logger's throat, and forced him to bend backward over the hardwood.

That had to be painful enough, but then, while the cowboy had his opponent pinned there, he reached down with his other hand and yanked a Colt from its holster on his hip. He raised the gun high, clearly intending to strike the logger with it.

Mac's sense of fair play boiled over inside him. He yelled, "Hey!" and when the cowboy involuntarily glanced at him, Mac threw the nearly full mug of beer right in the man's face with a flick of his left wrist.

He followed that with a straight right-hand punch that landed solidly on the cowboy's nose. Blood spurted over Mac's knuckles as the man's nose flattened. The cowboy reeled backward, tripped over somebody else that had been knocked down, and crashed to the floor.

Freed of the weight that had been holding him down, the logger straightened up just in time to catch a fist on the jaw from the other side. He collapsed, stunned, and the man who'd just walloped him loomed up in front of Mac.

It was Luke Jensen, and to Mac's great surprise, before his eyes even had time to widen, Luke hauled off and punched him in the face, too.

CHAPTER 8

The idea had come to Luke out of the blue, but he had learned over the years to trust his gut and follow his impulses, at least part of the time.

It had already occurred to him that it might be smart to act as if he and Mac didn't know each other. When the fight broke out, a way of possibly taking advantage of that idea had sprung to life in his mind.

"Take that, you tree-climbing ape!" he roared as the punch he'd thrown drove Mac back a couple of steps.

Luke hadn't pulled his punch. Well, not much, anyway. It must have looked genuine to anyone watching the fight, and some of the men actually involved in the brawl probably saw it, too. Luke certainly hoped so.

Mac caught his balance and yelled, "You no-good range-riding skunk!" He launched himself at Luke with his fists flying.

That shouted insult was enough to tell Luke that Mac had caught on to what he was doing. If Mac actually was angry, he wouldn't have been so specific in his reaction.

To anyone who didn't know better, it would seem that Mac

was aligned with the loggers, while Luke had thrown in with the Triangle 7 cowboys. That was exactly the impression Luke wanted to create.

He blocked two of Mac's punches but allowed the third one to slip past his guard and thump solidly into his solar plexus. The blow was hard enough to make Luke gasp for breath as he reeled against the bar.

Mac crowded in and looped a left to the side of Luke's head, knocking his hat off. That made the punch look like it landed with more force than it actually did.

Luke twisted to avoid another blow, lunged at Mac, and caught him around the body. He heaved upward so Mac's feet came off the floor. The bear hug put Luke's mouth close to Mac's ear. He whispered, "Good job."

"Try not to . . . break my ribs," Mac grated through clenched teeth as Luke increased the pressure.

Mac drove the sides of his hands against the spots where Luke's neck joined his shoulders. Again, it looked like a vicious counterattack, but Mac didn't put a lot of force behind the blows. Luke grimaced in fake pain and loosened his hold. Mac slipped out of it in convincing fashion.

They started swinging at each other again, standing toe to toe and apparently slugging it out. Luke tasted blood in his mouth after one of Mac's punches connected. That would just make the deception more believable, he thought, as he bounced a fist off Mac's left eye. Mac would have a shiner there by the next morning; a small one, but still noticeable.

The brawl was still going on. Nobody was left in the Lonesome Pine other than the men who were fighting, except Butler and the two bartenders. The aprons crouched low, peering over the hardwood, and were ready to duck if a piece of broken furniture or anything else came flying their way.

Butler still stood tall, however. He reached under the bar and brought out a sawed-off, double-barreled shotgun. Luke saw him bring the weapon to his shoulder and aim it at the wild melee.

That was going too far. Luke opened his mouth to yell at Butler to hold his fire, but he was too late. The shotgun boomed as flame spouted from its right-hand barrel.

Luke and Mac, who were close to the bar, stopped fighting and stared. They cast shocked gazes over the room, expecting to see that the shotgun blast had cut a bloody swath through the battlers.

Instead, even though some of the men were yelping and hopping around in pain, none of them seemed to be badly hurt. Between the scattergun's roar and the damage it had done, the fighting had stopped, although the air was still full of shouted curses.

"Shut up!" Butler bellowed at the men. "That barrel was loaded with rock salt, but the other one's got buckshot in it, and that's what you'll be getting next if you don't settle down!"

The way most of the men were grabbing at their legs indicated that Butler had aimed low with the rock salt, peppering the lower halves of their bodies. The impacts had to sting like blazes, but the stuff hadn't inflicted any significant injuries.

It would be a different story if Butler touched off the barrel loaded with buckshot, and every man in there knew that.

"Dang it, Butler, that hurt!" Rich Coburn said.

"Good!" the saloonkeeper snapped back at him. "It's a puredee miracle you idiots didn't bust another window. I see two broken chairs. You'll pay for them. But first, I want this place cleaned up. Put all the furniture back where it's supposed to be, pick up everything that got knocked off the tables, and mop up that spilled liquor."

"You can't make us do that," George Stanton protested. "We're not saloon swampers!"

Butler raised the shotgun to his shoulder again and squinted over the barrels. "Right now you are. Get busy!"

From the doorway, where he stood just inside the batwings, Marshal Abner Sundell said, "You'd better listen to the man and do what he says."

A faint smile lurked on the lips of the normally dour lawman.

One of the Triangle 7 hands pointed at Butler and complained loudly, "He threatened to kill us, Marshal!"

"A judge and jury might see that as justifiable," Sundell said. "I'm not sure but what I wouldn't agree. Now, clean the place up like Oren told you and pay him for the damages, or I'll lock the whole bunch of you up for a month."

"You can't do that," Coburn said. "Our boss wouldn't stand for it."

"Neither would ours," Stanton put in.

"They wouldn't have much choice in the matter. You know Judge Delavan will do whatever I recommend when it comes to passing sentence."

Evidently, the brawlers did know that, judging by the amount of resentful muttering that came from both factions.

Luke traded the briefest of glances with Mac, then drifted toward the assembled cowboys. The loggers had regrouped, too, and Mac edged toward them. Keeping some distance between them, both groups began straightening up the tables and chairs. The marshal talked briefly to Butler and then left.

As Luke set up an overturned chair, Coburn said quietly to him, "Did I see you pitchin' in to help us, mister?"

"I never did have much use for lumberjacks," Luke replied as he scowled toward the loggers. "Trees are for birds and squirrels, not real men."

"Can't say as I disagree with you there. We're obliged to you for the help." Coburn dragged a table back to where it had been and then stuck out a hand to Luke. "Rich Coburn's the name. I'm the ramrod over at the Triangle 7."

Luke shook with him. "Luke Jensen. I just rode in earlier today."

A look of surprise appeared on Coburn's face. He said, "Say, are you the fella who brought in those dead outlaws? We heard some talk about that before the ruckus started."

"That was me," Luke admitted. "I do a little bounty hunting

from time to time, although mostly I work with cows. I always prefer to have a riding job when there's one to be had."

He hoped he wasn't pushing his luck with that. While it was true that the rumor he'd heard had mentioned the possibility of Asa Dunnigan working as a logger, the notorious outlaw had done stints as a cowboy in Texas and Kansas as a young man. If Dunnigan was trying to lie low for a while, there was an outside chance he might have signed on with some ranch crew.

If nothing else, a job as a ranch hand would give Luke an excuse to move around the area and continue his search for the fugitive. It wouldn't look as suspicious as if he just sat in Pine Knob waiting for the reward money on the Bishop brothers.

And while he was doing that, maybe Mac could get a job with the logging company, which would put him in an even better position to look for Dunnigan.

Luke hoped that Mac would follow the same line of reasoning he had.

Meanwhile, Coburn was regarding Luke with a speculative look on his lean face. "You've done some cowboying, eh?" the foreman asked.

"Born to the saddle, as they say," Luke replied with a grin.

That wasn't strictly true. Growing up on the hardscrabble Jensen farm in the Missouri Ozarks, he had ridden plenty of horses and mules and, since the war, as a bounty hunter, he had spent most of his days in the saddle.

But he hadn't done all that much ranch work. He figured he could carry out the duties well enough to "make a hand," as the cowboys called it, but he would never be a top hand, especially at his age.

"Like I said, I'm the foreman at the Triangle 7," Coburn went on. "I believe in giving a break to a man who fights side by side with us. If the spread's owner doesn't have any objections, we maybe could find a place for you in our crew, Jensen."

"That would please me a whole heap," Luke replied without

hesitation. "At this time of year, I was hoping I might come across something where I could light for a while."

Coburn grinned. "Didn't I hear you say something about tree-climbin' apes?"

"Well, yeah, I reckon I did."

Coburn slapped him on the back. "Any man who feels like that is welcome on the Triangle 7."

Luke returned the grin and glanced across the room to where Mac was talking to one of the loggers. He hoped his partner had made as much progress as he had so far.

"What's your name, mister?" George Stanton asked.

"Dewey McKenzie," Mac replied. "But my friends call me Mac."

Stanton regarded him with suspicion. "My man Jack Miller says you stepped in and saved him when one of those blasted cowboys was about to stove in his head with a gun. Is that true?"

"Bare-knuckles brawling is one thing, but when a man figures on pistol-whipping the fella he's scrapping with, that goes too far," Mac declared. "At least to my way of thinking, it does. So yeah, I stepped in. Seemed like the thing to do at the time."

Stanton nodded solemnly. "I'd say it was, no doubt about that. I would never put any dirty trick beyond those cowboys." He paused. "But to be honest, from the way you're dressed, you look more like you ought to be on their side than ours."

"I'm just dressed to ride because that's the way I've been traveling," Mac said. "But to be honest with you, I've worked with cattle before. That was quite a few years ago, though."

Before he could say anything else, one of the loggers came up to Stanton and interrupted. "George, we got a problem."

Stanton turned to him and asked, "What is it?"

"I think Walt's leg is busted."

A look of surprise and worry instantly appeared on Stanton's face. He appeared to forget about Mac. Instead of continuing the conversation, he hurried back to the table where his men were gathered around someone sitting in a chair.

Mac followed, and as the crowd of loggers parted to let Stanton through, Mac saw a man sitting with his right leg propped up on another chair. The man's face was pale and haggard, and a glance at his leg explained why.

The canvas trousers were ripped and stained with blood, and the white, jagged end of a bone protruded from his thigh.

"What in blazes happened?" Stanton demanded.

"Sorry, George," the injured man said in a voice thin with pain. "I was wrestlin' around with one of those cowboys and we fell down. I landed wrong and he came down on top of me, and I knew right off that somethin' bad had happened."

Stanton turned to glare toward the bar, where the saloonkeeper had lowered the sawed-off shotgun but hadn't put it away.

"We need a doctor!" Stanton said. "I've got a man bad hurt here."

Butler turned to one of the bartenders and said, "Fetch Doc Abrams."

The bartender hurried from the saloon without removing his apron. Butler left the shotgun on the bar and came around to walk over to the table.

"What happened?" he asked.

"Walt Nichols has a broken leg, that's what happened," Stanton snapped. "And it's all the fault of those troublemaking cowboys."

"I'll admit Rich Coburn started this fight," Butler said, "but your bunch has stirred up plenty of trouble in the past."

Coburn and the other Triangle 7 hands—along with Luke, Mac noted—had withdrawn to the end of the bar closest to the door now that the tables and chairs had been put back in place. They hadn't mopped up, but Butler didn't appear to be interested in pushing that part of it.

Having heard what the saloonkeeper said, Coburn raised his voice and protested, "You can't blame this on us!"

"The devil I can't," Butler said. "Go on and get out of here, Coburn. Take your men with you. I just want you gone."

Coburn's eyes widened. "You're throwin' us out?"

"For now, I sure am. Go on. Get out!"

"Well . . . well, maybe we just won't come back!" Coburn blustered.

"Fine, if that's what you want."

Coburn jerked his head at his companions and said, "Come on, boys. We're not gonna stay where we aren't wanted."

The cowboys stalked out of the saloon, and Mac was glad to see that Luke went with them. He had a pretty good idea that was what Luke was after all along, otherwise he never would have punched his own partner like that.

Now Mac had to carry through on his part of the hastily formed plan.

He was trying to figure out how to go about that when the solution was dropped right in his lap.

"What are we gonna do about chow?" one of the loggers said in a plaintive voice.

Another man said, "Yeah, with his leg busted that bad, Walt's gonna be laid up for a long time."

The injured man groaned. "Don't remind me. You may be out a camp cook, but I'm out of a job!"

"No, you're not," George Stanton declared. "You were hurt defending the honor of the Empire Logging Company. That's got to be worth something, blast it. I'll talk to the boss and see if the company can't keep you on the payroll until you're back on your feet. You might not get your full wages, but it'll be better than nothing."

"Anything you can do, George, I'll sure appreciate it," Nichols said.

Mac said to Stanton, "Wait a minute. Did I hear right? This man's the cook for your outfit?"

Nichols himself answered the question instead by saying, "The best cook this side of the Cascades, if I do say so myself!"

"What's it to you, McKenzie?" Stanton asked.

"It just so happens that I'm a cook, too," Mac said. "I drove a chuck wagon thousands of miles on more trail drives than I can count. I've cooked an ocean of beans, a mountain of steaks, and bushels of biscuits!"

"A chuck wagon!" one of the loggers exclaimed. "That means he's a cowboy!"

Angry glares and muttered curses were directed at Mac, who held up a hand, palm out.

"Now hold on," he said. To Stanton, he went on, "I already told you I worked some with cattle, and it's true. I had to help out with the herds from time to time. But mostly I drove that chuck wagon and fed the crews. And even that was a long time ago. For years, I had my own café over in Wyoming. It would be a real stretch to call me a cowboy."

Stanton frowned at him and asked, "What are you saying? Do you want a job as camp cook, temporary-like, while Walt is recovering from that broken leg?"

Mac shrugged. "I need a job and you need a cook. Seems to me like the stars lined up for both of us."

A logger said, "How do we know this fella can even cook? His food may be awful!"

"It's not, I promise you," Mac said, "but I'll make a deal with you." He looked at Stanton. "I'll come with you back to your camp and cook supper for the whole crew tonight, and then you can have a vote on it. If the boys like my grub, I've got a job. If they don't, I'm plumb out of luck."

A moment of silence followed that suggestion. Then several of the loggers muttered agreement, and one said, "That seems fair."

Stanton was still frowning, but he nodded and said, "All right, McKenzie, you've got a deal."

Walt Nichols said, "I figured on buying supplies while we were in town today. Hadn't gotten around to that yet. If you're gonna feed that bunch, mister, you'll have to lay in some provisions. Nobody puts away food like loggers. You'll be cookin' all day every day just to keep up with them!"

Mac grinned and said, "Sounds good to me."

He just hoped that while he was at it, he'd have a chance to find out if the fugitive he and Luke sought was hiding among the crew. That was why he was doing this, after all.

But he had to admit, he was looking forward to firing up an oven and getting his hands covered with flour again!

CHAPTER 9

Luke retrieved his horse from the livery stable. The owner told him that Endicott's assistant had brought over the Bishop brothers' horses after the bodies were unloaded from them, and now the animals were being kept in a corral behind the stable.

"Hold on to them for now," Luke told the man. "I might keep one of them as a spare mount, but I'll want to sell the others. I'll make sure you get paid out of the proceeds."

Patterson nodded. "Sounds like a deal to me." He nodded toward the street where Coburn and the other cowboys waited. "Are you ridin' for the Triangle 7 now?"

"Looks like I might be. You know anything about the spread?"

"It's the biggest in these parts," the liveryman said. "Ben Harmon was one of the first cattlemen to settle in eastern Oregon. I don't have anything bad to say about the man. That crew of his . . . Well, they're a salty bunch."

Luke chuckled. "I've seen that for myself."

"No offense, mister, but aren't you kind of old to be cowboying?"

"A man does what he knows."

"I suppose. But I thought you were a bounty hunter."

"A man can know how to do more than one thing," Luke pointed out.

"That's true. You want me to see if I can find a buyer for those extra horses?"

"That would be much appreciated. Pick out the one you think is best for me to keep as a spare saddle mount, and if you can find someone to buy the others, I'll split the money with you."

Patterson grinned. "That sounds like an even better deal."

Luke nodded and led his horse out to join Coburn and the others. He swung up in the saddle and fell in with them as they rode out of Pine Knob, heading north on a well-used trail.

The settlement was located near the western edge of a broad basin that ran north and south. The heavily wooded hills and ridges to the west would be where the logging industry was concentrated, Luke thought as he rode along with the other men.

The basin, on the other hand, was cattle country, and anybody who knew much about cows would be able to tell that just by looking at it. Even this late in the season, the pastures through which the trail ran were still lush with grass.

Luke nudged his horse alongside Coburn's and said, "I haven't spent a whole lot of time in this part of the country. How do you get the cattle to market?"

"We drive over the mountains to The Dalles," the foreman replied. "There's a railhead there, and it's not as hard a drive as it sounds like. There's a decent trail. I'm not sayin' it's easy pushing hundreds of head through there, but it can be done. Easier than those big drives from Texas to Kansas, that's for sure."

Mac had been part of many of those drives. He had told Luke plenty of stories about the arduous journeys while they were traveling together, on the trail of some fugitive or another. Luke's life hadn't been easy, that was for sure, but he was glad he hadn't had to eat trail dust for thousands of miles. Mac, driving the chuck wagon, had been out in front of the herds most of the time, and that was much more pleasant.

"How big a crew do you have?" Luke asked, trying to sound idly curious.

Coburn squinted in thought. "I reckon it stands at sixteen men right now. Not counting you, since the boss hasn't officially taken you on yet. But I reckon there's a good chance he will. During roundup time, we sign on more grub line riders, so there's about twice as many men in the bunch then."

"Anybody else new besides me?"

Coburn frowned over at him and asked, "What does that matter?"

"It doesn't," Luke answered easily. "I was just wondering, that's all. Sometimes new men tend to partner up, since they don't know anybody."

"You don't have to worry about bein' a stranger, not after the way you pitched in to help us during that ruckus. You're one of us now, Jensen—assumin' Mr. Harmon goes along with that." Coburn chuckled. "*Tree-climbin' apes*. I still like that. I got a hunch the boss'll be tickled by it, too."

"So I'm the only new man?"

"Yeah, yeah. Hasn't been anybody else signed on in, oh, four or five months."

Luke nodded and didn't say anything else. It had been more than six months since Asa Dunnigan had dropped out of sight; the last report of him that Luke had seen was of a stagecoach robbery in Dakota Territory the previous winter. So the fact that there hadn't been any newcomers on the Triangle 7 in four or five months didn't rule out Dunnigan being one of them.

Right now, however, Luke didn't want to prod Coburn with any more questions. Once he was accepted as one of the crew, he could investigate without being obvious about it, and find out which of the other cowboys were the newest arrivals.

Assuming, of course, as Coburn had said, that the owner

approved of hiring Luke. Coburn didn't seem to think that Ben Harmon would give any trouble about that.

Luke changed the subject by asking, "What started all the trouble with that bunch of loggers, anyway? Just a natural dislike for fellas who clamber around in trees?"

The affable look disappeared from Coburn's face.

"That's something we don't talk about much," he said. "The boss has his reasons, and so do we. But I'll say this much. As far as I'm concerned, the biggest problem is what they're gonna do to this range."

Coburn swept a hand in the air to indicate the beautiful landscape around them and went on, "I've seen other spreads where loggers moved in next door and cleaned off all the hills around. They cut down every tree in sight, blast their hides. And then, when the big rains came, all the dirt washed down and fouled the streams and covered the graze. Just plumb ruined those ranches."

Luke nodded toward the western hills and said, "It doesn't appear that they're clear-cutting those slopes. There are still a lot of trees up there."

"For now, maybe," Coburn replied glumly. "Give 'em time. They'll get around to it." He shook his head. "An old cowboy once told me the saddest thing he ever saw was a bunch of cattle that got caught in a mudslide. None of us want that happening here."

"I can't blame you for that," Luke said.

Coburn was a proddy sort, no doubt about that, and Luke hadn't been sure what to make of him at first.

But listening to the man talk now, Luke felt a bit of an instinctive liking for him. He heard passion in the man's voice, passion for taking care of the land and of the animals in his charge. Luke couldn't help but admire that in a man, even one who'd start a saloon brawl by pouring whiskey over a fella's head.

At the same time, he couldn't help but wonder what motivated Ben Harmon's dislike for the logging company. Coburn made it sound as if the rancher had some other reason in addition to the potential damage to the range. Luke didn't have any idea what that reason might be, and of course it had nothing to do with why he was there, but he was curious anyway.

Maybe he would find out while he was working on the Triangle 7, but if he didn't, he figured he probably wouldn't lose any sleep over it.

After a while, he asked Coburn, "When will we be on Mr. Harmon's range?"

"We've been on it for a while now," Coburn responded with a laugh. "Headquarters is only about a mile away."

A few minutes later, they came in sight of a large frame house surrounded by outbuildings and corrals. The ranch headquarters was at the top of a rise overlooking a creek that twisted through the basin between banks lined with quaking aspen, black cottonwoods, and white alders.

As they came closer, Luke could see that the place was well-kept. The rambling, two-story main house appeared to have a fresh coat of whitewash on it. The big barn was painted red, as was the long bunkhouse. The fence rails on the pole corrals were tight. Evidently, Ben Harmon took a great deal of pride in his spread, and so did the men who rode for it.

Luke couldn't resist pointing out to Coburn, "You know, that ranch house, bunkhouse, and barn wouldn't be there if somebody hadn't cut down some trees and sawed them into lumber."

The foreman's head jerked toward him. An angry frown creased Coburn's forehead.

Then the frown went away and Coburn laughed. He reached over and slapped Luke on the shoulder.

"Well, I don't reckon I can argue with that. That's just a plain fact, now ain't it?" He grew serious. "It might be hard to get along without lumber, now that folks are used to it, but you know what? There are other places to get it besides right next to prime ranching land like this. Why, there are forests in other parts of the country where fellas could cut down trees for a hundred years and never make a dent! Nobody else's livelihood would be ruined by it, either."

Luke wasn't sure Coburn's estimate was exactly correct, but the man did have a point. Still, there had been advances in logging that meant the industry didn't have to be quite as destructive of the landscape. Whether the Empire Logging Company used those practices, Luke didn't know. He would be inclined to give the outfit the benefit of the doubt until he knew better.

Coburn went on, "I know you're just, what do they call it, playin' devil's advocate, Jensen, but I'd advise you not to say too many nice things about those loggers, especially around the boss. You'd be better off if you stuck to callin' 'em tree-climbin' apes."

"I appreciate the wise counsel, Rich, and I'll take it to heart."

A few minutes later, they reached the barn. Two men, both short and wiry and bowlegged, walked out of the cavernous structure to meet them.

"Howdy, Rich," one of them called as he raised a hand in greeting. "Good trip to town?"

"Good enough, I reckon." Coburn grinned. "We got into another fracas with those Elliott polecats."

"Dad-blast it!" the other man exclaimed. He smacked his right fist into his left palm. "Nothin' excitin' ever happens when we go to town."

"You just don't get to town often enough, Kaintuck."

The first man pointed at Luke and said, "Who's the new feller?"

"He pitched in to give us a hand during that scrap," Coburn explained. "Luke, meet Shorty and Kaintuck. They're our wranglers, because they're too old and decrepit to do any real work."

The old-timer called Shorty began sputtering belligerently, but Coburn overrode his outraged protest.

"Boys, this is Luke Jensen. Maybe a new hand, if the boss goes along with it. Where is he?"

"Mr. Harmon?" the one called Kaintuck asked. "He's in the house, I reckon. Said he was gonna be wrestlin' with some paperwork."

Coburn shuddered. Paperwork was the bane of most men who actually worked for a living, Luke knew. He felt the same way.

The foreman swung down from the saddle, and the rest of the men took that as a signal to dismount, as well. They handed their reins to Shorty and Kaintuck.

Luke shook with both of the old-timers before he turned his mount over to them.

"It's good to meet you," he said. "I can tell by looking at you that you'll take good care of my horse."

"Durned tootin' we will," Shorty said.

Kaintuck frowned at Luke and said, "Not meanin' no offense, Jensen, but while you ain't as long in the tooth as Shorty and me, you ain't exactly no spring chicken, neither."

Luke laughed. "I prefer to think of myself as a seasoned veteran of the frontier."

"You'll get some more seasonin' around here, that's for dang sure," Shorty grumbled. "There's always some sort o' ruckus goin' on."

Coburn said, "Leave these two old pelicans to their work, Luke, and come with me to the house. I'll introduce you to the boss and make sure he's all right with you hirin' on."

Luke hoped that would be the case. After the scrap with Mac back in the Lonesome Pine, he'd hate to think all that effort had been for nothing.

CHAPTER 10

George Stanton pointed out the general store to Mac and said, "That's where you'll need to get those supplies we were talking about. The company has an account there. But I suppose we'd better clear this whole thing about you taking over as camp cook with the boss first. I boss the crew, but I don't do the hiring and firing."

"You mean we'll have to go all the way out to your camp bcforc I can pick up the supplies?" Mac asked.

Stanton shook his head. "No, the main office is here in town. We can go over there and hopefully get everything settled right now."

He led the way across the street and up a block to a building that housed several businesses. One of them was the Empire Logging Company, according to a sign painted on the front window. A door with a glass pane in its upper half was next to that window. Stanton opened it and took Mac inside.

The front room had a couple of desks in it, but only one of them was occupied. The man who sat there marking down figures in a ledger wore a brown tweed suit over a white shirt. A string tie was cinched around his stringy neck. His graying brown hair was thinning and parted on the side. A bushy mustache of the same shade hung over his mouth. His eyebrows were equally bushy as he looked out from under them at the newcomers.

"Who's this, George?" he asked as he set down his pencil.

"A new man who's signing on if the boss agrees. Name's Dewey McKenzie. Mac, this is Carl Peters, the company's secretary and bookkeeper."

Peters didn't stand up or offer to shake hands. Instead, he said, "I didn't know we were going to hire any new men."

"I wasn't planning to," Stanton said, "until Walt Nichols went and broke his blasted leg."

Those bushy eyebrows jumped up on Peters's forehead.

"Broke his leg! Good gravy, how did he do that?"

"One of the Triangle 7 punchers fell on it while we were mixed up in a ruckus with them in the Lonesome Pine."

"The Triangle 7 again." Peters made a face, as if the ranch's name tasted bad in his mouth. "What started it this time?"

"Same as always, Rich Coburn being obnoxious and looking for trouble. We didn't have any choice but to fight back."

"Hmph." Peters sounded as if maybe he didn't quite believe Stanton's declaration of innocence, but he let that go and said, "Nichols has a broken leg, is that right?"

"Yeah. Doc Abrams took a look at it in the saloon and then had us carry Walt down to his house. The doc was able to set the leg, but he says Walt is going to be laid up for several weeks and has to stay there at Abrams's house so he can keep an eye on him."

"What a stroke of terrible luck."

"Yeah, but we may have had a stroke of good luck to balance it out," Stanton said. He nodded toward the man standing beside him. "Mac here used to be a chuck-wagon cook, and he owned a café for a while, too. He claims to be a fine cook and is willing to take the job on a temporary basis until Walt gets back on his feet."

"Literally speaking," Mac added with a smile.

Peters didn't seem amused. He grunted and said, "I wonder if we'd be able to hire Pop Channing away from the Blue Top for a short time."

"Pop would never abandon that granddaughter of his," Stanton said.

Mac said, "And to be honest, I'm as good a cook as Pop Channing, if I do say so myself. All I'm asking is a chance to prove that, Mr. Peters."

Peters looked skeptically at him. "Have you ever worked in a logging camp before?"

"No, sir, I can't say as I have."

"Or worked with loggers, period?"

Mac shook his head. "No, but I cooked hundreds of meals for tired, hungry cowboys, and I don't see how that could be any harder than cooking for loggers."

"You don't, eh? You think a man who sits in a saddle all day works as hard and builds up as much of an appetite as a man who swings an axe or bucks a saw or tops a tree does?"

"I wouldn't know," Mac replied honestly, unable to resist adding, "but there's a lot more to working cattle than just sitting on a horse all day. I don't know how it matters which job is tougher. They're both tough, and the men who do them have to eat."

"That's true as far as it goes, I suppose." Peters got to his feet. "It's not up to me to decide whether or not you work for the Empire Logging Company. It's not up to Mr. Stanton, here, either. Only one person can make that decision. Wait here."

He went to a door on the other side of the room, tapped on it, and then opened it without waiting for a response. He went in and closed the door behind him.

Mac looked over at Stanton and said quietly, "I don't think he likes me."

Stanton smiled. "Carl doesn't like much of anybody. But he's good at his job, and at the end of the day, that's all that matters, I suppose."

Mac wasn't sure he agreed with that statement. It seemed to him that how a man lived his life had some bearing on things.

But he didn't figure Stanton was interested in having a philosophical argument, and anyway, the door to what had to be an inner office opened again and Carl Peters reappeared.

"Come on in," he said. "Both of you."

Stanton motioned for Mac to go first. He walked into the office as Peters stepped back and to the side.

He hadn't gone very far into the room when he stopped short, surprised by what awaited him.

There was nothing unusual about the office itself. It was well-furnished, with a large, polished hardwood desk, a couple of leather chairs in front of it, some bookshelves full of dark, heavy, leather-bound volumes, two lamps on brass stands, a table with several maps spread out on it that were unrolled and held open by paperweights at the corners, and a portrait on one wall between bookshelves of a stern-looking man with gray hair and a neatly clipped mustache waxed to a point at each end.

It was the person standing up behind the desk, obviously waiting for Mac, who made him stop and stare.

She wasn't at all what he expected.

The woman was well past the first blush of youth, probably between thirty-five and forty, but her face was unlined for the most part, and Mac didn't see a single gray strand in the sleek, honey-blond hair that curved around her strikingly attractive face. She wore a plain, dark blue dress that was tight enough to reveal the well-curved lines of her figure, yet elegant enough not to be blatant about it. Her eyes, Mac saw, were a rich brown, although it took him a few seconds to get around to noticing that.

He realized he was staring and dropped his gaze for a moment. If his intent regard bothered the woman, she gave no sign of it.

Instead, she held out a slender, well-shaped hand toward the leather chairs in front of the desk and said, "Please, Mr. McKenzie, come in and have a seat. My name is Constance Elliott. I'm the owner of the Empire Logging Company."

"It's a, uh, pleasure to meet you, ma'am," Mac said as he took off his hat and held it with both hands in front of his chest. He stepped forward and took the chair on the right. He balanced the hat on his knee.

Constance Elliott sat down in the big chair behind the desk and clasped her hands together in front of her. She didn't offer to shake hands, and Mac didn't extend his paw, either. Constance Elliott gave off an air of being pleasant without being overly familiar with her employees—including potential employees.

"Carl tells me you have experience as a cook," she said.

"Yes, ma'am. I drove a chuck wagon for several years and also owned and operated my own café over in Wyoming, in a settlement called Hannigan's Hill."

He could tell by her faint smile that she had never heard of Hannigan's Hill, which was not surprising. She said, "Those chuck wagons you drove, were they on cattle drives from Texas to Kansas on what they're calling the Chisholm Trail?"

The fact that she knew about the Chisholm Trail surprised him a little. He wouldn't have thought the subject of cattle drives came up that often in the timber business.

"Most of them were," he said, "but some of the outfits I was with drove over to New Mexico and all the way up to Montana. I reckon you could say I've been around quite a bit."

Her voice had a keen edge as she asked, "Are you wanted by the law?"

Mac shook his head. "No, ma'am, I'm not."

"If I go over to Marshal Sundell's office and ask him to look through the wanted posters he has on file . . . ?"

"You won't find me," Mac said with a smile. He grew more solemn as he went on, "But I'll be honest with you, Mrs. Elliott. I suppose there's a slim chance the marshal might have paper on me, if he's been around for a long time and saves everything that comes in. You see, more than ten years ago, there were charges levied against me, but they were false ones and they've all been cleared up. I give you my word I'm not wanted by the law anywhere."

Constance Elliott leaned back in her chair and regarded him with interest.

"You could have maintained the lie, or rather, the lie of omission, I should say. Instead, you chose to put all your cards on the table."

Mac's shoulders rose and fell slightly. "You could have been bluffing about checking with the marshal. But you don't really strike me as the bluffing sort, ma'am, if you don't mind me speaking plainly."

"I not only don't mind, I insist upon it, Mr. McKenzie. And by the way, it's *Miss* Elliott, not Mrs. I'm not married and never have been."

"Begging your pardon, ma'am." Mac nodded toward the portrait on the wall. "I thought that might have been your late husband."

"That man was my father, Charles Davenport Elliott. You might have heard of him?"

Mac shook his head and said, "I'm afraid not."

"He was a rich man before he founded the Empire Logging Company, which made him even richer. But no man can ever be wealthy enough to command his own heart to start working again once it decides to stop."

"I'm sorry, ma'am."

She made a slight motion with one hand. "My father passed away a number of years ago. I remember him fondly, but the best thing I can do to honor his memory is to run this company successfully, as he would have run it."

It seemed to Mac that this conversation was a little personal for a potential employer looking to hire a temporary cook. But he certainly didn't mind talking to a woman as attractive as

Constance Elliott, so he just sat there and waited to see what she was going to say next.

She appeared to reach a decision. Clasping her hands again, she said, "Very well. You impress me as a trustworthy man. Whether you actually have the cooking skills to do this job is something that can't be determined until we've seen what you can do. Or tasted it, I should say."

She looked up at Peters, who was standing near the door with George Stanton, and went on, "Put Mr. McKenzie on the payroll, Carl. George, do you need supplies out at the camp?"

"Yes, ma'am, we do. That's why we came into town today. Well, that and I was rewarding some of the boys for excellent work lately."

She smiled. "I like to hear that. The crew always works better if they know they'll see some tangible benefits from their effort. Take Mr. McKenzie over to the store, and the two of you can figure out what he'll need."

"Yes'm, we sure will."

Constance Elliott looked at Mac again and said, "We haven't discussed wages."

"I'll work for free—today. And if the fellas like what I do, I'll work for whatever you were paying Walt Nichols."

Peters snapped, "Don't be presumptuous, young man. Miss Elliott will pay you what she sees fit."

"No, that's a fair enough proposal," Constance said. "But if the men don't like your cooking, you won't get a penny, Mr. McKenzie."

"I'll take that chance," Mac said.

"You're also risking having to walk back into town, because no one will take the time to bring you back in the wagon."

Mac's horse would need several days of rest to recover from its injury, the man at the livery stable had said. He needed to let the animal stay there for the time being, so he couldn't count on being able to use it any time soon.

Despite that, Mac nodded and said, "That's fine, too. A man never gets anywhere without running a risk now and then."

"That's true. And the same thing applies to a woman." Constance rose to her feet, prompting Mac to stand as well. This time she reached across the desk as she said, "Welcome to the Empire Logging Company, Mr. McKenzie—for now."

Mac clasped her hand, found her grip to be cool and strong, just as he expected it to be.

"Thank you, ma'am. I'll do my best not to let you and your men down."

"If you do, I'm sure they'll let you know about it."

Mac let go of her hand and said, "I don't figure they'll be any worse about hoorawing a fella than those cowboys I used to cook for."

Constance smiled and said, "I think you'll find, Mr. McKenzie, that loggers are an entirely different breed!"

CHAPTER 11

As Luke and Rich Coburn approached the ranch house, Luke saw just how well taken care of the place really was. The porch was swept clear of dust, and the glass in the windows was spotless. The front door, which was carved in elaborate patterns, gleamed from polishing.

Somebody went to a lot of effort to keep this ranch house looking good. That was something you didn't see on every spread. Most ranch houses were relatively clean and orderly, but some of them were downright pigsties, especially the ones with bachelor owners.

Of course Ben Harmon might not be a bachelor, Luke reminded himself. As far as he could recall, nobody had said anything one way or the other about the cattleman's marital status. There could be a Mrs. Harmon who was responsible for keeping the place so spick-and-span.

Or maybe not. As Luke and Coburn stepped up onto the porch, Luke spotted a figure on the other side of the glass in one of the windows, rubbing determinedly at the pane with a cloth as if trying to get some specks off it. The glass looked clean to

Luke, but obviously he wasn't seeing what the fellow in the house saw.

The man spotted Luke and Coburn and broke off what he was doing to hurry over and open the front door. He didn't bother with a polite greeting.

"Who's this?" he demanded with a suspicious frown directed at Luke as he planted himself in the entrance.

"A new rider, if the boss is agreeable to that," Coburn replied. "Luke, this is Alamo Paige. Alamo, meet Luke Jensen."

Luke nodded to the stocky, gray-haired man who, like Shorty and Kaintuck, appeared to be a former cowboy past his prime. He wore high-topped moccasin boots, fringed buckskin trousers, and a faded blue work shirt with a canvas apron over it.

"From Texas, are you?" Luke asked.

"Nope, not a bit," Alamo answered. "Born and raised in Arkansas. But my older brother went down there and fought ol' Santa Anna." His head jerked in a nod. "Died there, too."

"Sorry," Luke said.

"That was more than forty years ago. You want to see the boss, I reckon?"

"That's right," Coburn said.

Alamo jerked a thumb over his shoulder. "You know where the office is. I got things to do."

He turned and walked down a hallway toward the rear of the house, moving with the easy grace of a born horseman.

Quietly, Coburn said to Luke, "Don't let the apron fool you, or the fact that he's on the small side, neither. Alamo is one of the toughest hombres you'll ever meet. He rode for the Pony Express when he was a young man, and then, later on, he scouted for the army with Buffalo Billy Bates."

"I've heard of Bates," Luke said. "He's not as famous as Bill Cody, but he had quite a career as a scout."

"Alamo claims to be retired from all that adventuring and skalleyhootin' around, but I figure his fiddle-footed nature will get the best of him one of these days. In the meantime, he sort of runs things around headquarters for Mr. Harmon."

Coburn gestured for Luke to come with him along a hall that led to the right. They came to a door on which the foreman knocked. A deep, powerful voice answered from the other side, "What is it?"

Coburn opened the door and said, "It's me, Boss. You got a minute?"

"Sure, come on in, Rich. Whatever it is, it'll give me an excuse to get away from these dang numbers. After a while, they start swimmin' around on the page like they got minds of their own!"

Coburn swung the door wider, revealing a small, plainly furnished office. The best thing about it was a window that looked out onto the ranch yard and down the rise to the tree-lined creek and the beautiful basin beyond.

The man at the desk couldn't see that view unless he turned around, however, since his back was to the window. He had a ledger open in front of him with several stacks of papers surrounding it. He threw down the pencil he was holding, put his hands on the desk, and stood up.

He was the same height as Luke, broad-shouldered and impressive physically, although he was getting a little thick through the middle, more than likely a result of spending more time at this desk than he did on horseback.

However, he was dressed to ride the range in jeans and a work shirt, and the way his rugged face was weathered and tanned to the shade of old saddle leather spoke eloquently of all the time he had spent out in the elements. He was clean-shaven, and his dark hair was only lightly touched with silver. When he had spoken, Luke had heard the remnants of a Texas twang in his voice.

Ben Harmon was the genuine article, and any man who'd spent much time on the frontier would recognize that right away.

And like any such man, he was totally lacking in pretension. When he saw a stranger, he introduced himself without any hesitation, extending a rope-callused hand as he reached across the desk and said, "Ben Harmon."

"Luke Jensen," Luke replied as he returned the firm grip.

"What brings you to the Triangle 7, Mr. Jensen?"

"I thought you might have a riding job where I could settle in for a while."

Coburn said, "That's not the whole story, Ben. You know some of the boys and I went to town today."

Wind and weather had given Harmon's eyes a permanent squint, but they narrowed even more where they rested in deeply lined pits of gristle.

"Yeah, I know. I don't work you boys hard enough. You got too much time on your hands."

Coburn cleared his throat. "Well, we, uh, stopped in at the Lonesome Pine for a drink, and as it happens—"

"As it happens, my hind foot," Harmon said. "You were on the prod, and you went there lookin' for trouble with that Empire bunch, am I right?"

"Not necessarily," Coburn said, "but yeah, Stanton and half a dozen of his men were there, and things got a mite heated—"

Harmon sighed. "How much do I owe Oren Butler for the damages? You know I'll take it outta your wages."

"A couple of chairs got busted, but the amount sort of got lost in the shuffle. But that's all, Boss."

"I'll stop in there next time I'm in town and square things up with Oren for your half. I reckon Empire will pay half, too, even though Carl Peters throws around pennies like they weigh as much as one o' those blasted trees they cut down. His boss is too proud not to cover Empire's share o' the damages, though."

Harmon stepped out from behind the desk and went on, "None o' this tells me one danged thing about Mr. Jensen's part in the whole shebang, though."

"Well, Luke here, he was in the saloon when the trouble broke out, and he waded in and gave us a hand during the fracas. Never even hesitated before he started throwin' punches." Coburn grinned. "He even called those loggers tree-climbin' apes!"

Harmon frowned at Luke for a second and then burst out in a laugh.

"That's a pretty good description of that bunch," he said. "And I'm obliged to you for helpin' my men, Mr. Jensen."

"Make it Luke."

"And I'm Ben. We're not much for standin' on formality on the Triangle 7. By grab, I'm gonna shake your hand again, Luke."

The two men shook, and Harmon continued, "You say you're lookin' for a riding job?"

"I'll lay my cards on the table, Mr. Harmon—Ben. I have to stay around these parts for a while anyway, because I'm waiting to collect some reward money and Marshal Sundell had to write off to the state capital for it."

Harmon's jovial attitude disappeared. "Reward money," he repeated.

"Yes, sir. I brought in the Bishop brothers, some outlaws who were wanted."

"I know who the Bishop brothers are."

"Who they *were*, Ben," Coburn said. "All four of them were dead when Luke brought them into Pine Knob."

"Bounty hunter," Harmon said flatly. "And you killed the Bishops."

"They didn't give me any choice in the matter." Luke's voice hardened and went flat, too. "And every one of them was shot in the front, while they had guns in their hands, if you were wondering about that."

"Well, that makes things a little better, I suppose."

"I make no secret of the fact that I've brought in some wanted men from time to time and collected the rewards on them, but that's a hard life. I'd just as soon work cattle. And before you bring it up, I know I'm not a young man anymore. I can hold my own on any job that needs doing, though, and that's no brag."

"If it is, it won't take Rich long to find that out. He's my foreman, as you probably know, and he's a good one."

"Yes, sir. We talked quite a bit on the way out here, mostly about the trouble you've been having with those loggers."

He wanted to get Harmon talking about that subject in the hope of asking some careful questions about any new men who might be working for Empire. Harmon might not know anything about that, but it wouldn't hurt to find out, Luke hoped.

Instead, the cattleman shook his head curtly from side to side and stepped behind the desk again.

"I don't mind Rich chewin' the fat about such things, but you let me worry about the Empire Logging Company. That trouble with them doesn't have anything to do with what happens on this ranch."

"You know that's not strictly true, Boss," Coburn disagreed. "They may not have done anything to damage our range so far, but it's only a matter of time. They're already movin' closer and closer on those ridges above the basin. We ought to ride up there and—"

"I said let it go." Harmon's tone was sharp enough not to allow any argument. "Scrappin' with 'em in town is bad enough. I don't want Abner Sundell sayin' Pine Knob is closed to us. You stay away from their operation up there on the slopes, and make sure the rest of the crew knows that, too." He scowled. "This isn't the first time I've given these orders, Rich. I don't intend to have to give 'em again."

"Yes, sir," Coburn responded. His voice held an undertone of surly resentment, but Harmon appeared willing to overlook that, at least for the time being.

The cattleman looked at Luke. "You understand what I'm sayin', Jensen? Those lumberjacks are nothin' but tree-climbin' apes to me, too, but I don't want any of my men confronting them up there on the range they've leased."

"Sure, I understand," Luke said. "The men who ride for Triangle 7 mind their own business."

Harmon's head bobbed emphatically. "Darned right they do." His attitude eased slightly as he went on, "You're hired on a provisional basis, Luke. It'll be up to Rich to put you to work and see if you can do the job. No matter what he decides, you'll be paid for the time you put in."

"Fair enough," Luke said. "And I appreciate the opportunity."

Harmon relaxed enough to chuckle. "You might not be thankin' me once you've worked for Rich for a week. He pushes the crew hard, from can to can't."

"That's what I'm used to."

"Forty a month and found if we keep you on. Regular cowhand pay."

"Sounds good."

"You'll earn it," Harmon said as he sat down behind the desk again. He pulled the open ledger toward him and picked up the pencil again. This meeting was over.

Coburn leaned his head toward the door. Luke left the office first, with the foreman following him.

Alamo Paige was waiting in the corridor. "Get the job?" he asked Luke.

"On a provisional basis," Luke replied, using the same phrase Ben Harmon had.

"Meanin' the boss is gonna give you enough rope to see if you hang yourself."

"I'm not sure the situation is quite *that* dire."

"We'll see."

As they left the ranch house, Luke commented to Coburn, "I think Alamo wants me to fail."

"No, it ain't that. Alamo's a good hombre. He's just a mite hardheaded. Has to see a thing with his own eyes before he'll believe it."

"That's not a bad way to be." Luke decided to come right out with the question that had been nagging at him ever since before they left Pine Knob. "What's the real reason Ben doesn't like the Empire outfit? I get the feeling there's more to it than just being worried about the damage that logging up in the hills might be responsible for in the basin."

For a long moment, Coburn didn't answer. They continued walking toward the building Luke took to be the bunkhouse. The horses and the other cowboys were nowhere in sight now.

Finally, Coburn said, "You're right, Luke. There is more to it. I ain't sure it's any of your business."

"It's not my business at all," Luke agreed. "A man can't help but be curious about what's going on around him, though, when he takes a new job."

"That's true. Ben's got a grudge against Empire because of who runs the company."

"That fella Carl Peters he mentioned?"

Coburn shook his head. "Peters just keeps the books. The boss of the Empire Loggin' Company is Constance Elliott—and she left poor Ben at the altar."

CHAPTER 12

Mac and George Stanton left the Empire Logging Company after a brief stop in the front office, where Carl Peters wrote Mac's name in a book, adding it to a long list of other employees.

Mac tried to get a look at that list before Peters closed the book and put it back in the desk drawer where he had gotten it. That meant reading upside down, but Mac was fairly good at that.

However, none of the names he was able to make out meant anything to him. Anyway, if Asa Dunnigan actually was working for Empire, it wasn't very likely that he'd be using his real name.

From there, they walked to the general store, which was run by a man named Throckmorton. Stanton introduced Mac to the storekeeper, a portly, balding man who put his clerks to work gathering the order written on a piece of paper Stanton took from his pocket.

"Walt Nichols wrote down that list of things we need out at the camp before we came into town," Stanton explained, his words addressed to both Mac and Throckmorton.

"I heard about what happened to poor Walt in that brawl at the Lonesome Pine," Throckmorton said with a nod. "I hope he heals up quickly."

The man turned his attention to Mac and went on, "So you're taking over as the camp cook, eh?"

"Just temporarily," Mac said, "until Mr. Nichols gets back on his feet."

"You have some big shoes to fill. Walt is a good cook, from what I hear. I've never actually tried any of his food."

"Could I see that list?" Mac asked as he held out his hand.

Throckmorton passed it over. "Sure. You want to add some things to it?"

"I might." Mac looked over the list. "If you've got some cans of dried apples, I make a mighty good apple cobbler."

"I reckon we can do that."

Mac named some spices that weren't on the list—cinnamon, nutmeg, cayenne pepper, paprika, oregano, garlic, and cumin—causing Stanton to direct a skeptical frown toward him.

"We don't go in for anything fancy out at the camp," the logging foreman said. "Mostly just plain meat and potatoes, and beans and biscuits. I think regular salt and pepper are the only spices Walt ever uses."

Mac smiled. "Sounds like cooking for a bunch of cowhands, in spite of what Miss Elliott said about them being different. The outfits I worked for always seemed to like it when I changed things up a mite, though. You'd be surprised how much you can liven up the taste of things with just a few extra ingredients."

Stanton said, "If you want to wait here, Mac, I'll go fetch the wagon so Mr. Throckmorton's clerks can load up the order. I'd better round up the rest of the boys, too. They were going down to the Blue Top to have some pie—and to make calf eyes at Violet Channing, if I know them."

"Miss Channing's worth taking a good look at, that's for sure," Mac said. "Sure, I'll be here when you get back, Mr. Stanton."

"Make it George."

"Happy to, George."

When Stanton was gone, Mac made conversation with Throckmorton, who stood behind the counter in the back of the store and seemed more than willing to talk.

"Sounds like that was a pretty big ruckus over at the Lonesome Pine," the garrulous storekeeper said.

"From what I've heard, those two bunches go after each other pretty regular-like."

Throckmorton rolled his eyes.

"That's putting it mildly. Abner Sundell keeps threatening to lock up all of them on both sides if they can't behave themselves, but so far he hasn't done that. Abner likes to get along with folks, and I know he considers Ben Harmon a friend. He's a mighty fair man, too, and won't take sides even though he's known Ben a lot longer."

"He sounds like a good lawman."

"Oh, he is, no doubt about that." Throckmorton studied Mac for a moment, then said, "No offense, but you know, you look more like a cowboy than a lumberjack, Mr. McKenzie."

Mac grinned. "Just make it Mac. And you're not the first one to point that out. There's a good reason for it. I'm no lumberjack, that's for sure. I wouldn't have any idea how to cut down a tree, or what to do with it if I did. I'm just going out to the camp to cook. I figure one bunch of hungry hombres is pretty much the same as the next bunch, no matter what they do for a living."

"How'd you come to throw in with Empire?"

"They needed somebody else on their side to even up the odds during that ruckus in the saloon. A fight needs to be fair, as far as I'm concerned."

"That's a good way to look at it," Throckmorton said. "Empire and Triangle 7 are pretty evenly matched, overall."

"Do a lot of fellas come and go from those crews? Always some new men among them?"

Throckmorton rubbed his chin, frowned in thought, and said, "Well, not really. Not so's you'd notice, anyway. A new man comes along and signs on now and then, like you. You're the first one in several months, though."

"Nobody else new at Empire's camp?"

If Throckmorton found that to be an odd question, he didn't give any sign of it. Instead, he said, "No, not for a few months, like I just told you."

A few months was still in the time in which Asa Dunnigan had dropped out of sight.

"The two factions sure don't like each other much," Mac commented. "Not surprising, since cowboys and loggers usually don't get along very well."

"Maybe not, but it's more than natural hostility with Empire and Triangle 7. They have good reason to hate each other."

"Oh? Why's that?"

"I've heard it said that there's a thin line between love and hate. Constance Elliott and Ben Harmon have crossed that line, that's for sure."

"Harmon owns the Triangle 7, isn't that right?"

Throckmorton nodded. "That's right. And there was a time when it sure looked like him and Constance Elliott were gonna get hitched."

Mac's eyebrows rose. He hadn't heard anything about that. But it tied in with the veiled references he'd heard about the mysterious origins of the trouble between the cattle ranch and the logging company.

"They were engaged to be married?"

"Yep. The date was set for the wedding and everything. It was going to be a big deal. The ceremony was going to take place in the church up the street, and then they were planning to have a big dance and reception at the schoolhouse. Some of the men had cleaned the place up and pushed all the desks and tables to the back of the room so there'd be plenty of space to dance."

Throckmorton shook his head with a gloomy expression on his face as he continued, "And then the whole thing fell apart. Ben

Harmon stormed out of the church while Constance Elliott yelled after him not to come back. Ben told her he sure as blazes wouldn't."

"What in the world happened?" Mac asked.

"Nobody knows. Both of those two are too dang proud to go airing their dirty laundry in public. But whatever it was that set 'em off, it was like touching a match to a fuse attached to a bundle of dynamite."

"How's that?"

"Well, all the loggers from Empire were sitting on one side of the church, and Ben's whole crew from the Triangle 7 were on the other side. When Ben stomped out and Constance followed him, yelling at him, naturally all those boys took up for their own boss and started saying things across the aisle."

Throckmorton managed to look both appalled and amused at the same time as he went on, "Before you know it, there was a puredee battle royal right there in the church. Both sides went at it hammer and tongs, and the townspeople who had come for the wedding had to scramble to get out of there before they got in the way of all those flying fists. The innocent bystanders headed for the doors, and devil take the hindmost!"

"You sound like you were there," Mac said.

"Oh, I was. Some of the town's leading citizens, including me and Pastor Shotwell, we yelled and hollered at those boys, trying to get them to stop, but of course they were all caught up in the heat of battle and didn't pay no never-mind to us. Eventually, the fight spilled over outside, and from there it didn't take long to spread out, and the church was spared any real damage, thank goodness. There were a lot of bruised and bloody loggers and cowhands by the time it all petered out, but nobody was killed or even hurt too bad. Ben and Constance paid for the damages, even though they didn't amount to much that time."

"From the sound of it, they might go broke from paying for the damages their crews do."

Throckmorton threw back his head and laughed. "Not much danger of that, but I'm sure it's starting to seem like that to the two of them! I don't expect things to get better any time soon, either. Like I said, there's that thin line, and Ben and Constance have sure enough crossed over it."

That was interesting background, Mac thought, but it didn't bring him any closer to locating Asa Dunnigan. That was really the only reason he had wrangled his way into the job as camp cook.

"What do you think about the crew out at the Empire camp?" he asked. "Do any of them strike you as bad hombres that I ought to watch out for?"

"Well, loggers are pretty tough to start with, you know," Throckmorton said. "They work hard, every day, and when they come to town, they like to blow off steam. They've got plenty of it to blow off, too." The storekeeper shook his head. "But I wouldn't say any of the ones I've run into strike me as bad hombres, as you put it. I haven't met all the men who work for Constance, though."

"What about the cowboys who ride for the Triangle 7?"

Throckmorton frowned and looked confused. "You're asking me if any of them are troublemakers? Well, Rich Coburn, the foreman, can be proddy at times. Most of the fights that have broken out were started by Coburn picking at some of the loggers."

"How long has Coburn been working for the spread?"

"You're just full of questions, aren't you?"

"I like to know what I'm getting myself into," Mac said, hoping that answer sounded reasonable enough to keep Throckmorton from getting too suspicious.

"I don't suppose I can blame you for feeling that way. Rich has worked for Ben Harmon for, oh, four or five years now. He's had the foreman's job for the past couple of years."

That let Rich Coburn out as possibly being the fugitive Dunnigan.

Mac asked another question. "Do you think the trouble between the two outfits will ever come down to shooting?"

"I sure hope not," Throckmorton replied with what sounded

to Mac like fervent sincerity. "I like Ben and Connie both, and I'd hate to see a real war break out between them. That wouldn't be good for anybody around here. And speaking as a businessman, I'm happy to sell supplies to both crews. I wouldn't want anything interfering with that."

"The town pretty much stays neutral, eh?" Mac asked, recalling that Violet Channing hadn't expressed any leaning one way or the other when she told him about the friction between cowhands and loggers.

"That's right. I know I speak for myself, Oren Butler, and all the other businessmen in Pine Knob when I say that I wish they'd just keep their trouble out of town."

A heavy footstep from the open doorway at the front of the store made both Mac and Throckmorton turn their attention that way. George Stanton came in and walked toward them.

"The wagon's parked outside," he said.

Throckmorton waved a hand at the crates and bags stacked up at the end of the counter and said, "Your order is ready, too." He called to one of the apron-wearing clerks. "Alvin, you and Teddy get these supplies loaded in Mr. Stanton's wagon."

The two young men got started on that while Throckmorton entered an amount in an account book and then had Stanton sign it.

"Mac can sign for the goods next time if I'm not along," Stanton told him. "Assuming he gets the job."

"Oh, I'll get the job," Mac said with a smile, knowing that he sounded a little cocky. He preferred to think of it as being confident, though.

"I hope you're right." Stanton chuckled. "If the boys don't like your cooking, they're liable to kick your tail all the way back here to Pine Knob." He grinned as he clapped a hand on Mac's shoulder. "But don't worry. I'm sure you'll do fine."

Chapter 13

Luke looked at Rich Coburn in surprise.

"You mean a woman runs Empire?" he asked.

"Yep," the foreman replied. "Her father started the company, but he died a while back and she took over the whole shootin' match."

"It would take an unusual woman to run a company like that," Luke mused.

He thought about his brother Smoke's wife, Sally. His sister-in-law was probably the most capable woman he had ever met, not to mention the most strong-willed. Sally Jensen would be able to take over a company and continue operating it if she had to. She was probably the only female he knew of who could accomplish that, however.

"Oh, Miss Constance is unusual, all right," Coburn said. "She has plenty of backbone, and she's good-lookin', to boot. You don't want to ever get on her bad side, though. The boss found that out the hard way."

"He was engaged to be married to her, you said?"

"Yep. They made it all the way to the church and were even

standin' up in front of the preacher, but they never made it to the *I dos*. They said some things to each other that nobody else could hear, and then Miss Constance stomped off, mad as a wet hen. Ben stomped right past her, his face as dark as a thunderstorm comin' over the mountains. They fussed some at each other as he walked out of the church, and then she stood there yellin' after him. She even shook her fist at him a time or two."

"You were there to see that?"

"Sure. The whole crew went into town that day. If any wide-loopers had wanted to clean out our herds, there wouldn't have been anybody here to stop 'em. All those loggers had the day off, too, and they were there."

Luke cocked an eyebrow. "Sounds like the inside of that church was primed to explode like a keg of blasting powder."

Coburn laughed and said, "You're sure right about that. And it went off, too! The whole thing blew up."

"Not literally, I hope."

"Huh? Oh, you mean was there a real explosion? Well, no, but there was a big fight. We weren't gonna stand for Ben bein' treated like that."

"But you don't know what caused the disagreement between them," Luke pointed out. "You said so yourself. You said nobody could hear the conversation between them."

"Yeah, but it had to be her fault," Coburn insisted. "The boss never would have said or done anything to hurt her. He figured the sun rose and set on that lady. And she's the one who started to walk off first. That's proof, right there."

Not necessarily, Luke thought, but he could tell it wouldn't do any good to say that to Coburn. Instead, he asked, "When the fight between Triangle 7 and the loggers started, who threw the first punch?"

"Well . . ."

Luke chuckled. "I thought so."

"What would you expect me to do? Like I said, we couldn't

just stand by and let that sort of behavior pass. Besides, those loggers were just askin' for it."

Luke didn't argue. He knew he would never convince Coburn of the rightness of the cowboys' cause. They reached the bunkhouse and went in. Luke had already met the members of the crew that had been in Pine Knob; now Coburn introduced him to the others, and told Luke to claim one of several empty bunks.

Trying not to be too obvious about it, Luke took a good look at the men as he shook hands with them. Only two of them came anywhere close to matching Asa Dunnigan's description when it came to height, hair color, and age. He made a mental note to talk to them later, and try to elicit more information about them, especially how long they had been riding for the Triangle 7.

However, his gut told him that neither man was actually the fugitive he sought. He had a hunch that going to work for the ranch wasn't going to pay off.

But it was something to do while he waited for the reward money to arrive, and despite Ben Harmon's order for his men to avoid the hills to the west, where the Empire Logging Company was operating, that was exactly where Luke intended to do some scouting. He needed to figure out a way he and Mac could get word to each other as Mac searched among the loggers for Dunnigan.

Of course, before Mac could do that, he'd have to establish himself as the camp cook. Once he'd done that, he could carry out his investigation without arousing suspicion.

The wagon was crowded as it rolled west out of Pine Knob toward the Empire camp several miles away. The supplies from Throckmorton's store took up enough room in the back that two men had to ride on the lowered tailgate while the others perched on the sideboards around the pile of crates, boxes, and burlap bags.

George Stanton handled the reins hitched to the team of four mules. Mac rode beside him on the driver's seat, a privilege that drew a few resentful glances from the other men.

They would decide he'd earned that privilege once they had eaten some of the meals he prepared. He was already thinking about the stew he was going to cook for the evening meal, along with some corn bread.

The apple cobbler would have to wait until the next day; he didn't think there would be time for it today.

The trees grew thicker on both sides of the trail as it wound into the hills. Pines crowded close to one another and soared toward the blue sky overhead. The fragrance they gave off filled Mac's nostrils. It was a clean, fresh scent that made a man feel like maybe the world wasn't such a bad place after all.

Then the memory of some of the humans who walked the world tempered those good feelings. Betrayal and greed had made Mac's life pure misery for several years. He tried not to dwell on those bad times, but he didn't figure the memories would ever go away completely.

For now, he pushed them aside and chatted with Stanton to pass the time. The boss of the logging crew was interested in Mac's experiences driving a chuck wagon. Mac spun some yarns about his adventures, trying not to exaggerate *too* much.

"Why do you want to know about those trail drives?" Mac asked after a while. "I thought you loggers didn't like cowboys."

Stanton glanced over his shoulder at the other men and lowered his voice as he said, "Don't tell anybody, but there was a time when I wanted to throw a saddle on a horse and head up the trail myself."

"Really?"

Stanton nodded. "Yep. I was a youngster down in East Texas at the time when those cattle drives were just getting started good after the war. I thought the idea of getting out of the woods and riding through the wide-open spaces sounded mighty fine. Those piney woods down yonder can be sort of dark and gloomy, you know."

"I know," Mac said. "I'm from Louisiana, and I've spent some time over in East Texas. I can understand why you'd feel that way."

"But growing up surrounded by pines, I learned about cutting them down and hauling them to the sawmills and cutting them up into lumber. My pa and all my brothers worked at that." Stanton shrugged. "It was sort of taken for granted that I would, too, when I got big enough. And so I did. Been at it ever since."

Mac eyed the other man speculatively and said, "I reckon you might have made a good cowboy."

"Hush your mouth! I don't want these other boys knowin' anything about that."

Mac smiled and said, "Sure." After a moment's pause, he changed the subject and went on, "I never would have figured that a woman would wind up running a logging company."

"I wouldn't get in the habit of saying things like that, either. Miss Constance wouldn't take kindly to it. She's not the sort who believes there's anything she can't do." Stanton chuckled. "If we'd let her, she'd be out at the camp in work boots and a flannel shirt, leaning on a cross-cut saw."

"What do you mean, if you'd let her? She owns the company, doesn't she? Isn't she the boss?"

"Yeah, she owns Empire," Stanton replied, "but she knows the boys wouldn't like it if she bulled her way in on their territory. She visits the camp pretty often, just to make sure everybody remembers who's really in charge, but she doesn't try to intrude on the way I run things, or how the fellas do their jobs."

Mac nodded slowly and said, "Sounds like a smart woman."

"She is, and you'd be wisely served not to forget it."

After a few minutes of silence, Mac said, "That fella Throckmorton told me about how Miss Elliott and Ben Harmon at the Triangle 7 almost got hitched."

A frown corrugated Stanton's forehead. "Henry Throckmorton likes to flap his jaws a mite too much. What's past is past, and there's no point in thinking about it all the time."

Given Mac's own checkered history, he agreed with that

sentiment. He was too curious to let the subject go entirely, though.

"I can see how something like that would cause some bad blood and leave behind a whole heap of hurt feelings."

Stanton blew out a disgusted-sounding breath. "If you ask me, the boss was lucky things blew up when they did. She didn't need to get herself tied up with somebody like Harmon. He'd have just held her back. Now she can go on and build Empire into the biggest and best logging outfit in this part of the country, just like her pa set out to do. He'd be proud of her."

"I'm sure he would," Mac said.

He wondered, too, if maybe Stanton was glad Constance Elliott hadn't married Ben Harmon because his feelings for the lady weren't strictly those of an employee for a good boss.

Mac could understand if that were the case. Meeting Constance Elliott had stirred some unexpected feelings inside him, too.

He wasn't going to think about that as long as he had a job to do. A short time later, the wagon trail started up a long slope. The mules had to lean hard into their harness to make the pull as George Stanton cracked a whip over their heads and shouted encouragement—and curses—at them.

The team carried on valiantly until the wagon reached the top and rolled onto a large, open shelf that backed up to an even steeper ridge.

The area was open, Mac realized, because most of the trees that had once covered it had been cut down. A few stumps still stood here and there.

"You had to clear this off before you could build the camp, didn't you?" Mac asked Stanton.

"That's right. This is the best piece of level ground around here." Stanton pointed to the north. "And about half a mile that way is a natural flume where a creek comes down out of that notch you can see up in the hills."

"That's how you get the logs down," Mac guessed.

"Yep. Down below, the creek runs into an even bigger stream. We have a depot of sorts there, where men lash the logs together and then float them all the way to the sawmill just outside of Pine Knob."

"I didn't see a sawmill when I was there."

"It's on the other side of the settlement from where you were," Stanton explained. "You would have heard it, except it wasn't working today while the crew there does some repairs on it. From there, the rough lumber is transported over the mountains to a finishing mill at The Dalles, where it's loaded on train cars and shipped to the coast."

"That sounds like quite an operation."

"It is," Stanton agreed. "Lots of people have to do their jobs correctly in order for it to work. But it starts right here, with these fellas and the trees they cut down and trim."

After hearing this place referred to as a camp, Mac had expected a scattering of tents, maybe a crude shack or two.

Instead, as he looked around he saw a much more impressive layout, dominated by a large, log building with a wood-shingled roof. It was big enough to contain half a dozen rooms, he estimated.

In addition, there were several smaller log cabins, a shed and corral for the mules, a small, square, windowless structure that was probably a smokehouse, and a couple of storage buildings.

These were men who had spent their lives working with trees he reminded himself. It wasn't surprising that they knew how to erect sturdy log buildings.

"This is a nice place," he commented.

"There's an actual kitchen inside the main house," Stanton said. "Probably a little better than what you were used to working with on those chuck wagons."

"Don't underestimate what a skilled man can do with a campfire and a Dutch oven," Mac said with a smile. "But it does look like you live better than I expected."

Three men came out of the largest building. Each lifted a hand in greeting as Stanton brought the wagon to a halt in front of the steps that led to a covered porch.

Mac heard a faint sound coming from the ridge that rose above the camp. It took him a moment to figure out what it was.

Axes biting deep into wood as other members of the crew worked on felling trees. A couple of hours of daylight were still left, and the men who worked for Empire would put that time to good use, obviously.

Stanton wrapped the reins around the brake lever and jumped to the ground next to the wagon. The men who had come out of the main house ambled over. They studied Mac with keen interest, especially one man with a lean frame, a bald head, a hawk nose, and a dark mustache that curved down on both sides of his mouth.

"I don't see Walt," this man said to Stanton. "And who's this fella?"

"Walt's replacement," Stanton said. "Meet Dewey McKenzie. Goes by Mac."

Resting a hand on the side of the driver's box, Mac vaulted to the ground, too, and gave the bald man a friendly nod.

"Mac, this is Alec Lafferty," Stanton went on.

Mac extended his hand. "Good to meet you, Alec."

Lafferty shook with him but looked wary. "Why are you our new cook?" he asked.

Stanton answered the question for Mac. "Because Walt went and got his leg broken during a ruckus in the Lonesome Pine with the Triangle 7 bunch."

"Those blasted, troublemakin' cow nurses!" one of the other men exclaimed. "I hope you broke a few of their arms and legs."

"We did our best, Pete," a man called from the back of the wagon. "I think they all got off with just cuts and bruises, though."

"Well, that's a shame," the man named Pete said. He thrust out a paw to Mac and introduced himself. "Pete Newton."

The third member of the trio, a short, stocky man with impressive handlebar mustaches curling up on each cheek, shook Mac's hand as well.

"Frank Rigoni," he said. "Pleased to meet you, McKenzie."

With a grin, Stanton said, "Frank is half Irish, half Italian, and all trouble."

A booming laugh came from Rigoni, followed by, "George speaks the truth."

"He also has the appetite of two men," Alec Lafferty said dryly, "so you may have your work cut out for you satisfying his appetite, McKenzie."

"Just call me Mac. I'm happy to be here and meet all you fellas. And before anybody mentions it . . . I know I look a little like a cowboy. I used to drive a chuck wagon. That's how I learned to cook."

Rigoni threw an arm around Mac's shoulders and steered him toward the building.

"I hold no man's past against him," he said. "Not even one who used to associate with cowboys!"

CHAPTER 14

The stew Mac served for supper that night was greeted with wariness by the men who gathered around the big table in the main house's dining room. He knew the smell was probably a little different from what they were used to.

But once they dug in and tasted it, they ate eagerly and with obvious enjoyment, grabbing biscuits from a huge mound on a platter in the center of the table and using them to sop up the last of the juice in their bowls.

Then they demanded more.

"I don't want to say anything bad about Walt," Frank Rigoni declared, "but his stew was a little bland compared to this. This tastes like something that might come from an Italian's kitchen."

"It's the garlic," Mac said from where he stood near the table with his arms crossed over the apron he wore. "I don't use it as heavy as some people do, but it's there."

"Mighty tasty, too," Pete Newton said. Several other men echoed that sentiment.

George Stanton sipped from his cup and said, "Even the coffee tastes a mite different."

"I put a little nutmeg in it," Mac said. "Gives it a richer flavor."

"I'm sorry Walt broke his leg, but it was a stroke of good luck that you happened to be in the Lonesome Pine when it happened, Mac."

"Good luck for me, too," Mac said. "I was looking for a job, and I'm happy to be here with you fellas."

Looking for Asa Dunnigan, that was what he'd actually been doing, of course, and so far the search hadn't paid any dividends—but it was early yet.

The men ate heartily and polished off everything Mac had prepared, right down to the last biscuit crumb and last drop of coffee. They sat around the house's big main room for a while after that, some of the men playing cards while others read old newspapers or just sat and talked while smoking their pipes. It was a warm, convivial atmosphere, and Mac enjoyed being part of it once he had cleaned up the kitchen.

The men began to drift off to bed, and Mac returned to the kitchen. He had to prepare the dough for biscuits first thing in the morning. He put a pot of beans on to soak, as well, before he headed to the small room adjacent to the kitchen where the camp cook slept. The bunk there was comfortable, although the furnishings were far from fancy.

Over the next few days, Mac settled in as one of the crew. He divided his time between cooking and planning and preparing future meals. The men continued praising his food, especially the apple cobbler, which some of them declared to be the best they had ever tasted.

Stanton had told Mac that every now and then, he might be called upon to help out with other chores around the camp. Mac had said that he would do his best, although he knew nothing about logging.

So far nothing like that had come up, and Mac had his fingers crossed that it wouldn't, even though pitching in and working with the other men would have given him the opportunity to see more of them and get to know them better. That might help him determine whether the fugitive outlaw he and Luke sought was hiding in plain sight among them.

He couldn't apprehend Asa Dunnigan, though, if a giant tree fell on him, so he'd just as soon avoid any chance of that happening!

Anyway, he saw the men at every meal and talked to them every chance he got. So far, he hadn't found any clues to tell him if the man he was after was there.

He had been at the camp a little less than a week and wondered how Luke was getting on at the Triangle 7. He had stepped out of the house's rear door and was dumping a pan of dishwater when he heard hoofbeats approaching. He went back through the house and had just emerged onto the porch when a buggy reached the top of the trail. As it rolled closer, Mac recognized Carl Peters, Empire's bookkeeper and secretary, at the reins.

Next to Peters sat Constance Elliott. Her head was uncovered, and the sun shone on her honey-gold hair. Mac felt his heart pick up its pace a bit as he recognized her.

Peters handled the team fairly skillfully for a man who spent most of his days inside, hunched over a desk. He brought the buggy to a halt in front of the main house.

Mac started to raise a hand in greeting, then realized belatedly that he was still wearing his apron. He untied it quickly, took it off, and bunched it in his hands before tossing it through the open door behind him.

Then he waved and called, "Howdy, Miss Elliott! Welcome to camp!"

"It's my camp, Mr. McKenzie," she said from the buggy seat. "I've been here before, you know."

"Well, sure, of course. I just meant that it's good of you to visit."

"This isn't a social call." While Peters was setting the brake, she didn't wait for him or Mac to assist her from the vehicle. She stepped down lithely from it and went on, "I've come to talk to

George Stanton and make sure everything is running smoothly. Problems just get worse if they're not addressed promptly, so I like to get frequent reports on the operation."

"I think George is in the office. I'll let him know you're here."

"No need," Constance said. "He's expecting me."

Mac couldn't help but admire the way she looked as she strode confidently toward the building. She wore canvas trousers that probably would have been considered scandalous on a female anywhere except in the woods like this, along with high-topped boots and a corduroy jacket. She carried a felt hat in the planter's style that Mac had seen so often in Louisiana. Despite that, it didn't seem out of place here in this northern forest.

He stepped into the house as Constance started up the steps. He grabbed the apron that had landed on the floor and stuffed it under his left arm. With his right arm, he gestured for her to come in.

She wasn't waiting for an invitation. She was already halfway in, her attitude slightly imperious, as befitted the owner of an outfit called the Empire Logging Company.

"I reckon you know where you're going," Mac said.

"Certainly." She turned and started along a hall that led to the small office where George Stanton worked part of the time, keeping up with the camp's production and figuring out if they were on schedule. He worked out in the woods with the other men, too, but spent part of most days in the office as well.

"How about some coffee?" Mac called after Constance.

She paused and looked back over her shoulder at him. "Is it fresh?"

"I put a new pot on to boil right after the men finished breakfast."

A slight smile appeared on her face. "In that case, I wouldn't mind. It's a long enough ride out here that I could use something to brace me up a bit."

"My coffee'll do it," he promised. As he headed for the kitchen, out of the corner of his eye he saw Carl Peters come in, the bookkeeper having taken the time to tie the buggy team to the hitching post outside.

He would bring a cup for Peters, too, Mac decided, as well as for Stanton.

And maybe one for himself. If nobody ran him off, he might just linger in the office for a spell while Constance and Stanton were discussing the business.

When Mac got back to the office carrying a tray with four cups of coffee on it, Constance was sitting behind the desk going over a couple of open ledger books and several documents that were spread out before her. Stanton stood in front of the desk, ready to answer any questions Constance had for him. Peters sat in a chair to one side, studying another ledger book.

The desk was cluttered enough that there was no room for the tray, so Mac set one of the cups near Constance's right hand and let Stanton and Peters take their own cups from the tray. He lifted the one remaining cup and leaned against the doorjamb with the tray held down at his side.

He already knew the coffee was good, but it was gratifying anyway when Constance took a sip and then smiled up at him.

"This is excellent," she said.

"Thanks."

Stanton said, "I suppose we have to give Walt his job back once he's up and around again, but I don't reckon anybody around here would be upset if Mac stayed on permanently. We've been eating mighty good since he showed up."

"I agree, we have to be loyal to Walt Nichols," Constance said. "It's the only fair thing to do. But I understand what you're saying, George."

Stanton shrugged. "It's a dilemma, all right."

Mac said, "No offense, but I didn't figure on taking anybody's job away from him permanent-like. Also, to be honest, I've never been the sort of fella to put down roots." He chuckled. "I reckon that's a pretty appropriate way to put it since we're in the middle of a forest."

Constance didn't laugh, but Mac thought he saw a brief twinkle of amusement in her eyes. She said, "I checked on Mr. Nichols before I drove out here today, and the doctor says it'll still be a while before he's able to resume his normal activities. So no decision has to be made right now. That is, if you're all right with letting the status quo continue, Mr. McKenzie?"

"Mac," he said. "And yeah, that's fine with me." He took a sip of his coffee and nodded. "You folks go on with your meeting. Don't let me stop you."

Peters said, "It's not necessary for the cook to be here."

"No, it's all right," Constance said. "Mr. McKenzie—Mac—can stay. He's not bothering me. You may be bored by all our business talk, though, Mac."

"Actually, I think the whole operation is kind of interesting," Mac said. "I don't know much about logging. I guess I figured lumber just appeared somehow."

Stanton said, "It's a lot of hard work."

"Yep, I've been seeing that for myself."

The superintendent went on, "I can tell you the thing the crew is most interested in right now, Miss Elliott."

"No need," Constance said. "I have a pretty good idea. They want to know if this month's payroll is still on schedule, don't they?"

"Well, yeah, that's right. They do."

She nodded. "It's coming in on today's stagecoach from The Dalles. Carl and I will be back in Pine Knob before the stage arrives, and he'll see to it that the money is put safely in the bank overnight. The men can come into town in shifts, as usual, and draw their wages starting tomorrow morning."

"I'll pass that news along to them this evening at supper. They'll be happy to hear it."

Constance leaned back in the chair and said, "I'm not sure why they were concerned. I've never missed a payday, have I?"

"No, ma'am, you sure haven't. You've been about as steady a boss as anybody could ever hope to work for. But things happen sometimes, and when a fella's out in the woods all day swinging an axe or wrestling a saw, he likes to know his efforts are going to be rewarded."

"They will be," Constance said with a decisive nod. "The money will be here, and nothing's going to happen to it."

Chapter 15

Because of the rugged terrain between The Dalles and Pine Knob, the stagecoach required two days to make the journey. The road went through the same mountain pass that the Triangle 7 and the other cattle spreads in the basin used to drive their herds to the railhead town on the Columbia River.

The mountains weren't the only obstacle. The landscape was covered with wooded hills and ridges and the trail snaked through them, seldom following a straight line for more than two hundred yards. Small creeks ran alongside many stretches, and here and there the stagecoach had to ford one of those shallow, fast-flowing streams. The water was usually less than half a foot deep.

Today, the stagecoach was still ten miles northwest of Pine Knob when the driver, Fred Carter, hauled back on the reins and brought his six-horse team to a stop in the middle of one of those fords. The horses lowered their heads to drink.

Beside Carter on the seat atop the driver's box was Arch Whitehorse, who held a double-barreled coach gun with the butt propped against his right hip and the twin barrels angled toward the sky.

Whitehorse's grandfather, an Umpqua Indian from the Cow Creek Band, had fled the troubles during the Rogue River Wars and wound up settling on a farm near the Columbia. He'd married a white woman, and their son was young Arch's father. Arch's one-quarter Umpqua heritage was visible in his long, raven's-wing-dark hair and eaglelike visage. He wore a black, flat-crowned hat and a black duster over canvas trousers, suspenders, and a bib-front shirt. A .44 caliber Remington revolver was holstered on his hip, and a Winchester rested on the floorboards at his feet. He hadn't been working as a stagecoach guard for very long, but he took his duties seriously, and being well-armed was a part of that.

Fred Carter had been a jehu for a lot longer. He was a small, slightly built man who was a lot stronger than he looked, especially in the arms and shoulders, from years of handling stagecoach teams. He had a gray brush of a mustache and sharp eyes that darted, birdlike, everywhere around him as he drove.

Now, with the coach stopped, Carter relaxed for a moment. He pulled a briar pipe from a pocket of the vest he wore and packed it with tobacco from a pouch he took out of another pocket. He fished out a lucifer, snapped it to life with his thumbnail, and puffed on the pipe until he had it alight. He flicked the spent match into the creek.

Whitehorse thumbed back his hat, but his attitude remained vigilant. He wanted a smoke, too, but he wasn't going to distract himself by fumbling with the makin's. There would be time for that when they reached Pine Knob and turned the strongbox over to the manager of the local stage station.

That strongbox was closed up in the compartment under the bench where he and Carter sat. Nobody knew it was there except their boss in The Dalles, the bank messenger who had turned it over, and the station manager in Pine Knob who was expecting it.

Well, that wasn't strictly true, the shotgun guard reflected. Miss Constance Elliott knew about the box, because it was her money packed away in it. She would be distributing it to the lumberjacks who worked for her.

Both banks of the creek were fairly open for at least a quarter of a mile on both sides. That was why Carter was in the habit of stopping at this ford to let the horses drink and rest for a few minutes. There were no rocks or trees close by where would-be stage robbers could hide.

No passengers were inside the coach today. That wasn't unusual; this run carried more mail than it did people, along with the occasional important shipment such as the Empire Logging Company payroll currently in the strongbox.

Carter was puffing contentedly on his pipe when Whitehorse stiffened on the seat beside him. With his teeth still clamped on the briar, Carter asked, "Something wrong, Arch?"

"Somebody's comin'," the guard said.

Carter had been regarding the rumps of the two horses closest to the coach as he smoked. He didn't really see them; that was just the way his gaze was pointed while he mused on other things.

He lifted his head now and looked the same way Whitehorse was looking. He saw a wagon that had just emerged from some trees about two hundred yards away and was rolling slowly along the trail toward them. A man handled the reins, while a woman sat next to him. Both were stoop-shouldered, and their heads sagged forward so their eyes were downcast.

They had such an aura of weariness about them that it would make a man tired just to look at them for very long.

Carter grunted and said, "Couple of sodbusters, from the looks of 'em."

"This isn't very good farming country," Whitehorse said.

"That's probably why they're leavin'. They've given up and are goin' somewhere they can start over."

Whitehorse frowned. "Maybe. But if they're looking for better farmland, shouldn't they be headed East?"

"Back to the Plains country, you mean? Well, maybe. But maybe the fella's had enough of wrestlin' a plow and figures on givin' something else a try."

"I suppose that's possible." Whitehorse lowered his coach gun and laid the barrels across his left forearm while he gripped the stock with his right hand. They pointed in the general direction of the approaching wagon.

"You're not gonna threaten those folks, are you?" Carter asked.

"Not as long as they just drive on past without stopping or giving us any trouble."

"We can at least give 'em a friendly hello. An encouragin' word can mean a lot to folks who are down on their luck."

"I'd be more inclined to be encouraging if we didn't have all the money riding right underneath us."

"Yeah, there's that to consider," Carter allowed. He shifted on the seat and pulled his gun belt around so the holstered Colt on his hip was easier to get to.

The slow-moving wagon was only about twenty yards away now. The two mules pulling it looked just as tired and dispirited as the humans on the seat. As they plodded closer, the man looked at Carter and Whitehorse and gave them a curt nod. His gaunt, rawboned face was stubbled with dark beard. He wore a pair of threadbare trousers over a set of faded red long underwear.

The woman beside him wore a sunbonnet and a patched dress. She kept her head down as the mules splashed into the creek.

"Howdy, fella," Carter called as the wagon came abreast of the stagecoach about a dozen feet away. The back of it was piled with blanket-covered bundles, obviously all the worldly goods of this downtrodden couple.

The farmer, if that's what he was, suddenly pulled back on the reins. The blanket-covered shapes in the wagon bed came alive as two men threw the coverings aside, leaped to their feet, and pointed shotguns at Carter and Whitehorse.

Even out in the wide-open spaces like this, the booming reports were deafening as the gunmen blasted four loads of buckshot at the stagecoach.

Whitehorse was on the far side of Carter from the wagon when the scatterguns went off. The guard felt a couple of pellets rip fiery wounds on his back as the deadly storm of lead slammed into Carter and drove him sideways on the seat into Whitehorse.

Carter's luckless body took the brunt of the attack. Whitehorse wasn't seriously wounded yet. He thrust the coach gun's barrels past Carter's bloody, twitching form and pulled both triggers. The recoil was violent enough that, firing one-handed like that, it jolted the weapon right out of Whitehorse's grip. The coach gun thudded to the floorboards.

The young guard had tried to aim so that both bushwhackers in the back of the wagon would be hit, but he'd had to hurry too much. Both charges of buckshot struck the man on the right. That double impact shredded his chest into raw meat and slammed him backward off the wagon. Water flew high in the air as he splashed into the creek. Crimson began to spread quickly through the fast-flowing stream.

The other man dropped his empty shotgun and clawed out a revolver. On the wagon seat, the "farmer" was up on his feet and had pulled a gun from somewhere, too. Both men blazed away at the stagecoach.

Even more surprising, the person Carter and Whitehorse had taken to be the farmer's wife bolted upright, swept the bonnet back to reveal the rough, beard-stubbled face of a man, and brought a Winchester to his shoulder to join the others in the deadly attack on the stagecoach.

Carter had gone limp as he slumped against Whitehorse. The young man felt the driver's body jerk as bullets pounded into it. Whitehorse realized that trying to pick up his own Winchester would expose too much of him to all the lead flying around, so he yanked his Remington from its holster and kicked himself backward off the seat.

He landed in the shallow creek on the far side of the coach from the ambushers. Using the vehicle for cover, he ignored the pain from the wounds on his back and ran to the rear of the coach. Angling his gun around the luggage boot, he snapped off a shot at the dress-wearing varmint with the rifle.

Whitehorse was a decent shot, but with his heart slugging like crazy in his chest and blood trickling down his back under his shirt, he knew it was pure luck that guided his bullet to the gunman's shoulder. The man yelled in pain and twisted halfway around as he dropped the Winchester. He fell back onto the wagon seat as he clutched his bullet-shattered shoulder.

Whitehorse sent two more shots under the hooves of the mules and shouted at them. The mules might have been tired, but they spooked at that and lunged forward. The sudden jolt threw both of the remaining ambushers off their feet.

Unfortunately, the stagecoach team, equally skittish from the gunfire and the smells of powder smoke and blood in the air, chose that moment to bolt as well, in the opposite direction.

That was going to leave Whitehorse standing out in the open, exposed to the fire of the two men who still wanted to kill him.

As the stagecoach lurched away from him, he leaped after it with his left hand outstretched. He managed to grab the canvas cover over the rear boot and hung on for dear life as he was jerked off his feet. Gritting his teeth, he jammed his Remington back in the holster and hoped it wouldn't fall out. Then he groped for the canvas with his right hand and got hold with it, too.

He was lying on his belly, soaked from the creek and instantly covered with mud as the coach dragged him through the dust of the trail. Luckily, it was fairly level and smooth right there, so he was able to hang on without being battered too much.

Whitehorse twisted his neck to look back over his shoulder. The wagon was still going the other way. The man who'd dressed like a down-on-his-luck farmer was struggling to bring the mules under control. The other man was on his knees in the back, firing the Winchester after the stagecoach. As far as Whitehorse could tell, though, none of the bullets were coming close.

Dust from the churning wheels billowed up into Whitehorse's face, blinding and choking him. He squeezed his eyes shut and tried to pull himself onto the boot. He had to let go with one hand and reach higher for a better grip, and that split second was terrifying as he thought he might lose his hold entirely.

But his fingers dug into the canvas, and he grunted with the effort as he heaved himself upward. He shifted his other hand and got a good hold with it. With agonizing slowness, he climbed onto the boot. His arms quivered with relief when he finally got his feet under him and took his weight with his legs.

A bullet spanged off the brass rail that ran around the coach roof, a couple of feet above his head.

Whitehorse grimaced and looked back. The "farmer" had gotten the wagon turned around, and the two remaining killers were coming after him now. The man with the Winchester fired over the back of the wagon seat. The shot must have missed entirely; Whitehorse didn't see or hear it strike the stage.

He couldn't stay here, he realized. He was too exposed. Dangerous or not, he had to keep climbing.

He reached up and grabbed that brass rail.

Whitehorse had always been good at climbing trees when he was a kid. He wasn't sure how helpful that experience was now; those trees hadn't been bouncing and jolting around like this stagecoach. But he supposed it didn't hurt. He hauled himself up and over and sprawled on top of the stage.

From here he could see the horses as they galloped frantically along the trail. At least they were staying on the road instead of careening off across open country.

He couldn't see Fred Carter. The driver might have tumbled off, and with all the dust flying in his face and his body being jerked around, Whitehorse hadn't seen Carter fall. He knew the jehu was dead; no man could absorb so much buckshot and so many rifle and pistol bullets and survive.

But he was still alive, Whitehorse told himself, and he still had that strongbox to protect. He didn't think he was too badly wounded, even though his back ached and burned where the buckshot had ripped across it.

He began crawling toward the driver's box.

It took him only a moment to reach it, and when he did, he saw that Carter's body had slipped down onto the floorboards. The old reinsman was dead, all right. His shirt was soaked with blood, and a fist-sized chunk of his head had been blown away.

Whitehorse slid over the seat back and onto the bench. He made a face as his booted feet came to rest on Carter's corpse.

"I'm mighty sorry, Fred," he muttered as he reached for the reins. They were caught under Carter's bloody torso. That was a stroke of grim luck. If they had slithered off the box and fallen under the team, Whitehorse wouldn't have been able to recover them.

He pulled the leather lines loose, grimacing again at the sticky feel of Carter's blood on them.

Pine trees flashed by on both sides of the trail now. The road had entered the woods once again. Whitehorse yelled at the team and flapped the reins against their backs, urging them on to as much speed as they could muster.

A glance over his shoulder told him that the wagon was gaining on the stagecoach now. But even though they were pulling a greater weight, the coach's six sturdy horses could outrun the two mules.

Whitehorse continued the mad dash toward Pine Knob. He thought that if he could get close enough to the settlement without the pursuers catching him, they would give up and turn back rather than chasing him all the way into town.

As he drove, he thought about what had happened. Clearly, the four men were after the payroll in the strongbox. He didn't believe they would have gone to so much trouble and prepared such an elaborate ruse just on the off-chance something valuable might be in the mail pouch.

No, they *knew* that money was there, Whitehorse thought, but how they had found out about it was a mystery to him. He had believed that no more than a mere handful of people were aware the payroll would be on the stagecoach today.

A sudden glimpse of motion up ahead made Whitehorse forget all about pondering that question. Half a dozen men on horseback had just rounded a bend a hundred yards away and were coming toward him. At the sight of the stagecoach, they spurred ahead. Puffs of gray smoke appeared in front of them, spurts of powder smoke that disappeared as the riders galloped through them.

They were shooting at him, Whitehorse thought wildly. He had almost gotten away from one bunch that wanted to kill him, and now here he was with another bunch of bloodthirsty owlhoots charging right at him!

He gathered the reins in his left hand and reached for his holster with his right. A groan escaped from his lips as he found the leather scabbard empty. His Remington had fallen out somewhere, just as he had worried that it might. His Winchester still lay on the floorboards under Carter's body. If he stopped the coach, he could retrieve it and at least put up a fight.

But if he stopped the coach, the two men in the wagon might catch up to him. They were still back there somewhere behind him.

Before the young guard could make up his mind what to do, fate stepped in. The right-hand leader in the team suddenly stumbled, lost its footing, and fell. One of those wild shots the outlaws in front of him were throwing had found the unfortunate animal, Whitehorse thought.

When the stricken horse fell, the other leader tangled up with it and went down, too. The other horses piled up with them in a welter of flailing hooves. The coach, out of control now, slewed sideways.

Whitehorse jumped for his life, rather than wait to be thrown.

He sailed through the air, praying that he wouldn't dash his brains out against a pine tree trunk. Somehow he missed the trees and crashed to the ground, rolling over and over. He came to a stop on his belly and lifted his head, shaking it groggily. He'd wound up in some brush, and while he couldn't see the riders anymore, he still heard the swift hoofbeats from their mounts.

Unarmed and wounded, Whitehorse did the only thing he could.

He squirmed backward, deeper into the brush, trying to stay hidden. The strongbox with the Empire payroll inside it was lost; he couldn't do anything about that now. But with luck, maybe he could stay alive.

For a while longer, anyway.

"Where'd that hombre go?" a man shouted, not too far away. "Spread out! Find him!"

They didn't want to leave any loose ends dangling, Whitehorse thought. They wanted him just as dead as Fred Carter was.

He heard booted feet thudding on the ground, accompanied by the crackling of branches as they searched for him. If they found him, all he could expect was a quick bullet. He stayed low, crawling as long as his nerves would stand the strain.

Then he clambered to his feet and started to run, once again hoping he wouldn't blindly smash into a tree trunk or a low-hanging branch.

"Hey, I thought I heard something over there!"

"Go check it out!"

The voices spurred Whitehorse on. He tried to look behind him but couldn't see anything except tree trunks and underbrush.

Then, with no warning, there was nothing under his feet except empty air as he plummeted like a stone into one of the many ravines that clawed their way across this forest wilderness.

CHAPTER 16

Luke reined to a stop alongside Rich Coburn and three other cowboys from the Triangle 7. The little group had come to a stop in front of the Lonesome Pine.

Coburn rested crossed hands on the saddle horn and studied the other horses tied up at the hitch rack in front of the big saloon. After a moment, he nodded in satisfaction.

"I don't see any Empire mounts," he said. "Anyway, that bunch usually comes to town in a wagon, and there aren't any of those parked along here, either." He turned his head and spat with obvious contempt. "Those blasted tree-climbers ain't comfortable in a saddle, like real men."

"You're not sayin' you'd be scared to go in there if some of those loggers were havin' a drink, are you, Rich?" one of the cowboys gibed with a grin on his face.

Coburn scowled and demanded, "What in blazes do you think? I ain't no more afraid of them than I would be of a squirrel or any other tree rat!"

Luke paid little attention to the back and forth. Without dismounting, he said, "I'll catch up to you fellows in there later.

I want to see the marshal and find out where things stand with that reward money."

Coburn suddenly looked genuinely concerned. "If the reward has come in, are you gonna quit the spread, Luke? You haven't been around long, but I can tell already you're a fine hand. Especially for somebody your age."

Luke let that comment about his age pass, knowing the foreman probably didn't mean anything by it. In truth, he actually was quite a few years older than the other members of the Triangle 7 crew.

But as he had demonstrated in the past week, he didn't mind hard work and could handle a horse and a lasso with considerable skill.

He hadn't set out to remain a cowboy for any significant length of time, but he hadn't found any clues to tell him whether Asa Dunnigan was in the area or not. Nor had he been able to establish contact with Mac to find out what his partner had discovered, if anything.

"I don't think I'm ready to move on just yet," Luke said. "I've enjoyed working on the Triangle 7, and Mr. Harmon seems like a good boss. I think I'll stay around for a while, whether the reward money is here or not."

Coburn looked relieved as he nodded. "I'm glad to hear it."

Luke swung his horse away from the hitch rail and walked the animal up the street toward Marshal Abner Sundell's office. Behind him, Coburn and the others dismounted, tied their horses, and went into the saloon.

The hitch rail in front of the marshal's office was empty. Luke looped his horse's reins around it and stepped onto the shallow boardwalk. The door wasn't locked, so when he opened it, he wasn't surprised to see Sundell sitting behind the desk, puffing on a pipe, and apparently content to just sit there with his hands laced together on the little mound of his belly.

Sundell nodded to his visitor and added a verbal greeting. "Howdy, Jensen."

Luke thumbed back his hat and said, "Hello, Marshal. You look like you're taking life easy."

"If you were a real lawman, you'd know to take advantage of every moment of peace and quiet you can grab."

"I like to think I serve the forces of law and order in my own way." Luke took hold of a ladder-back chair, turned it around, and straddled it with his arms resting on the back. "Speaking of which, any word on the rewards for the Bishop brothers?"

"No, I'm afraid not," Sundell replied with a shake of his head. "I'm expecting to hear something any day now, though. As a matter of fact, there's a stagecoach due today. Might be some news in the mail pouch."

A frown creased the marshal's forehead, as if something had just occurred to him. He reached for his vest pocket and took out the turnip watch attached to a chain that looped across his midsection to the other vest pocket. He thumbed the watch's catch and it opened.

"Actually, that coach should have been here by now," he went on. "I wonder why it's late."

"Plenty of things can happen to delay a stage."

"Yeah," the marshal agreed with Luke's statement, "but they usually don't when Fred Carter is handling the reins. He's driven stagecoaches in this part of the country for nigh on to twenty years, and he had plenty of experience as a jehu in other places before that. He's generally so punctual you can set your watch by him."

He snapped the turnip closed to emphasize his words.

"Even so," Luke said, "accidents happen. The terrain between here and The Dalles is pretty rugged, I understand."

Sundell waved that off. "It's not as bad as you might think, considering there's a mountain range between the two places. But the pass isn't too steep and difficult, and the road is good all the way through. You can't rule out an axle cracking or something like that, but generally there aren't any problems."

Luke's eyes narrowed. "If that reward money is on the stage and owlhoots got wind of it, they might try a holdup."

"The approval and the money wouldn't have been sent together," Sundell said. "I'd get a letter from the chief marshal's office first, and then the money would be shipped to the bank here. But I was expecting something else—"

Sundell's mouth clamped shut and his lips thinned, as if he had realized he was about to say too much. Had, in fact, already said too much.

Luke's suspicions were aroused, and he was about to seek some answers from the lawman when quick, heavy footsteps sounded on the boardwalk. A moment later, the door swung open and a somewhat agitated voice asked, "Marshal, are you in here?"

The man who came into the office on the heels of that question was a gangling, rawboned fellow dressed in rough work clothes and a battered old hat. He wore an alarmed expression on his face.

Sundell came to his feet behind the desk. Luke stood up, too, and turned toward the newcomer.

"What's wrong, Cooley?" the marshal asked.

"I got a man outside in my wagon who's bad hurt, Marshal. He says he's the guard on the stagecoach that was supposed to be here today."

Sundell let out a startled exclamation and hurried from behind the desk. All three men left the office quickly, with Cooley leading the way.

When they got outside, Luke saw that a crowd had collected already around the wagon parked in front of the marshal's office. Anything out of the ordinary attracted a lot of attention in a frontier settlement.

"Stand back!" Sundell ordered, raising his voice. "Give us room."

Some of the townspeople moved aside, forming a path for Sundell, Luke, and Cooley to approach the wagon. Luke saw that part of the wagon bed was filled with neatly stacked firewood, split and cut into suitable lengths for hearths or stoves.

An area on one side had been cleared, and a man lay face down on a blanket spread there. Another blanket had been folded and placed under his head to serve as a pillow. His head was turned to the side so his face was visible. He was pale and haggard with strain. His dark hair, high cheekbones, and hawklike features seemed to indicate that he was part Indian.

The back of his shirt was dark with dried blood. His left leg was twisted at an unnatural angle. Scrapes and bruises covered his face and hands. He had taken some punishment recently, there was no doubt about that.

The young man was conscious, though. His dark eyes were open. He lifted his head at the sound of Sundell's voice as the marshal said, "Arch Whitehorse, is that you?"

"M-marshal?" Whitehorse rasped. "Marshal Sundell?"

"Yeah. What in blazes happened, kid?"

"B-bandits . . . held up . . . stage. Killed . . . Fred."

That sent excited, horrified murmurs through the crowd. A heartfelt curse escaped from Sundell's mouth. He leaned forward, gripping the top of the wagon's sideboards, and asked, "The strongbox?"

"G-gone."

Sundell looked over at Cooley. "Where'd you find him?"

"I was on my way along the trail from my woodyard to the stage road when I heard yellin' from somewhere in the trees," the man answered. "The fella sounded like he was in a bad way, so I stopped my wagon and went to look for him. He'd fallen in a ravine and was callin' for help. I couldn't get to him with the wagon, but I unhitched one of my mules, climbed down, and got a rope on him, and then the mule pulled him out." Cooley made a face and shook his head. "I hope I didn't wind up hurtin' him worse'n he already was."

"You couldn't go off and leave him there like that," Sundell said. "You did the right thing. Did you see the stagecoach anywhere?"

Cooley shook his head again. "Nope. But you know the trail

from my place hits the main road just a couple of miles northwest o' town. It could've been farther on up toward the pass."

Sundell leaned over the wagon's side again and asked, "Can you tell me what happened, Arch?"

Luke said, "This man needs medical attention, Marshal. He's lost a considerable amount of blood and his leg is clearly broken."

The marshal shot a sharp glance at him. "Blast it, I know that, but I've got a job to do, too. I have to find out about that stagecoach robbery."

In a weak voice, Arch Whitehorse said, "That's . . . all right . . . Marshal. I want you to find . . . the varmints who killed Fred."

"How many were there, kid?"

"F-four . . . starting out. Then I . . . ran into . . . half a dozen more."

In halting sentences that obviously cost him a considerable effort due to the shape he was in, the young shotgun guard explained about the ruse the outlaws had tried originally, followed by the chase, and then the unfortunate encounter with the second group of robbers.

"After . . . the coach crashed . . . I was just trying . . . to save my life," Whitehorse said. "I lit out . . . into the woods . . . and then fell in that hole." Tears squeezed out of his eyes. "I'm sorry, Marshal. I should've . . . tried to save . . . the strongbox."

"Don't you think that for a second, Arch," Sundell told him. "Against odds like that, you wouldn't have accomplished a thing except to get yourself killed."

By this time, one of the townspeople had gone to fetch the doctor. The small, birdlike man carrying a black medical bag bustled up, took one look in the back of the wagon, and unleashed a blistering torrent of abuse.

"Why didn't you bring this man directly to my office?" he demanded of Cooley.

"I figured the marshal would want to know—"

"Never mind, just get on down there with him now. And be careful! Don't jostle him around anymore than you have to."

Cooley climbed onto the wagon seat, Sundell waved the crowd back, and the vehicle rolled away slowly. The doctor had climbed into the back with Arch Whitehorse and was already conducting a preliminary examination of the injured young man.

Sundell watched them go with a disgusted look on his face, then raised his voice again and ordered the bystanders to go on about their business.

"But the stage was held up, Marshal," a man said. "Ain't you gonna form a posse and go after the robbers?"

"I'm going to find out exactly what happened, you can bet a hat on that," Sundell snapped. "I'll take a few men with me in case we're able to trail the skunks who did this."

"I'll come with you, Marshal," Luke said without hesitation.

"The boys and me will, too," Rich Coburn added. The commotion had drawn him and the other Triangle 7 hands from the Lonesome Pine. Luke had noticed them when they drifted up to the crowd a few minutes earlier.

"No, you won't," Sundell said. "I don't want a bunch of trigger-happy cowboys riding with me. You hotheads are more trouble than you're worth."

Coburn looked like he wanted to argue, but before he could say anything, Luke said, "I insist on coming along, Marshal. I have a stake in this, you know. The mail pouch could have contained a response about the rewards I have coming, and I have a right to know if the thieves took it, too."

Sundell considered the demand for a moment before nodding in agreement.

"All right, you can come along, Jensen," he said. "But not you other fellas. Go on back to Harmon's spread."

Coburn and the other punchers complained a little about being left out of the excitement but didn't kick up too much of a fuss. Sundell pointed out two men from among the townspeople and asked them to come along. Both agreed readily and hurried off to fetch guns and horses.

"Matt Rand is the local blacksmith and has served as a part-time deputy for me in the past," Sundell told Luke. "Cliff Campbell is a printer and publishes the newspaper. He and Matt are two of the most levelheaded hombres I know. That's why I want them to come along."

"Sounds like a good idea," Luke said, nodding.

The marshal eyed him. "And you've got manhunting experience."

"More than I like to think about."

"I reckon the four of us ought to be able to deal with that bunch if we catch up to them." Sundell sighed. "I'm not holding out a lot of hope that we'll be able to do that, though."

Now that the marshal had selected the men for his posse, the rest of the crowd drifted off No one was standing nearby as Luke asked quietly, "Just what was in that strongbox the robbers were after, Marshal?"

"What makes you think anything special was?"

"The way that young guard was so upset about losing it."

"Arch takes his job seriously, that's all."

Luke ignored that and said, "Also, back in your office, you were about to say something concerning what the stagecoach was carrying today, but then you stopped yourself, as if you didn't want to give away too much."

"Noticed that, did you?"

"I'm in the habit of paying attention to most things. It helps me stay alive."

"Yeah, I can see how it would, in your line of work." Sundell rubbed his chin and then went on, "Empire's payroll was coming in today from the bank in The Dalles."

Luke raised his eyebrows. "That must be a considerable amount of money."

"Yeah, it is. And those loggers won't be happy when they find out that it's gone. In fact, they're liable to raise holy Ned about it."

"Will the stage line make the loss good?"

"More than likely they will. Eventually. But they'll drag it out as long as they can, and that'll just give the loggers time to stew about it even more."

"So, for the sake of keeping the peace around here, it would be best if we were able to track down those robbers and recover the money."

"That's right."

"And the mail pouch as well, of course, and whatever's in it."

"Like I told you, it wouldn't be your reward money. You don't really have a stake in this, Jensen, if you want to change your mind and not come along."

"I never said that," Luke replied. He chuckled. "Who knows, the stage line might be willing to pay a reward to whoever recovers the strongbox in order not to have to make good on the whole loss."

Sundell looked askance at him, as if he couldn't decide whether Luke was joking or not.

CHAPTER 17

The posse followed the stage road northwest out of Pine Knob. They hadn't gone very far when Marshal Sundell pointed out a narrow trail angling into the road from the west.

"That's the trail from Jed Cooley's wood-cutting camp," the lawman said to Luke. "It winds up through the hills and forms a rough *V* with the stage road. The area in between is pretty rugged, covered with trees and thick brush and ravines like the one young Arch Whitehorse fell into while he was running away from those outlaws."

"So the stagecoach itself ought to be somewhere ahead of us," Luke said.

"Yeah. Judging by what Arch said, we'll probably find it in another mile or two."

"Pretty daring, pulling a robbery that close to town."

Sundell shook his head and said, "It wasn't really that much of a risk. This road isn't heavily traveled, so it wasn't like somebody was bound to come along."

Luke turned his head from side to side as he studied the landscape around them. He waved a hand toward the northeast.

"The Triangle 7 and Empire's camp are both off in that direction from here, isn't that right?"

"Yep. But different trails lead into town from both of those, so there wouldn't be any reason for anybody from either of them to use this road."

"What about the cattle trail leading to the pass that the ranchers in this area use?"

"That starts farther north, swings southwest along the foot of the mountains, then turns again and parallels this road." Sundell frowned a little at Luke. "You really do like to study on a thing, don't you?"

"I've found that the conscientious use of a keen brain is just as valuable as a fast gun hand, if not more so."

The marshal grunted. "I haven't run into all that many bounty hunters in my life, Jensen, but I think it's safe to say that none of them were like you."

"I'll take that as a compliment."

"Take it however you want, because I'm not quite sure how I meant it."

As Sundell had predicted, they found the wrecked stagecoach a quarter of an hour later. The coach lay on its side at the edge of the road. The six-horse team was still hitched to it, but two of the animals were down. One was dead, while the other was still moving around in obvious pain from the broken leg it had suffered.

"Matt, get those other horses unhitched and move them away from here," Sundell said.

Rand said, "Sure, Marshal," and swung down from his saddle. He was a burly, broad-shouldered man, like most blacksmiths, and had a reddish-blond beard.

Cliff Campbell, on the other hand, was a lean, gray man, gray from his suit to his hat to the hair beneath it.

Rand got the uninjured horses loose and led them away so they wouldn't spook when Sundell drew his revolver and put a bullet through the head of the injured animal.

"I hate a man who'd hurt an animal," Sundell muttered as he pouched the iron. "And this isn't the worst thing they did."

Luke knew what the marshal meant. Several yards away lay the bullet-riddled body of the driver, Fred Carter, crumpled in the short grass at the side of the trail where it had been thrown when the coach wrecked.

"Would you like me to check on Fred, Marshal?" Campbell asked.

Sundell shook his head. "No need. You heard what Arch Whitehorse said about the shooting. Fred got hit with four loads of buckshot and no telling how many pistol and rifle rounds. There's no way a man can absorb that much lead and live."

The lawman dismounted and approached the wrecked vehicle. Luke swung down and followed him. The door into the box underneath the driver's seat was closed but not latched. Sundell pulled it back and revealed the empty cavity behind it.

"The strongbox and the mail pouch are both gone, just like I expected," he said. "I reckon they took them somewhere else to open them up and go through them."

Luke stood at the edge of the road and studied the hard-packed surface intently. The dust was disturbed in places by the wheels of the stagecoach and numerous hoofprints, many of them from the team but some from saddle mounts, as well. Luke moved closer to those and hunkered on his heels to get a better look at them.

Sundell joined him. "Any distinctive markings?"

"Not really. You can see the nails are bent over quite a bit on some of the shoes." Luke pointed out what he was talking about. "That's not unusual, but these seem to be bent more than normal."

Matt Rand had come up behind them and was peering over Luke's shoulders. He made a disapproving noise and said, "Somebody didn't do a very good job. Those shoes are liable to come loose too easy."

Sundell looked over at him and asked, "That's not your work, is it, Matt?"

"It sure isn't. I take more pride in what I do. This is slipshod work."

Sundell rubbed his chin. "So the robbers aren't from around here."

"That's too big a conclusion to jump to, Marshal," Luke said as he straightened from where he'd crouched in the road. "Mr. Rand, are you the only blacksmith in Pine Knob?"

"I am, but I see what you're getting at, Mr. Jensen. Other fellas besides me might shoe a horse. A man might take care of that chore for his own mount, and some of the cattle spreads in the basin handle their own shoeing, as well."

Luke nodded. He didn't mention it, but the hoofprints had struck him as familiar, and he had a pretty good idea why they did.

He had seen similar prints around the Triangle 7. At the time, he hadn't really paid attention to them, but he had filed away that information in his brain without being consciously aware of it.

He had a hard time believing, though, that any of the men he had met on Ben Harmon's ranch would hold up a stagecoach and wantonly murder the driver.

But Harmon had a grudge against Constance Elliott and the Empire Logging Company, Luke reminded himself, and Empire's payroll had been in the stage's strongbox. . . .

Luke pushed that thought out of his mind for the moment. At this point, it was nothing but mere conjecture. He'd need to see a lot more evidence before he would believe such a thing.

Sundell said, "Before we left town, I sent word to John Endicott and told him to head out this way with his wagon. He ought to be here before too much longer. I hate to leave Fred like that, but there's nothing we can do for him."

"Perhaps we should put his body inside the coach just to make sure no scavengers bother it," Campbell suggested.

"That's a good idea," the marshal agreed with a nod. "Come on, Matt, give me a hand."

Luke climbed on top of the coach and opened the door on

that side while Sundell and Rand carried over the body. It took all three men on the ground and Luke on top of the stage to lift the corpse. Luke lowered it into the wrecked vehicle and let it slump onto the opposite door as gently as possible.

Luke grimaced at the blood on his hands and then climbed down.

This was hardly the first time he'd had the sticky, dark red stuff smeared on his hands.

Even so, he cleaned them as best he could in the dust of the road.

"That man you mentioned is the local undertaker, as I recall?" he said to Sundell.

"Yeah, Endicott will take care of Fred. I want to see if we can follow the trail of the men who killed him."

That sounded like a good idea to Luke. The posse mounted up again and continued northwest toward the mountains, leaving the four uninjured horses from the team tied to the stagecoach.

Luke was able to establish a couple of things from the tracks of the gang that had looted the stagecoach. They had ridden up from the southeast, the direction of Pine Knob, but after taking the strongbox and mail pouch, they had continued northwest, the direction the coach had come from.

The road twisted and turned a great deal as it followed the contours of the land. That meandering made it difficult to be sure how much ground they had covered. Luke thought they had traveled for a mile or so when they came to a straight stretch where the road crossed the shallow creek Arch Whitehorse had mentioned.

"That'll be where the outlaws first jumped them," Sundell said as he nodded toward the stream they were approaching. "Arch said he killed a couple of the bunch, or at least badly wounded them. I don't see any bodies around here, though."

"Their friends carried them away," Luke said. "Either out of the goodness of their hearts and a desire to do the decent thing—or else they were afraid someone might come along and recognize them."

"You mean they were from around here?"

Luke shrugged. "It's a possibility, that's all. But it makes sense."

"Yeah, it does." Sundell looked around. "Well, it doesn't appear that we're going to find anything here, so we might as well see if we can keep tracking them."

Luke found the marks in the road left by the supposed farm wagon used by the four men who had ambushed the stagecoach. Its wheels were slightly larger than those on the coach, and that allowed him to tell the difference.

When he pointed that out to Sundell, the marshal said, "You're pretty good at this sort of thing, aren't you?"

"I've had a considerable amount of experience," Luke allowed. "I'm not as good a tracker as my brother, though, and the man who taught him is even better. Maybe the best at it there ever was."

"Oh? Who might those fellas be? Have I heard of them?"

"My brother is Smoke Jensen. His mentor was an old mountain man called Preacher."

Sundell's eyes widened as the names visibly impressed him. Rand and Campbell, riding close behind Luke and Sundell, heard the conversation, too, and pressed their mounts forward.

"Smoke Jensen," Rand repeated. "The famous gunfighter?"

Luke said, "Smoke's just a rancher these days. Has a big spread down in Colorado."

"Smoke Jensen is hardly just a rancher," Campbell said. "Don't forget, I publish a newspaper. I see stories from all over the West. Smoke Jensen is still quite famous as an adventurer! Why, he seems to get mixed up in some sort of trouble on a regular basis."

"That's true," Luke admitted. "Ruckuses do seem to sort of follow him around."

"And that fellow Preacher you mentioned was a famous mountain man, like Jim Bridger or Kit Carson."

"Not was," Luke corrected the man. "Is."

"Preacher is still alive?" Campbell sounded skeptical.

Luke nodded. "And kicking. Or at least he was the last I heard. He pays a visit to Smoke's ranch now and then."

"He must be ancient by now."

"He's no spring chicken, that's true. But he seems to have reached a point where he never gets any older. He still looks about sixty." Luke paused, then added, "He's still spry enough that I'd hate to have to tangle with him, too."

"That's really surprising. If anyone had asked me, I would have said I was sure he had passed away." Campbell got a thoughtful look on his face. "You don't think he'd consent to be interviewed sometime, do you?"

Luke laughed and shook his head. "Not Preacher. He's never been one to talk about himself."

"The stories he must have to tell about the adventures he's had. What an amazing life."

"I can't argue with that."

Sundell said, "It's none of my business, but I can't help but wonder how you wound up being a bounty hunter, Jensen."

"You're right, Marshal, it's none of your—"

The high-pitched wind rip of a bullet passing close by their heads interrupted Luke. At the same instant, the sharp crack of a rifle shot came from their right. The four riders reined in hurriedly and looked for the source of the shot.

Another report sounded as a bullet kicked up dirt from the road a few yards in front of them. Luke spotted a spurt of grayish powder smoke from some boulders near the top of a knoll about fifty yards away.

"Spread out!" Marshal Sundell shouted. "Don't bunch up and give him an easy target!"

The four men scattered, urging their mounts to move fast. Sundell charged ahead, Rand and Campbell headed back along the trail the way they had come from, and Luke sent his horse lunging toward the knoll, going directly at the bushwhacker.

It wasn't uncommon for outlaws on the run to leave a man or two behind to discourage any pursuit. Luke was hard to discourage. He leaned forward in the saddle to make himself a smaller target as he pulled his Winchester from its scabbard.

He worked the rifle's lever as he straightened and brought the weapon to his shoulder. His horse was accustomed to the sound and smell of gunfire, so it continued running forward smoothly as Luke opened up on the rocks, cranking off five rounds as swiftly as he could work the Winchester's lever and squeeze the trigger.

The roll of gun thunder and the lead storm bouncing around the boulders must have spooked the ambusher. Luke spotted a figure dashing out of the rocks and heading for the top of the knoll as fast as his legs would pump.

The distance was too great for Luke to make out any details about the man and his clothing. He threw two more shots after the fleeing rifleman, but the man never slowed down or broke stride. He flung himself over the knoll's crest and disappeared.

Luke rammed the Winchester back in its sheath and concentrated on riding as he swung his horse to the right. He intended to get around that knoll and confront the ambusher. The fellow already had demonstrated that he wasn't a crack shot. Luke figured as long as he kept moving fast, there was a good chance no bushwhacker's bullets would find him.

A glance over his shoulder told him that Sundell and the other two posse members had regrouped and were galloping after him, but he had a good lead on them and knew he couldn't count on them catching up in time to help him in a showdown with the ambusher. Luke was going to try to take the man alive so they could question him and maybe find out who else was in the gang.

As Luke rounded the knoll, he saw movement on its far slope. The bushwhacker's horse must have been waiting just over the crest. The man was most of the way down and riding at a reckless, breakneck pace, leaping the horse in great bounds. He was lucky that the animal appeared to be sure-footed. The horse stayed up, reached level ground, and raced northward.

The bushwhacker's mount had speed and stamina to spare, Luke realized, as it began to pull away. His own horse was fast and had plenty of sand, but he wasn't sure he could match the other man's pace. The ambusher was already closing in on a stretch of trees. Once he got into that thick growth, the chances of Luke catching him would diminish greatly.

Luke reined in and yanked out his rifle again. The hurricane deck of a galloping horse was no place for accuracy with a gun. He lifted the Winchester to his shoulder, aimed, and fired three times.

The fleeing man reached the trees and vanished into them. Luke bit back a frustrated curse. He knew all three of his bullets had missed.

A moment later, Sundell, Rand, and Campbell pounded up on their lathered mounts to join him.

"He got away?" the marshal asked.

"That's right."

"You didn't hit him with any of those shots?"

"I can't be certain," Luke said, "but I don't think so. In fact, I'm pretty sure I didn't."

"You figure he was part of the bunch that held up the stagecoach?"

"No one else would have any reason to ambush us, would they?" Luke said.

Sundell grunted. "Not likely."

Luke tugged his earlobe as he frowned in thought. After a moment, he said, "They overplayed their hand. He's likely to run right back to the rest of the bunch."

"And we can follow him!" Matt Rand said with excited anticipation in his voice.

"That's right," Sundell said. "Unless he gives us the slip, he'll lead us right to the others." The marshal lifted his reins. "We'd better get moving. And keep your eyes open in case that varmint tries to double back and ambush us again!"

CHAPTER 18

When Constance Elliott and Carl Peters concluded their meeting with George Stanton, Constance came to the kitchen in the main house and found Mac working on that evening's supper.

"How do you like it here so far, Mr. McKenzie?" she asked.

"Why, I'm liking it just fine, ma'am," he replied. "And you can just call me Mac."

"Not Dewey? That's your first name, isn't it?"

He tried not to make a face but didn't quite succeed. "Yeah, but I've never really cared for it. That's what my mother called me when I was in trouble."

Constance laughed. "Well, I certainly don't want you thinking of me like your mother."

"Not much chance of that, ma'am," he assured her, then wondered if maybe the comment was pushing things a little too far. She didn't seem to mind, though, or even to notice the possible implications of what he'd said.

"How are the supplies holding up out here?" she went on. "Do you need anything from town?"

"Since you said that about the payroll coming in today, I figure some of the boys will be heading into Pine Knob tomorrow. I thought I'd go along with them and take the wagon. I could use a few things from Mr. Throckmorton's store."

Constance nodded. "That's a good idea. And you'll stop by the office to pick up your wages while you're there?"

"I wasn't sure I had any pay coming just yet," Mac said. "I've only been working for Empire for a week. I figured I might not get paid until the job is over."

"That's not the case at all. I'd rather you be paid at the same time as everyone else in the crew. It's simpler to keep up with it that way. Although your wages will be adjusted for the difference in time of employment, of course."

"Of course," Mac agreed.

"But I've spoken to Carl and made it clear to him that you can draw your pay tomorrow, too."

"How did he feel about that?" Mac asked.

The question seemed to surprise Constance. "What do you mean? He agreed with me that it would be better that way."

Peters had been cool to the idea of hiring Mac in the first place, so he wouldn't have assumed the bookkeeper would just go along with Constance's suggestion. But it wasn't really a suggestion, he reminded himself. She was the boss, and she didn't let anybody forget that for very long.

"I hope things continue to work out well," she said. "George has said the men are very pleased with the meals you've been preparing for them. We're all appreciative of your talents." She smiled. "It was fortunate for us you were available when Walt Nichols broke his leg."

"A lucky break, so to speak?" Mac asked with a grin.

"Well, not for poor Walt. But he'll be all right." Constance reached out and rested the fingertips of her right hand on Mac's forearm for a second. "I'll see you when you come by the office tomorrow."

"Yes, ma'am," he said.

For a moment, he thought she was about to say something else, but then she left the kitchen. Mac regarded the stove and the pots that were sitting on it. A puzzled expression settled over his face.

He was pretty sure he wasn't mistaken about Constance's attitude. She'd been flirting with him.

Mac was glad Stanton hadn't been here to see that. Given the man's own interest in Constance, the way she'd been playing up to Mac might have been a definite burr under his saddle. Mac didn't really need any complications like that when he was just here to hunt down a fugitive, that was all.

He figured he ought to keep telling himself that so he wouldn't forget it.

Mac heard the buggy leaving a few minutes later as Constance and Peters headed back to Pine Knob. Shortly after that, Stanton came into the kitchen and said, "Seems like you've made quite an impression on the boss lady, Mac."

"Just trying to do my job," Mac said without looking up from the biscuit dough he was mixing.

"She never has been quite the same after that big dustup with Ben Harmon. I sure wouldn't like for anything else to happen that might upset her."

"I don't want that, either," Mac said, wondering if Stanton was trying to warn him off. He felt a natural resentment at that possibility, but he wanted to keep things at the logging camp as smoothed over as possible while he continued searching for Asa Dunnigan, so he went on, "You don't have to worry, George."

Let Stanton interpret that any way he wanted to, Mac thought.

"All right," Stanton said with a nod. "I just figured—"

What Stanton figured was destined to remain a mystery, because at that moment, one of the loggers burst into the kitchen and said, "Come quick, George! Trouble at the rollway!"

Stanton swung around. "What happened?"

"Don't know, I just heard a big racket and then some of the fellas yellin'."

Stanton cursed and ran out of the kitchen close behind the man who had summoned him. Over by the stove, Mac hesitated, then grabbed a rag and wiped the flour off his hands as he followed the two men. He didn't take the time to remove his apron.

Stanton and the other man were already running along a path leading from the camp toward the stream that the lumberjacks used to get logs down from the upper slopes. Mac trotted after them. He wasn't sure exactly what the rollway was; he knew that it had something to do with transporting the logs, but that was all.

And he was no timberman, he reminded himself. No matter what was wrong, he might just get in the way. But if there was anything he could do to help, he wanted to pitch in. He got along well with these rough, hardworking men. Although they were different in many ways from the cowboys with whom he had gone up and down the cattle trails, they also reminded him of those rannies.

The path twisted and turned through the woods and trended generally downhill. Trees pressed in close on both sides. That muffled sound to a certain extent, but after a few minutes, Mac heard men shouting somewhere ahead of him.

Shortly after that, the trail rounded a bend and came out in a large clearing. The creek ran along the clearing's edge to Mac's left. Straight ahead of him was a pile of logs stacked about five feet tall. Beyond the logs, the ground sloped down to a larger stream running left to right. Thick, rough-hewn beams rested on that slope, laid out so that they were perpendicular to the lower stream.

Mac's agile brain grasped the logistics of the setup right away. He had believed from what Stanton said that the logs floated all the way down the smaller creek and into the larger one. Evidently, that wasn't the case, for some reason unknown to Mac at the moment.

Instead, the logs were taken out of the smaller creek at this point, hauled over here to this slope, and then rolled down it to land in the larger stream. The beams were there to give the logs something to roll on so they wouldn't bog down in the dirt, especially when it had been raining and the ground was muddy.

Continued shouting drew Mac around the pile of logs. Several logs were scattered at the bottom of the slope, resting partially in the creek. From the looks of them, they had tumbled down there in haphazard fashion.

One of the logs was hung up part of the way down the slope, and that was where half a dozen men were gathered. As Mac made his way down toward them, being careful not to lose his balance and go tumbling himself, he saw that the men were trying to lift the log, but it was stubbornly resisting their efforts.

He cast a nervous glance over his shoulder as he realized that he was now in the path of the logs if any more of them should happen to come sliding down. He figured they built up quite a bit of speed once they started moving.

Enough to smash anything—or anyone—who got in their way with devastating force.

When he came closer, Mac felt a surge of horror go through him as he saw that a man lay trapped underneath the log angled across the slope. The beams that the logs used as a sliding surface were about a foot square, and there were narrow gaps between them. The injured man lay in one of those gaps, with his feet toward the creek and his head toward the top of the rollway. The beams were all that prevented the log from crushing him to death, but there was enough weight on him to keep him pinned down.

"Heave!" Stanton yelled as Mac arrived on the scene of the accident. The men trying to lift the log threw their backs, shoulders, and legs into the effort.

Nobody stood at the end of the log closest to Mac, so he grabbed it and heaved. The log was long, thick, and heavy. It was hard for Mac to conceive just how much it weighed.

It didn't budge, either, despite the sweating, red-faced men trying to lift it.

"It's . . . all right . . . George," the man trapped under the log said in a croaking voice. "You fellas . . . did your best."

Mac recognized him now as Frank Rigoni, the jovial, stocky logger he had met on his first day here in camp. He saw that Alec Lafferty and Pete Newton were part of the group of would-be rescuers, too.

As the men let go of the log and straightened to catch their breath, Stanton said gruffly, "You can go to blazes, Frank. We're getting you out of there."

One of the other men said, "We need to get the mules and rig a pulley—"

"Rig it to what?" Stanton asked. He waved his hand at the long, open slope. "There's nothing above us to fasten a pulley to."

Mac stepped over a couple of the sliding beams as he approached the spot where Rigoni was trapped. The logger was pinned down almost exactly in the center of the thick trunk.

"Can you push it enough to make it roll on down the hill?" he asked Stanton.

"Maybe," the superintendent said grimly, "but if we do, it'll crush every bone in Frank's leg to powder."

He gestured toward Rigoni's left leg, which stuck out from under the log at an angle that placed it atop the beam on that side. Mac grimaced as he saw that Stanton was right. Sliding the log might save Rigoni's life, but it would cost the man his leg, at the very least. It might inflict so much damage that Rigoni would bleed to death before anybody could do anything to stop it.

Stanton put a hand on top of the log and leaned over it so that he could see Rigoni's face. "What happened, Frank?"

"I don't know," Rigoni replied in a voice that carried all the strain he was feeling. "I was crossing the slope . . . a stupid thing to do, I know . . . an amateur mistake . . . when the rope holding the logs in the stack let go. I heard it and knew I couldn't get out of the way in time . . . so I got down between these beams and tried to burrow as deep as I could . . . they went over me and scraped me up some . . . but I thought it was going to work. The last one . . . the very last one . . . had to hang up and trap me here."

"You're lucky you're still alive."

"Yeah, I know . . . but I think the weight's settling some . . . it's getting really hard to breathe, George . . . if you don't get it off of me . . . soon. . . ."

Rigoni couldn't go on. He didn't have to. Every man there knew what he meant.

An idea stirred in Mac's brain. He said, "The log's too heavy to lift. How about if we lighten it?"

"How are we going to do that?" Stanton asked.

"Get some saws and cut it on both sides of these beams it's resting on." Mac pointed to indicate what he was talking about. "Then you could roll the two end pieces down and just have to lift the middle part enough for somebody to pull Frank out from under it."

Alec Lafferty made a disgusted noise. "Do you have any idea how long that would take?"

"No, I don't," Mac answered honestly, "because I'm not a timberman. But I don't see any other way to get any of the weight off, and it seems like that has to be done."

Stanton rubbed his jaw and frowned in thought as he studied the situation.

"George, you can't be thinking of going along with this . . . this cook!" Lafferty protested. "He doesn't know a blasted thing about logging, and he admits it!"

"Maybe looking at it as an outsider is good in this case," Stanton said. "A fresh eye sometimes sees things that somebody too close doesn't. And for the life of me, I can't think of any other way to get Frank out from under there."

Rigoni said, "It's not for . . . the life of you, George. It's . . . the life of me . . . we're talking about here."

Stanton jerked his head in a nod and ordered some of the men, "Go fetch a couple of bucking saws. Hurry!"

They ran up the slope and disappeared around the pile of logs.

Mac eyed that stack warily and asked, "What are the chances of the rest of those logs rolling down here?"

"It's not impossible, I can tell you that," Lafferty snapped.

"But it's not likely," Stanton added. "The logs lower in the pile are well-settled. It's the ones on top that were more precariously balanced. That's why we use a heavy rope on them to keep them from toppling." A frown creased his forehead. "It shouldn't have snapped. Are you sure that's what happened, Frank?"

"I heard the dang thing . . . twang when it gave out," Rigoni replied. He sounded like he could barely find the air to form the words.

After a few minutes that seemed longer, the men Stanton had sent to bring saws came back carrying the long, sharp-toothed tools. The saws had handles on each end so that two men could use them. These experienced loggers were skilled in the process, and in a matter of moments, Stanton had two teams positioned and working. To Mac's eyes, it seemed as if the saws were practically flying back and forth. Sawdust sprayed in the air from the long cuts they were making.

Time dragged. The men took turns on the saws, switching out so fresh muscles were always pushing and pulling on the blades. These loggers were veterans and their timing was good, so they got the maximum effect from their efforts. The saws bit deeper and deeper into the log on both sides of where Frank Rigoni was trapped.

When the saws were far enough through, men used wedges and mauls to spread the cuts and keep the blades from binding. Eventually, it was no longer safe for men to be on the lower side. With only one man on each saw, that slowed down the rescue attempt, but they had no choice.

The scrape of the saws, the pounding of the mauls, the harsh breathing of the men—all combined to form a rough harmony. As Mac listened to it, he watched Frank Rigoni. Like the others, Mac had moved around to the upper side. He could see Rigoni's face, which was now pale and still. His chest rose and fell slightly, just enough for Mac to be able to tell that he was still alive.

The sharp crack as one end of the log came loose made Mac jump. The man using the saw pulled it out and tossed it aside to put his shoulder against the log. Several others joined him.

"Shove it out of there!" Stanton bellowed.

A couple of remaining strands of wood holding the pieces together gave way with a rending sound. The piece of log tipped forward, and its weight did the rest. It began rolling and skidding down the beams toward the creek.

As that was happening, the other end broke loose as well. Mac was among the men who put his shoulder into the effort to dislodge it. It followed the first piece down the slope, leaving only the section that had Frank Rigoni pinned down.

Men swarmed around both ends of that piece, got their hands under it, and heaved upward. Mac was the closest to Rigoni, so he dropped to his knees just above the trapped logger and grabbed him under the arms.

Rigoni yelled in pain as Mac tried to haul him upward. There was still too much weight on him.

"Again!" Stanton called. "Don't drop it!"

A chorus of strained grunts came from the men as they lifted the log. Mac pulled again, and this time Rigoni slid toward him. Mac put all the strength he could muster into the effort. He halfway stood, digging in his heels, as he dragged Rigoni out from under the piece of log.

"He's clear!" Mac shouted.

The men lifting the remaining piece of log shoved it instead, and it began skidding and bouncing down the beams to land at the edge of the creek with a huge splash.

Mac was sitting down again with Rigoni lying half on top of him. The burly logger groaned in pain. Mac didn't see any blood on his clothes, but there was no telling how much damage the log's weight had done to him internally.

Stanton dropped to a knee next to Rigoni and carefully probed his torso with surprisingly gentle fingers. Rigoni caught his breath and cried out.

"He has some busted ribs for sure," Stanton said. He looked up at the men gathered around them. "Bring a blanket and we'll make a sling to carry him. We need to get him to Pine Knob so the doctor can examine him. Looks like Frank is going to be spending some time in town recuperating along with Walt."

Rigoni's eyelids fluttered open. "I'd argue with you, George," he said, "but I just don't . . . have the strength!"

Stanton laughed and squeezed Rigoni's shoulder. "That doesn't hurt, does it?"

"It's just about . . . the only thing . . . that doesn't!"

"Get the wagon ready," Stanton ordered. "Put plenty of blankets in the back! We want to make it as comfortable for Frank as we can."

They placed Rigoni on a blanket and used it to carry him up the slope and back to the camp as carefully and gently as they could.

Mac lingered behind as the men took Rigoni back to camp. He stood there looking at the pile of logs and at the piece of rope lying on the ground in front of them. The rope was tied to an iron ring attached to a metal stake driven deep into the ground. A similar arrangement was behind the stack, also with a piece of rope tied securely to it. Those two pieces of rope had been one length before it parted and allowed the logs to slip.

Mac spent only a moment studying those things, then followed the group carrying Rigoni toward the camp.

The wagon was ready by the time they got there, its bed covered by a thick pile of blankets. The men eased Rigoni onto the makeshift pallet.

Stanton turned to Mac and said, "You've got a lot of experience handling a wagon, Mac. How about doing the driving?"

"I never had a man hurt this bad in the back of a chuck wagon," Mac pointed out.

"Maybe not, but I trust you to do the job. I'll come with you, of course. Pete, climb in back with Frank. As easy as you can, mind. We don't want this thing bouncing around too much."

"It'll make supper late if I go into town," Mac pointed out.

"I don't figure any of us care much about that right now," Stanton said.

Mac untied his apron. "I'll drive the wagon, then, if that's what you want."

He took off the apron, handed it to one of the men, and asked him to put it back in the kitchen. Then he and Stanton climbed onto the driver's seat and Mac took up the reins.

Stanton turned his head to look into the wagon bed. "All right back there?"

"As all right as we're gonna get, George," Newton said. "Frank's passed out."

"He's still breathing, isn't he?"

"Yeah, but he sure looks gray."

Stanton nodded to Mac. "Let's go."

Mac flapped the reins and called out to the mules, urging them firmly to start moving but not being emphatic enough about it to startle them and cause a jolt. A little jerk was inevitable, though, and as the wagon began rolling, Rigoni moaned again even though he didn't regain consciousness.

Mac kept the team moving at as steady a gait as he could manage. As they followed the trail down the hill and the camp fell behind them, Stanton scrubbed a hand over his face wearily and said, "I sure don't see how such a thing happened."

"I do," Mac said quietly, keeping his eyes on the trail ahead of them. "I took a look at the rope that's supposed to hold the logs in the stack. Somebody went to some trouble to work on it and make it look like it just frayed and snapped—but I've got a pretty strong hunch it was cut enough to weaken it until it was only a matter of time until it gave way."

Stanton drew in a sharp breath. He kept his voice equally low as he asked, "You mean somebody wanted to kill Frank?"

"No, him getting caught in front of the logs like that was an accident. Nobody could have predicted that." Mac glanced over at Stanton. "But somebody was sure trying to cause trouble for you, George. As my cowboy friends say, you can bet a hat on that."

Chapter 19

Luke had to put all his tracking skill to work as he, Marshal Sundell, Matt Rand, and Cliff Campbell followed the man who had tried to ambush them. Luke was convinced the rifleman was part of the gang that had held up the stagecoach and stolen the Empire Logging Company payroll.

The trail led generally north, although it veered from side to side at times to avoid ravines and other obstacles. Trampled grass, broken branches, and overturned rocks all pointed the way.

After a while, Luke realized that even though it took some effort on his part to follow the signs, the man they were after hadn't gone to any trouble to hide his trail. It appeared he had been more concerned with getting away quickly than with concealing his tracks.

Speed was what the man had achieved, too. The posse wasn't able to close the gap on him.

Luke began to notice that the landscape around them looked familiar. He recognized the trees, the hills, the wide, flat, grassy stretches. They were well up into the basin where the Triangle 7 and the other area ranches were located.

Marshal Sundell was aware of that, too. As he and Luke rode in front of the other two men, the marshal said quietly, "I think we're on Triangle 7 range by now."

"You're absolutely right, Marshal," Luke said. "I've ridden through these parts in the past week while working for Ben Harmon. This is part of his spread, no doubt about it."

"It seems to me that the trail we're following leads toward Triangle 7 headquarters, too."

Luke nodded slowly. "It does."

Sundell looked over at him and asked, "What do you reckon that means?"

"At this point, I don't want to speculate."

"Well, I don't mind speculating, and I can't help but wonder why somebody would try to bushwhack us and then light a shuck straight for Ben Harmon's ranch."

Luke's mouth tightened to a grim line, but he didn't say anything in response to the marshal's comment. He was going to keep an open mind—for the moment.

However, he couldn't help but think about the history between Ben Harmon and Constance Elliott. Clearly, there was no love lost between those two anymore, despite the close relationship they'd once had. In fact, these days they were mortal enemies, plain and simple.

Luke had a hard time believing that Harmon would try to get back at Constance by stealing her company's payroll, though. And certainly, none of the men Luke had been riding with for the past week struck him as the type to wantonly gun down a veteran stage driver like Fred Carter, either. After decades of dealing with outlaws and killers, Luke trusted his gut when it came to evaluating a man's potential for such behavior.

But there was no doubt the tracks were headed in the direction of the Triangle 7 headquarters.

Before the posse came in sight of the ranch house and the other buildings, the tracks disappeared. The trail led onto a ridge that was bare rock, so the ground wouldn't take any prints.

Sometimes in a situation such as this, it was possible to spot places where a horse's shoes had chipped the rock, but Luke didn't see any of those telltale marks.

"Wait here," he told Sundell and the others. He dismounted to take a closer look. Leading his horse, he ranged back and forth along the ridge for several hundred yards in both directions.

"Find anything?" Sundell called to him.

Luke shook his head and continued searching. He found one thing he considered interesting, but no actual tracks that would allow them to keep following the mysterious bushwhacker.

He returned to where Sundell, Rand, and Campbell waited. Pointing to a brown pile on the ground nearby, he said, "Those are fairly fresh horse droppings. The man we're after stopped here long enough for his horse to do that."

"Why would he stop?" Sundell asked.

"No tracks lead away from here in any direction," Luke said. "My hunch is that he stopped here and tied some pieces of blanket around his mount's hooves so the horseshoes wouldn't leave any marks on the rock. Then he went on up and over the ridge."

Sundell frowned. "So you're saying that after not taking the time to cover his trail from the spot where he ambushed us to here, he suddenly got careful?"

"That's what the evidence indicates to me."

Campbell asked, "Why would he do that?"

The marshal snorted and said, "Because he finally realized he was leading us right back to the rest of the gang, that's why!" Sundell pointed. "Ben Harmon's ranch house is only half a mile on the other side of that ridge."

"Wait a minute," Matt Rand said. The blacksmith frowned. "I've known Ben Harmon more than ten years. You don't really believe he's connected to that gang of stagecoach robbers and killers, do you, Abner?"

"I hate to think so, but I can only go by what I see with my own eyes. We've been on Triangle 7 range for a while now, and that bushwhacker's trail has been leading straight toward the ranch headquarters."

"That doesn't mean Ben's in on it," Rand insisted. "Could be some of his men have gone lobo."

Luke had considered that possibility, too, but he had met the whole crew and he didn't believe any of them were the sort to turn bad like that.

It was impossible to know what actually went on inside a man's head, though—and in his heart. A man could live a law-abiding life for a long time and then do something beyond the pale, if the circumstances were right to lead him into it.

"Maybe Mr. Jensen could pick up the trail on the other side of the ridge," Cliff Campbell suggested.

"That ridge runs for several miles through here," Sundell said. "It would take a while to search the whole thing, and in that time, the fella we're after would have an even bigger lead." A bleak expression settled over the marshal's face as he shook his head. "No, it's a bitter pill to swallow, but it looks like the varmint has given us the slip. Unless . . ."

"Unless what?" Luke asked.

Grim determination was in Sundell's voice as he said, "Unless we ride on to the Triangle 7 and see if Ben Harmon can give us any answers."

"If you ride in and accuse Harmon of ramrodding a bunch of outlaws and murderers, he's going to start bucking like he's got a whole cactus under his saddle, not just a burr."

"I know that, but it's my job to get to the bottom of this, find those owlhoots, and recover what they stole from that strongbox, no matter what else happens." Sundell's jaw tightened. "Don't forget, Matt, Ben and I have been friends for a long time, too. I don't like accusing him any more than you do."

"Yeah, I reckon I see that," Rand admitted. "You're the marshal. You're in charge of this posse. I reckon if you say we're riding to the Triangle 7, we're riding to the Triangle 7."

"That's the way I feel about it, too, Abner," Campbell said.

Sundell looked at Luke. "How about you, Jensen?"

"I have a hard time believing it," Luke said, "but I think we have to check it out."

He mounted up, and the four men started up the ridge, their horse's shoes clinking against the rock. Luke continued to watch for signs that their quarry had come this way, but he didn't see any. Covering the horse's hooves with pieces of blanket would prevent them leaving any sign. By the time they reached the crest and started down the other side, Luke was more convinced than ever that was what the bushwhacker had done.

He was also convinced this trip to the Triangle 7 wasn't going to do any good—and might, in fact, just make things worse—but he agreed with Sundell that they had no other option.

A short time later, they came in sight of the ranch headquarters. Everything looked normal around the place. Luke didn't see anybody moving at first, but as he and the others approached, Shorty and Kaintuck ambled out of the barn. The two old wranglers must have heard the horses.

They were surprised to see the marshal and the other two men from Pine Knob; Luke could tell that from the expressions on their weather-beaten faces.

"Didn't expect to see you back without Rich and the other boys, Luke," Shorty said.

"They haven't gotten back from town yet?"

"Ain't seen hide nor hair of 'em," Kaintuck answered. "Marshal, what are you doin' here?" The old-timer's frown deepened as he looked at Rand and Campbell. "And with the blacksmith and the newspaper fella, to boot."

"Looks mighty like an official delegation to me," Shorty drawled.

Kaintuck grunted. "Yeah, or a posse. A mite on the small side for that, though."

Sundell ignored the questions and leaned forward in his saddle. "Has anybody else ridden in here in the past hour?" he asked sharply.

"Who might it be you're lookin' for?" Shorty asked.

"Never mind about that. Just answer the question."

That was the wrong tone to take with these two old pelicans, Luke thought. He could practically see their hackles rising.

"If you're askin' as the marshal of Pine Knob, you can go climb a stump," Shorty said. "You got no, what do you call it, *jurisdictation* out here."

"I think *jurisdiction* is the word you're lookin' for, Shorty," Kaintuck added, "but whatever you call it, you're right, Abner here ain't got it."

Sundell glowered at the wranglers and said, "You two know good and well that the county sheriff doesn't object to me investigating matters outside the town as long as I send him a report."

Shorty sniffed and said, "That ain't official."

Luke figured he'd better step in. "I'm giving the marshal a hand with this, men, and it's important. A matter of life and death, in fact."

"Well, why in blazes didn't you say so?" Kaintuck demanded. "We ain't seen a soul since you and Rich and them other boys rode out earlier, Luke. Ben and Alamo are in the house, the rest o' the crew is out on the range, and nobody else has been here."

Shorty jerked his head in a nod. "That's right, if it's any o' your doggone business, Marshal."

"It's my business, all right," Sundell snapped. "The stagecoach from The Dalles was held up and robbed. The outlaws shot Fred Carter to pieces and wounded young Arch Whitehorse, who was riding shotgun."

The two wranglers gaped at the marshal. They couldn't find their voices for a moment, and then Shorty said, "Ol' Fred's dead?"

"As can be."

Kaintuck let out an explosive oath. "Fred was as fine a jehu as ever picked up a set o' reins!" he said.

"A dang good checker player, too," Shorty said. "I can't believe he's gone." He got a confused look on his face. "If you're huntin' the owlhoots who done that awful thing, Marshal, what in blazes are you doin' here?"

"While we were trying to track the bandits, somebody ambushed us," Sundell explained. "The trail led here."

The wranglers began to cloud up and look like they were fixing to rain again.

"That ain't possible," Shorty said.

"We done told you, nobody's ridden in here except you fellas," Kaintuck added.

"We followed the tracks to within half a mile of this place, and they were headed straight in this direction."

"Half a mile's a long way," Kaintuck drawled. "The fella you've been chasin' could've turned and gone any which-a-way."

"You reckon the Triangle 7 hires owlhoots and killers?" Shorty demanded in a heated voice. He was the proddier of the two old-timers, Luke knew.

"I didn't say that—" Sundell began.

Shorty interrupted him. "Sure as blazes sounded like you was implicatin' it!"

Luke moved his horse forward slightly. "We're not accusing anybody," he said. "We're just trying to find out who's responsible for what happened today."

"Well, it sure wasn't anybody from this ranch." Shorty turned his head toward the house and bellowed, "Boss! Boss, get out here!"

"Settle down," Sundell ordered with a growling edge in his voice. "We wanted to talk to Ben anyway. No need for you to yell, you leather-lunged old coot."

"Old coot, is it!" Shorty bristled up like a banty rooster and looked like he wanted to fight. Kaintuck frowned and moved to put himself between his friend and Sundell, just in case Shorty decided to charge the lawman.

The front door of the ranch house banged as Ben Harmon thrust it open and stalked out onto the porch.

"What's all the yelling about?" he demanded. "Abner? Is that you?" Harmon started down the steps from the porch. "What are Matt and Cliff doin' out here with you? And Jensen? I thought you went into Pine Knob with Rich and some of the other boys."

"I did," Luke said. "But the marshal got word of trouble while I was there in his office, checking on that reward money."

Clearly, Harmon was baffled by what was going on, but he said, "What are you fellas doing still in the saddle?" He frowned at Shorty and Kaintuck. "We got visitors. How come you didn't invite 'em to light and sit?"

"Might have," Shorty said sullenly, "if they hadn't accused us o' bein' a bunch o' murderin' owlhoots, and the Triangle 7 o' being the new Hole in the Wall!"

"What are you talkin' about?" Harmon looked at Sundell. "What's this all about, Abner?"

"The stagecoach from The Dalles was held up today," Sundell said. Without wasting any words, he filled the rancher in on everything that had happened, including how the bushwhacker's trail had led them to the Triangle 7.

Harmon's face tightened into grim lines as he listened. When Sundell was finished, Harmon said, "It sure sounds like you're accusing me of bein' behind that robbery and killing, Abner."

"The trail led here."

"Like blazes it did! You said yourself that Jensen lost the trail on the other side of the ridge."

"That's true," Luke said.

Sundell didn't look convinced. "Why would the bushwhacking skunk come this way if he wasn't heading home?"

"How the devil would I know? All I know is that you don't have a lick of proof that anybody on the Triangle 7 was mixed up in that deviltry, and I don't savvy why you'd even think such a thing in the first place. It's loco!"

Sundell said, "This month's payroll for Empire was in that strongbox, Ben."

"So? What does that have to do with—" Harmon broke off

and stared at Sundell. He looked flabbergasted and then angry. "You think I had my boys steal that payroll to get back at Constance for what she did to me!"

"I've got to consider all possible motives," Sundell said stiffly.

"What better motive could an outlaw have than getting his filthy hands on a strongbox full of loot?"

From the porch, the stocky cook called across to the men, "Hey, boss, you want me to fix somethin' to drink for our guests?"

Harmon turned and said, "Forget about that, Alamo. They're not guests. They're . . ." He searched for a word. "Interlopers!"

Then he swung his furious gaze toward Luke and went on, "You're part of this, Jensen?"

"I rode with the marshal because I have experience tracking lawbreakers," Luke replied coolly. "Also, the thieves took the mail pouch, and it's possible there was a message in it regarding those rewards."

"Yeah, you wouldn't want to take a chance on losin' that blood money, would you?"

Anger welled up inside Luke at Harmon's bitter, contemptuous tone, but he tamped it down. Losing his temper at this point wouldn't accomplish anything.

Instead, he said calmly, "When I offered to ride with the marshal, I didn't have any idea what we were going to find. I was surprised when the trail led in this direction. And to tell you the truth, after getting to know everybody here, I have a hard time believing anyone from the Triangle 7 was involved with that robbery and killing."

Harmon snorted in disgust. "Well, thank you 'most to death for that, Jensen. I've got half a mind to fire you."

Kaintuck surprised Luke by speaking up. "You shouldn't ought to do that, Boss. None o' this is Luke's fault."

"He led 'em here, didn't he?" Shorty said.

"He just followed some tracks. He didn't make those tracks."

"That's true," Harmon admitted grudgingly. The looks he shot toward Luke remained fairly unfriendly, however.

Sundell said, "Your men claim nobody has ridden in here during the past hour."

"That's true," Harmon said. "I've been in my office with the window open. If anybody had ridden up, I would've heard 'em. There's been nothing around here but peace and quiet. I'm sure Alamo Paige will tell you the same thing if you want to go and ask him."

"I don't reckon that's necessary. I'll take your word for it."

Harmon didn't look like that did much to soothe his ruffled feelings.

"I still have plenty of questions," the marshal went on, "but there's one thing I'm sure of: The man who took those shots at us was on your range not long ago, Ben. I don't know why or where he went. But if outlaws are hanging around your place, you'd probably be wise to tell your men to keep their eyes open."

Harmon jerked his head in a nod. "You can be sure I'll do just that. And if we catch anybody up to no good on this spread, we'll deal with 'em, I can promise you that."

"If you or your men see anything suspicious, you need to let me know," Sundell said. "Don't go taking the law into your own hands."

Harmon frowned. "Something else occurs to me," he said. "If you were so quick to figure I had something to do with this, those blasted loggers are liable to jump to the same conclusion."

"I suppose that's possible."

"Tell that Elliott woman I didn't steal her payroll. I would never stoop to anything that low-down and dirty. That hardheaded female probably won't believe you, but there's nothing I can do about that." Harmon sighed, and at that moment, the rancher didn't look angry as much as he looked tired and disappointed, Luke thought. "I just don't want any more trouble with that bunch."

"I don't want trouble, either." Sundell looked at Rand and Campbell. "Let's keep this to ourselves, gents, at least for now.

When we get back to Pine Knob, we'll just tell folks that we lost the gang's trail. All right?"

Rand nodded, but Campbell looked uneasy. "I'm a newspaperman, Abner," he said. "It goes against the grain for me to keep the truth from the public."

"Just give me some time to get this sorted out, Cliff. That's all I'm asking."

"Well, all right," Campbell said with obvious reluctance. "You know how word gets around in a small town, though. It's hard to keep anything quiet for too long."

Luke said, "I think I'll ride back with you, Marshal, just to see if anything else has happened." He looked at the rancher. "Do I still have a job here, Mr. Harmon?"

Harmon appeared to think about for a couple of heartbeats, but then he nodded.

"I reckon you do. I don't have any complaints about your work, Jensen, and you've fit in well with the crew. I suppose I can't hold it against you that you tried to give the law a hand—even if it did lead to this star packer throwin' accusations around."

Now Sundell looked angry, but when Luke turned his horse away, so did the marshal.

"I'll be back this evening," Luke said. "Thanks, Boss."

"Hold on a minute," Harmon said. "I've heard that you're supposed to be pretty good at trackin' down outlaws."

"I've had a considerable amount of experience at it," Luke allowed.

"Then do me a favor: Find this bunch. Then when Constance Elliott starts accusin' me of being a crook, as she's bound to sooner or later, I can rub the truth right in her face!"

CHAPTER 20

Frank Rigoni hadn't regained consciousness by the time the wagon reached Pine Knob, but he was still breathing, Mac saw to his relief when he brought the vehicle to a stop and looked back over his shoulder into the wagon bed.

The injured man's arrival stirred up interest among the townspeople and attracted a crowd. Several people gathered around and asked questions as Mac and George Stanton climbed down from the wagon.

"Don't just stand there flappin' your jaws," Stanton barked at them. "Some of you men give us a hand here. We need to take Frank in to see the doctor."

Mac had brought the wagon to a stop in front of Dr. Abrams's neatly kept house, which also served as the medico's surgery. One of the townies ran up on the porch and pounded on the door to summon the doctor, while others helped Mac and Stanton lift Rigoni out of the wagon bed.

The doctor came out of his house and said, "Careful, there, careful! What's wrong with that man?"

"He got pinned on the rollway by a log, Doc," Stanton said.

"He has some busted ribs for sure, and I don't know what else might be wrong with him."

"Well, bring him in, bring him in. And I repeat, carefully. You might do irreparable damage if you start jostling around a man with internal injuries."

As gently as possible, Mac and the others carried Rigoni into the house. They placed him on a sturdy table in Abrams's examination room.

"All right, get out of here and give me a chance to look him over," the doctor ordered. "But stay close, because I'll probably need you to move him to one of the bedrooms when I'm finished."

"We'll wait out on the porch," Stanton said.

The men filed out. Stanton stood at the porch railing and heaved a tired sigh. Mac could see how heavily the responsibility for the safety of his men weighed on the burly superintendent.

One of the townsmen lingered on the porch with Mac and Stanton and said, "This has been a mighty bad day for Empire, I reckon."

Stanton frowned and asked, "How do you figure that? I mean, I'm sorry to have a man injured, of course—"

"I was talking about the payroll," the townie said.

"What about the payroll?" Stanton demanded.

The man looked surprised, but then he said, "Yeah, I guess you wouldn't have heard about it, since you've been out at the logging camp. The stagecoach from The Dalles was held up earlier today. The driver was killed and the guard wounded, and the outlaws made off with the strongbox with your payroll in it."

For a long moment, Mac and Stanton just stared at the townie in shock. Mac found his voice first and asked, "Does anybody know who did it?"

The man shook his head. "Nope. The marshal and a few other fellas have ridden out to where it happened to have a look around. Marshal Sundell said they'd try to pick up the robbers' trail. That fella Jensen was one of the hombres who went with him. You know, the bounty hunter who brought in the Bishop brothers."

Stanton recovered from his surprise enough to unleash a torrent of profanity. That outburst helped Mac conceal his reaction when he heard that Luke had joined the marshal's posse. That made sense, he supposed; Luke was a professional outlaw hunter, after all.

The townsman drew back defensively as Stanton ranted obscenely. He held up his hands and said, "Whoa there, friend. I didn't have anything to do with it."

Stanton ran out of steam with a frustrated sigh. "Sorry," he said. "That cussing wasn't directed at you, mister. I just wonder when this run of terrible luck we're having is gonna end, that's all."

"Well, I can't blame you for that, I suppose. If I'd stopped to think about it, I should have known you hadn't heard the news."

"No, no, that's all right. You didn't do anything wrong. We were going to find out sooner or later." Stanton rubbed his temples wearily. "I can't help but wonder what's going to happen next."

Mac felt the same way. The camp cook, Walt Nichols, breaking his leg was just pure bad luck, as Stanton had said. But the accident that had befallen Frank Rigoni, coming as it had on the same day the company's payroll was stolen . . .

Mac had to wonder if those things were just coincidence. A suspicious hunch stirred inside him and whispered to him that they weren't.

The sound of hoofbeats from the street made Mac and Stanton look in that direction. Several mules from the camp were being used as saddle mounts. Alec Lafferty was one of the riders.

"What are those fellas doing here?" Stanton muttered. "I gave orders before we left for everybody to get back to work."

"They're probably worried about Frank and decided to ride in and check on him," Mac said.

Stanton scowled. "I didn't tell 'em they could do that."

"Even if you had, they might have ignored those orders if they were worried enough about a friend."

"Yeah, you're right about that." Stanton blew out a breath. "Loggers are a hardheaded bunch if there ever was one!"

The handful of riders reined in the mules and dismounted in front of the doctor's house. Lafferty came up the walk to the porch, trailed by the other two men.

"How's Frank doing? He's still alive, isn't he?" Lafferty asked.

"He was alive when Mac and I left him in there," Stanton said. "Doc Abrams is taking a good look at him now, tryin' to decide how bad he's hurt and what to do about it."

The door opened behind them as if the physician had been waiting for that cue. He stepped onto the porch, wiping his hands on a piece of cloth.

"What's the patient's name again?" he asked as Mac and the others turned quickly to look at him. "He told me, but I can't recall it."

"Frank Rigoni," Stanton said.

The doctor nodded. "That's right. I believe Mr. Rigoni will live."

"Thank the Lord for that," Lafferty said.

Abrams went on, "He has four broken ribs, but it doesn't appear that any of them punctured anything vital. I've bound up his torso to keep everything stable. That's really all I can do for him except to make sure that he remains as still as possible while the fractures heal. He's also badly bruised and will be quite sore for a few days. Rest is going to be the best thing in the world for him."

"He doesn't have any other internal injuries?" Mac asked.

The doctor looked at him with interest. "You know about internal injuries?"

"I drove a chuck wagon over plenty of cattle trails," Mac explained. "Out there on the prairie, the cook generally does any doctoring that needs done. I've picked up a few things out of necessity."

"Then you're probably aware that it's difficult to know for certain about internal injuries. If they don't cause any symptoms, we can't know about them because there's no way to look inside a man's body and see them for ourselves. But at this point, Mr. Rigoni isn't showing signs of anything else being wrong. I'll keep him under close observation while those ribs are healing. That's really all I can do."

"We appreciate it, Doc," Stanton said.

"Actually, I'd say that Mr. Rigoni is extremely lucky to be alive. A log the size of the ones you men work with could easily crush a man to death if it rolled over him."

Lafferty said, "You mean somebody tried to use that log to murder poor Frank, don't you, Doc?"

Abrams frowned. "I never said that. I don't know how the accident occurred."

"Pete Newton and I figured it out," Lafferty went on. "Somebody sabotaged that rope so it would break and turn loose the top layers of the log stack. They were tryin' to kill Frank."

Stanton said, "Now hold on. Nobody could have known that Frank would be walking where he shouldn't have been at exactly the wrong moment. Even if somebody monkeyed with the rope, they wouldn't have any way of knowing the precise time it would break."

"Yeah, yeah, sure," Lafferty said. "Maybe not, but that doesn't mean it wasn't sabotage."

"I'll have to look at the rope for myself," Stanton said, not mentioning that Mac had already told him the same thing, "before I'll believe it. What would be the purpose of sabotaging that log stack?"

"Somebody could've done it just on the chance one of us would get hurt," Lafferty said. "And just letting those logs loose like that would cause trouble and extra work for us."

"Maybe," Stanton said, slowly nodding. "But who would do such a thing?"

"You know good and well who'd do something like that, George," Lafferty snapped. "Those blasted cowboys from the Triangle 7."

There it was, Mac thought. The kind of thinking that could set off a full-scale war between Triangle 7 and the Empire Logging Company—and complicate his and Luke's search for Asa Dunnigan.

One of the other timbermen said, "I think I spotted some of their horses down at the Lonesome Pine. They're probably in the saloon celebrating how they nearly killed poor Frank!"

"Maybe we should go down there and let them know their dirty trick didn't work," Lafferty said. "And teach them that they'd better not try such a low-down thing again!"

Stanton held up his hands. "Hold on, hold on," he said. "Nobody's gonna go down there to the saloon and start a brawl with Harmon's men."

"But you know they did it," Lafferty insisted. "Nobody else has any reason to want to hurt our outfit. You know how bad Harmon hates the boss lady, George. He'd do anything to get back at Miss Elliott for kicking him aside instead of marrying him."

Stanton glared at him and said, "For one thing, all that trouble happened before you came into these parts and signed on with Empire, Alec, so you don't know what really went on between them."

Lafferty snorted. "I've heard enough stories to have a pretty good idea."

"And for another thing," Stanton went on, as if he hadn't heard Lafferty's comment, "I'm the boss of this crew, and if there's any getting even to be done, I'll be the one to give the order. I'm not gonna do that until I've had a better chance to look things over."

"Looking things over is just a waste of time," Lafferty said.

That brought growls of agreement from the other men. Their jaws tightened as they stared defiantly at Stanton.

Dr. Abrams cleared his throat and said, "If you're going to do battle with Ben Harmon's men, try not to break any bones or inflict any other serious injuries. I have three rooms for recuperating patients, and they're all full, or they will be once some of you men come back inside and move Mr. Rigoni to a bed."

"Hear that?" Stanton snapped at the loggers. "Frank needs us to do something that'll actually help him instead of just stirring up more trouble. Come on."

Grudgingly, the other men followed Stanton into the doctor's house. Lafferty and another logger stayed on the porch.

So did Mac. As angry as Lafferty seemed to be, Mac didn't trust him not to head for the Lonesome Pine Saloon despite Stanton's orders.

"It would be better if you kept a cool head until we find out for sure what's going on, Alec," he said.

Lafferty gazed at him with obvious resentment. "You've been part of the crew even less time than I have, McKenzie. I'll thank you to keep your opinions to yourself. Besides, you don't know that Triangle 7 bunch like I do. They're no good—"

"Here they come now, Alec," the other logger said, breaking into Lafferty's condemnation of Ben Harmon's men.

Mac and Lafferty swung around to look along the street where the other man was pointing. Sure enough, four men were riding slowly in their direction. Mac recognized one of them as Rich Coburn, Harmon's foreman. The other three looked familiar, leading Mac to think they must have been involved in the ruckus in the Lonesome Pine a week earlier.

Lafferty headed abruptly toward the steps. Mac said, "Wait a minute, Alec. Stanton said—"

"I don't care what he said," Lafferty responded without turning around. "I'm gonna give those cowboys a piece of my mind—and anything else they want!"

CHAPTER 21

The other logger was right behind Lafferty and just as eager for trouble judging by the look on his face. Mac might have been able to grab one of them and force him to listen to reason, but not both. All he could do was follow them down the steps and along the short walk to the street.

Rich Coburn had seen them coming. He reined in as he reached the front of the doctor's place. The other three cowhands followed suit. Coburn rested his hands on the saddle horn and smirked down at Lafferty as the man planted himself, rested his balled fists on his hips, and glared.

"You want something, mister?" Coburn drawled.

"I want to let you know that your little trick didn't work," Lafferty said. "One of our men was hurt when those logs rolled down the hill, but nobody was killed—no thanks to you and your dirty work!"

Coburn shook his head. "I don't know what you're blatherin' about. Somebody got hurt out at your camp, you said?"

Lafferty's jaw jutted out. "Actually, no, I didn't say that. I didn't mention the camp. But you'd know where it happened, since you were responsible for it, wouldn't you?"

Mac had been watching Coburn's face during the exchange. His instincts told him that the ranch foreman was genuinely confused and didn't know anything about what had happened to Frank Rigoni.

"Mister, you must've fallen out of one of those trees and landed on your head," Coburn said. "We didn't do anything to your bunch. My pards and I have all been down in the saloon for the past couple of hours."

"How did you know something happened at Empire's camp, then?" Lafferty shot back at him.

"It's a reasonable guess, ain't it?"

That was true, Mac thought. Coburn could easily have jumped to that conclusion based on what Lafferty had said. However, he had a hunch that the loggery was in no mood to listen to reason.

"Get down off that horse," Lafferty insisted. "Your boss has got a grudge against our boss, and you cowboys hate us because of it. Let's settle this between us. No more skulking around and trying to wreck our operation."

Through clenched teeth, Coburn said, "I told you, I don't havc any idea what you're talkin' about. But Mr. Harmon told us we could come to town as long as we didn't start any ruckuses, and I intend to do what he said."

"Fine," Lafferty bit off. "You're not starting it. *I am*!"

Before Mac could grab him and hold him back, Lafferty leaped at Coburn's mount. The horse shied away as Coburn yelled in surprise. But Lafferty was still able to lunge close enough, reach up, grab the front of Coburn's shirt, and haul the cowboy out of the saddle.

Coburn howled in outrage, a protest that was cut off sharply as he slammed to the ground on his back. Lafferty stepped away from him but appeared to do so in order to position himself for a kick aimed at Coburn.

He didn't get to attempt that because one of the other cowboys left his saddle in a diving tackle that drove Lafferty off his feet and sent both men crashing to the ground.

The other logger yelled, "Hey!" and started after them, but a Triangle 7 hand dropped to the ground and intercepted him. The cowboy hit the logger with a looping right that staggered him, but the timberman recovered his balance and slugged the cowboy in the belly as the man tried to rush in on him.

The remaining cowboy threw his leg over the saddle and hit the ground, charging toward Mac.

"Whoa!" Mac said as he twisted out of the way. He grabbed his attacker's arm and used the man's own momentum against him, swinging him around so that the cowboy lost his footing, fell, and rolled in the street.

As the man came back up on one knee, Mac raised his hands in front of him, palms out. He was about to tell the cowboy that this wasn't his fight, but then he realized that would make him an outcast in the logging camp.

Instead, he put a mocking grin on his face, changed the defensive gesture to a beckoning one, and said, "Come on, mister, if you're bound and determined to get a whipping."

The cowboy's face turned dark red with rage. He surged up from the ground and charged Mac like a maddened bull.

Mac tried to twist out of the way again, but the cowboy wasn't as out of control as he appeared to be. The rush turned out to be a feint, and when Mac started to step aside, the cowboy changed course and drove a punch at his face. Mac jerked his head aside just in time to avoid the blow's full force. It scraped his ear painfully, anyway.

Mac jabbed a left into the man's face to slow him down and then landed a right cross on his jaw. For a second, Mac thought he might go down, but the cowboy kept his feet and came in close, hooking punches that hammered Mac's midsection. Mac grimaced in pain as he bent forward.

The cowboy tried an uppercut then, but Mac pulled his head

back out of the way just in time. He felt the wind from the man's fist as it shot upward in front of his face, missing by no more than an inch.

That left the cowboy wide open. Mac's right fist sank into his belly up to the wrist. An instant later, Mac's left whipped around and caught the man on the chin. The impact slewed the cowboy's head to the left. Mac chopped a blow to the spot where the man's neck met his right shoulder. That was finally enough to knock him to the ground and keep him there for a while.

Mac turned to see how the other battles were going. Lafferty and Coburn were both on their feet, slugging away at each other. They appeared to be evenly matched, and it was likely that the winner of their struggle would be determined by luck. Whoever made the first misstep would wind up stretched out on the ground, senseless.

The other contest wasn't nearly as fair. Two cowboys had closed in on the remaining logger, one of them getting behind him to grab his arms and hold him while the other slammed brutal punches into his face and body.

The one doing the beating had his arm pulled back to launch another blow when Mac clamped a hand on his shoulder and hauled him around. The cowboy wasn't expecting that, so he wasn't braced to stop Mac from pulling him away. Mac threw a punch with all of his weight behind it. His fist cracked against the cowboy's jaw with a sound like an ax biting into a block of wood.

At the same time, the logger stamped a hobnailed work boot on the foot of the man holding him from behind. The cowboy's riding boot saved his foot from any significant damage, but it must have hurt because he let out a bellow of pain. That caused his grip to slip, and the logger was able to wrench himself free.

He whirled around, grabbed the shoulders of the cowboy whose arms he'd just escaped from, and shoved down as he lifted his knee. The knee cracked into the cowboy's jaw and rocked his head so far back it looked like it was about to come off his shoulders. The cowboy crumpled bonelessly to the ground, out cold.

A few yards away, Rich Coburn and Alec Lafferty seemed to be tiring, which was understandable after all the punches they had thrown at each other. Coburn launched another one now, but it was a hair too slow. Lafferty twisted out of the way and got behind Coburn as the Triangle 7 foreman lost his balance for a second. The logger's arm looped around Coburn's neck. Lafferty grabbed that wrist with his other hand and locked his forearm in place across Coburn's throat like an iron bar.

"Now we'll see how you like not bein' able to breathe," Lafferty snarled in Coburn's ear. "I'll choke you to death like that log almost crushed poor Frank!"

Lafferty looked like he meant every word of the threat. His hawklike face was merciless. Coburn's face quickly turned red, and although he flailed his arms, he couldn't dislodge the hold Lafferty had on him.

Mac knew it wouldn't be a good idea to just stand there and allow Lafferty to kill Rich Coburn. He was about to move in and try to get Lafferty to let go when he heard the rapid patter of running footsteps coming up behind him.

Constance Elliott shot past him, holding up her skirts so she could move faster. Farther down the street, puffing and trotting considerably slower, came Empire's bookkeeper, Carl Peters.

"Lafferty!" Constance cried as she came to a stop not far from where Lafferty stood choking Rich Coburn. "Let that man go! *Now!*"

Lafferty didn't follow the order right away. He stood there for a moment longer, his face still dark and contorted with fury.

But then he jerked his arm away from Coburn's throat and stepped back. Coburn's knees buckled and dropped him to the ground. He rolled onto his side and lay there gasping for air, his chest heaving with the effort. Gradually, the dark red color faded from his face.

"You should've let me finish him off, ma'am," Lafferty said. "He had it coming. All those blasted cowboys do."

"I heard that one of our men is hurt," Constance said. "What happened?"

Mac would have explained, but at that moment, George Stanton and the other man who had gone inside to help Dr. Abrams get Rigoni settled in bed emerged from the house. Seeing the group in the street, Stanton rushed forward.

"What in—" he began, then stopped short rather than blurting out any profanities in front of Constance. After a second, he looked at Mac and said, "I heard a commotion out here. What's going on, McKenzie?"

Mac didn't feel much like explaining. It seemed to him that it ought to be obvious what was going on.

But he said, "Coburn and those other fellows from the Triangle 7 were riding by. Things turned into a fracas."

Alec Lafferty had provoked that fracas, but Mac didn't point that out. Lafferty was fairly well-liked among the logging crew, and blaming the trouble on him would just cause problems for Mac in the long run.

"Who's the injured man?" Constance asked. "All I heard was that an Empire man was brought in and taken to the doctor."

"Frank Rigoni," Stanton told her. Quickly, he filled her in on the accident at the rollway.

But he didn't mention the possible sabotage, Mac noted. Stanton probably wanted to look into the situation more himself before he gave Constance that information.

"Is he going to be all right?" Constance asked when Stanton was finished.

"Doc Abrams thinks so. He says he's done everything he can for Frank right now. It'll just take time and rest for him to recover."

Constance nodded. "The company will pay for all his expenses, of course."

Rich Coburn was still a little red-faced, but he had caught his breath and now pushed himself to a sitting position.

"Lady . . . Miss Elliott . . . your man accused Triangle 7 of bein' behind what happened to that Rigoni hombre. It ain't true."

Lafferty clenched his fists and stepped toward Coburn.

"Shut your lying mouth," he said. "You saddle tramps aren't fit to talk to Miss Elliott."

"That's all right, Lafferty," Constance said. She looked at Coburn and nodded. "Go on."

Coburn held up a hand to one of the other cowboys. They clasped wrists and the man helped Coburn to his feet.

"We've been here in town most of the afternoon," he said. "There ain't no way we could have caused any trouble out at your camp."

"Ben Harmon has more men working for him than just you four," Constance said.

"All due respect, ma'am, but do you really believe Ben would stoop to doin' anything as dirty as whatever it is this fella is talkin' about?"

For a long moment, Constance didn't answer. Then she said, "No. No, I have a very hard time believing that." She drew in a deep breath. "This day has already been difficult enough without having to come to grips with something like that." She turned to Stanton. "You've heard that we lost the payroll to robbers, George?"

"Yes, ma'am, one of the fellas from town mentioned it."

"The news was waiting for Carl and me when we got back to town. We can only hope that Marshal Sundell and the men who went with him are able to track down the thieves and recover the money."

One of those men with the marshal was Luke Jensen, Mac thought. That meant Sundell had more of a chance of success than he would have had otherwise.

Constance squared her shoulders and lifted her chin, obviously gathering her strength after the multiple assaults on her business today. She said to Stanton, "Is there anything else we can do for Frank right now?"

"No, ma'am. I reckon he's in good hands."

"Then you and the other men should get back to camp. Empire still has contracts to fulfill, after all, despite the troubles that have befallen us."

Stanton nodded. "Yes, ma'am."

Coburn cleared his throat and said hoarsely, "Beggin' your pardon, Miss Elliott, but ain't you gonna do anything about these men o' yours who jumped us?"

Constance's voice and expression were chilly as she said, "I apologize, Mr. Coburn. I think you're going to have to be satisfied with that."

Coburn looked like he wanted to say something else but, perhaps wisely, he didn't. He just picked up his hat, slapped it against his leg to get some of the dust off it, and nodded as he said, "Ma'am."

The men from the Triangle 7 might have mounted up and ridden on back to the ranch, and Mac and the other members of Empire's crew might have returned to the camp, but just then they all noticed that a new group of riders had come into view, heading into the settlement from the northwest. Mac caught his breath as he recognized Luke riding next to Marshal Sundell. Two men followed fairly close behind them.

This was the posse that had gone out after the stagecoach robbers, Mac realized.

And from the dispirited look of them, they hadn't been successful at rounding up the owlhoots.

The riders came on at a deliberate pace until they were only a few yards away from the gathering in the street. They reined in as Sundell regarded the group with a frown.

"What's going on here?" the lawman asked. "Not more trouble, I hope."

"You could say that, Marshal," Constance replied. "One of my men was hurt in an accident out at our camp."

"It was no accident," Lafferty said.

Coburn added hotly, "These varmints accused Triangle 7 of bein' behind it, but we didn't have anything to do with it!"

"Triangle 7, eh?" Sundell grunted. "That's where we just came from."

Constance was surprised enough to ask, "What were you doing out there?"

The marshal looked like he didn't want to answer, but after a moment, he said, "That's where the trail of a man who tried to bushwhack us led. We figure he was one of the gang that held up the stagecoach and killed Fred Carter."

"And stole Empire's payroll!" Carl Peters exclaimed.

Sundell nodded. "And stole Empire's payroll."

Lafferty said, "That means those blasted cowboys are behind that, too!"

Mac and Luke exchanged a glance. Both of them were well aware of what this latest news could mean.

With everything else that had happened, this was enough to spark an all-out war between Empire and Triangle 7, Mac thought for the second time today.

CHAPTER 22

Luke could tell there had been quite a brawl here a short time earlier. The clothes on Mac and some of the other men were disheveled, and several of them were covered with dust and dirt, as if they'd been rolling in the street—which Luke had no doubt was the case.

None of them appeared to be hurt too badly, though. Was it just a coincidence that the battle had taken place in front of Dr. Abrams's house and office?

It probably had something to do with that accident Constance Elliott had mentioned.

"There's no proof that Triangle 7 had anything to do with the stagecoach robbery," Sundell said in response to the timberman's accusation. "And I don't want you going around town making such inflammatory claims, Lafferty. That'll just stir up more trouble, and by grabs, I don't need it!"

"Well, we need the wages that are coming to us," Lafferty said, "and the way I see it, there's a good chance Harmon and his bunch are responsible for us not getting them."

"That's enough, Alec," Constance said as she stepped forward.

"As you can guess, Marshal, something else has happened while you and your posse were gone." She turned to look at Stanton. "Tell the marshal about it, George."

Stanton did so, not casting any blame, just laying out the facts of the mishap that had left a logger named Frank Rigoni with some broken ribs—and it sounded like he'd been very lucky to get off that lightly.

When Stanton was finished with the story, Marshal Sundell asked, "So, was what happened an accident or not?"

"I honestly don't know," Stanton replied with a shake of his head. He glanced at Mac and then added, "It's possible somebody sabotaged the rope holding the logs in place above the rollway. I'm going to take a look at it when we get back out there and see if I can tell."

"Keep me informed. I don't know how you'd ever be able to prove something like that, let alone figure out who did it, unless somebody happened to see it." Sundell turned his head so that his stern gaze took in everyone in the street. "But no more brawling, understand? Both sides have been at each other's throats for too long now, and I'm sick and tired of it."

"We're tired of it, too, Marshal," Constance said, "especially since it seems that all the real harm has been done to one side and not the other."

The cool, unfriendly look she directed toward Rich Coburn made it clear what she was talking about.

"Triangle 7 ain't done nothin' wrong—" Coburn began.

Sundell held up a hand to stop him. "I said to quit it. Coburn, you and your men mount up and move out. You're not welcome in Pine Knob for a few days."

"That ain't fair! Not unless you put the town off-limits to them tree-climbers, too."

"Empire's office is here," Sundell said. "I can't very well kick Miss Elliott and Mr. Peters out of town." He looked at Mac, Stanton, Lafferty, and the other loggers. "But you men had better stick close to your camp for a few days, too, until things have had a chance to cool off."

"Tomorrow was supposed to be payday for us," Lafferty said bitterly.

"Well, your boss doesn't have that payroll right now, does she?" Sundell pulled his horse to the side to ride around the clump of people in the street. Over his shoulder, he said, "Everybody go home!"

Constance said to Stanton, "You heard the marshal, George. Go on back to camp."

"Somebody's gonna need to check on Frank pretty regular," Stanton protested. "Not to mention Walt."

"Don't worry, Carl or I will look in on both of them and make sure they're being properly cared for. If we need you for anything, I'll get word to you."

Stanton sighed and nodded. "Yes, ma'am." He jerked his head at the other men. "Come on."

Mac said, "Actually, Miss Elliott, would it be all right if I picked up a few things at the store since I'm already here in town anyway?"

"I don't think the marshal would begrudge you that opportunity," Constance said. "George, you go on back to the camp with the other men. I'm sure Mr. McKenzie can handle the wagon by himself."

"Mac and I came in together on the wagon," Stanton said with a frown. "I don't have a horse."

"Get one of the company's saddle mounts that we keep at the stable. You can bring it back into town another time." She glanced at Lafferty, Newton, and the others. "I'd feel better knowing that you're back at the camp looking after things."

In other words, Luke thought, she didn't trust the loggers to ride out and keep going back to camp without Stanton accompanying them to make sure they didn't stir up any more trouble.

"Sure, I suppose I can do that," Stanton allowed. "You'll be all right, Mac?"

"There shouldn't be any problem," Mac said.

"Yeah, but problems are what keep croppin' up, even when they shouldn't."

Nobody could argue with the bleak sentiment Stanton expressed.

By now, Coburn and the other Triangle 7 hands had swung up into their saddles and were riding away without looking back. They had reached the edge of Pine Knob and went out of sight along the trail that led to Ben Harmon's ranch and the other spreads in the basin. Coburn hadn't asked Luke if he was coming back to the ranch with them, perhaps thinking that the marshal wasn't through with him yet.

Stanton stalked off toward the livery stable. Lafferty and the other loggers climbed onto the mules they had ridden into town. Matt Rand and Cliff Campbell nodded to Luke and headed back to their own businesses. Both men looked disappointed, perhaps because the posse's efforts hadn't done any good.

That left Luke sitting on his horse with his hands crossed on the saddle horn. A few yards away, Mac started to climb onto the wagon and paused as Constance said to him, "You'll tell Mr. Throckmorton to put whatever you need on the company's account, Mr. McKenzie?"

"Sure," Mac said with a smile. "That Mr. McKenzie business sure sounds odd in my ears, though. I'm just Mac."

"All right, Mac. Carl and I are going back to the office. You can find us there if you need us."

"Yes, ma'am."

Constance smiled wearily. "I hope nothing else happens today. I think plenty has gone wrong already."

"Yes, ma'am," Mac said again, returning the smile. "It sure has."

He had been paying no attention to Luke—at least, he'd been pretending to pay no attention. But as Mac climbed onto the driver's seat and took up the reins, his eyes met Luke's for a second, and the message conveyed by that glance was clear.

They needed to talk.

Luke swung his horse around and rode slowly toward the general store. Mac took his time about getting the wagon turned and heading in the same direction. Well before Mac got there, Luke had dismounted, tied his horse at the hitch rack, and gone inside.

"Something I can do you for, Jensen?" Henry Throckmorton asked from behind the counter at the back of the store.

"A couple of boxes of .44s for these Remingtons of mine," Luke answered. "And I believe I'll browse a bit, too."

"Help yourself. That ammunition will be waiting back here for you when you're done."

Luke nodded his thanks and drifted along the aisles to a rack where several sheepskin-lined coats were hung. He examined them closely, as if thinking of buying a new one, and was still there when Mac came in and gave Throckmorton a short list of supplies he wanted to pick up and charge to Empire's account.

"I'll just look around while you're getting that order ready," Mac added. The storekeeper nodded and bustled off to see to it.

Mac dawdled along an aisle, pausing here and there to look more closely at some of the goods displayed there, but it didn't take long for his apparently idle path to bring him to the same area where Luke stood in front of the coats.

"Doing any good?" Mac asked in a voice low enough that only the two of them could hear it.

"Not a bit," Luke replied. "I don't think Dunnigan is at the Triangle 7 or any of the other spreads in the basin. I've asked about new men working on the other ranches, and there don't seem to be any." He paused. "Of course, somebody could have ridden in that Coburn and the other hands out there don't know about. How about you?"

"Nothing that points to Dunnigan," Mac replied. "But there are several men I can't rule out. How long are we going to keep this up?"

"Until we feel sure the man we're after isn't around these parts, I suppose."

Mac didn't say anything for a moment. Then he went on quietly, "There's something else to consider now."

"The trouble between Empire and Triangle 7, you mean?"

Mac started to look at him, then stopped short before the reaction gave away that they were talking.

"I've never been one to turn my back on trouble and just ride away from it," he said after a moment.

"This business has nothing to do with us," Luke pointed out. "We don't have any stake in it."

"Not when it comes to reward money, maybe, but I've been cooking for that crew for a week now. Some of them seem like pretty good fellas to me."

"And you don't like abandoning them when trouble is brewing."

"You didn't see Frank Rigoni lying there with a log nearly crushing the life out of him," Mac said. "I'd like whoever was responsible for that to get what's coming to them."

Luke sighed. "I didn't like seeing that stagecoach driver's body after four loads of buckshot hit it, either."

"Some of the hotheads in the Empire crew will blame the Triangle 7 bunch for that, too." Mac paused and then asked, "Do you think there's any chance Harmon could be behind it, Luke?"

"My gut says no." He smiled faintly. "I guess it depends on whether you trust my gut."

"You've never given me any reason not to. But somebody's sure stirring up trouble. I'd like to find out who."

"Chances are it won't pay us anything."

"Maybe not, but I'm still mighty curious."

"So am I," Luke admitted. "All right, we'll each stay where we are for the time being and see what we can find out. Just be careful out there that no trees fall on you."

"That's not likely to happen while I'm in the kitchen. And you probably ought to keep an eye out for bushwhackers."

"I always do." Luke frowned. "There's something else we

probably ought to do before we head back where we're going, though."

"What's that?"

Luke turned, put a hand on Mac's shoulder, and gave him a shove.

"Watch who you're crowding, you blasted tree-climber," Luke said, raising his voice so that Henry Throckmorton, the store's two clerks, and the other two customers in there at the moment couldn't help but hear him. That was an elderly couple who stopped their squabbling to turn and stare at the source of the sudden commotion.

Mac caught his balance, glared, and responded, equally loudly, "I wasn't crowding you, cow-nurse. I wouldn't even get close to you because I'm used to the smell of pine trees, not the cow dung you reek of."

Luke was glad that Mac had caught on to the deception right away, but he wasn't surprised. Mac was a pretty smart fellow, not to mention a fine cook. Luke sort of envied the logging crew; old Alamo Paige wasn't a bad cook, but his food wasn't at the same level as Mac's.

The loud, angry voice brought Throckmorton out from behind the counter. He hustled up the aisle toward Luke and Mac, holding his hands out in front of him beseechingly as he approached.

"Now, fellas, take it easy," Throckmorton said. "We don't want any trouble in here, do we?"

"I don't like being crowded," Luke snapped as he sent a dark look in Mac's direction.

"And I don't like being around somebody who's been tramping through cow dung," Mac said. "Is my order ready, Mr. Throckmorton?"

"As a matter of fact, it is," the storekeeper said. "My clerks loaded it in your wagon a few minutes ago."

"Well, I'll just take it and go, then," Mac told him with a curt nod.

"Yeah, go back to the woods where you belong," Luke said as

Mac and Throckmorton walked toward the back of the store. Mac threw one more hostile glare over his shoulder but didn't say anything else.

After that angry confrontation, nobody would suspect they had just been exchanging information, Luke thought. But even though he was glad they had just been able to seize the opportunity for a quick conversation, the bleak mood that had settled over him during the ride back to Pine Knob still had him in its grip.

He and Mac had made no progress in their hunt for Asa Dunnigan, and now, despite their own best intentions, they were embroiled in the hostilities brewing between Triangle 7 and the Empire Logging Company. On numerous occasions in the past, Luke had seen such tensions escalate to the point that bloodshed was inevitable.

In this case, he sensed that it was rushing toward them, and he knew that both he and Mac would feel compelled to stop it somehow, even though it was none of their business. They just weren't the sort of hombres who could stand by and watch innocent people get hurt.

Maybe they would get lucky, and the spark it would take to set off the explosion wouldn't come. . . .

CHAPTER 23

Somewhat to Luke's surprise, the next few days passed peacefully, at least on the ranch. He and the other men went about their range chores without anything unusual happening.

He couldn't help but wonder, though, what was going on in Pine Knob and out at the Empire camp.

He had no excuse for riding into the settlement to find out, so he told himself to be patient. It probably wouldn't be long before something came up to give him a reason to visit Pine Knob. While he was there, with any luck he could pick up some gossip about Empire.

Today, he and another Triangle 7 hand named Clint Douglas were riding up a narrow trail in a brush-choked canyon on the northwestern edge of Ben Harmon's range. Recently, a couple of the other men had reported seeing a few head of Harmon's stock up here, so today Rich Coburn had sent Luke and Douglas to comb those cattle out of the brush and move them back down with the rest of the herd.

Douglas was a garrulous youngster with a shock of red hair

that tended to fall down over his forehead because he habitually wore his steeple-crowned hat thumbed back.

"A cow critter with the wanderlust is the stubbornest varmint on the face of the earth," Douglas was saying as he and Luke rode along a trail that was wide enough for two horses side by side but no more.

Off the trail on both sides, the ground was covered with sagebrush, antelope brush, rabbitbrush, and stubby junipers. It wasn't the sort of growth that clawed mercilessly at man or animal, but it grew so thickly that pushing through it was difficult, and it could inflict some injuries.

The trail meandered roughly down the center of the canyon, which was about a hundred feet wide. Rugged, forty-foot-high rimrocks reared up on both sides. According to Douglas, who had ridden this part of the spread before, the canyon wandered all the way up into the mountains.

"Could be we'll have to go off Mr. Harmon's range to find those cows," Douglas went on, "but as long as they're wearin' Triangle 7 iron on their hides, it don't matter."

"We won't be encroaching on somebody else's territory?" Luke asked.

"Naw. All the spreads up here in the basin get along pretty well, and I'm mighty thankful for that. I been mixed up in range wars down in Texas and New Mexico Territory, and I hope to smile, I'd just as soon never do that again! It's plumb nerve-rackin', not knowin' if you're gonna make it through the day without gettin' ventilated."

Luke chuckled and said, "You're not old enough to have been in two range wars, Clint."

"Two? Try four! I been cowboyin' for a long time, Mr. Jensen. I started packin' iron and ridin' the range at the tender age o' fourteen, down yonder along the Lavaca River. I had to make my way in the world, so it was that or clerk in a doggone store in Hallettsville, and I sure as blazes didn't want to do that!"

Luke grinned and shook his head. "I don't suppose I blame

you. When I was fourteen, I was ready to get out and see the world, too. Never managed to do it, though, until the war came along. By the way, you can call me Luke."

"No, sir. My folks might've passed on when I was just a younker, but I was with 'em long enough to be raised to respect my elders. And no offense, Mr. Jensen, you're dang near old enough to be my grandpaw!"

Luke laughed and said, "You're right about that, Clint. You just call me whatever you're comfortable with."

"I sure will, Mr. Jensen." The young cowboy pulled a bright blue bandanna out of his pocket and mopped sweat off his face. "It's hotter than usual for this time o' year. I figured this far north, the weather would be cool all the time, but that ain't the case. It gets hot up here, too. Not like Texas, o' course."

"Of course," Luke agreed.

"I don't know why in tarnation Hamlin and Merrill didn't go ahead and round up them critters when they spotted 'em up here a few days ago. They said they was busy with other chores, and I guess maybe they were, but if they'd gone ahead and choused those cows outta the brush, then we wouldn't have to be doin' it today. I wonder how far we're gonna have to ride to find 'em."

"Those are the hands who reported the strays?"

"Yep. Hamlin Daly and Merrill Lewis. Good fellas."

"Have you known them long?" Luke recognized the two names and knew he had been introduced to the men, but he didn't know much about their backgrounds. He didn't figure it would hurt to find out more.

"I think they come from over in Montana. They been ridin' for the Triangle 7 for a year or so, same as me. They signed on a couple o' weeks after I did."

"Together?"

"Yeah. I think they knowed each other for a spell whilst they was ridin' the chuck line."

Luke nodded. It wasn't unusual for a couple of drifting cowpokes to form an unofficial partnership, although they would split up without hesitation if they got hired on at different spreads.

The canyon wall up ahead bulged out toward the trail, and the rimrock at its crest had a saw-toothed appearance because of several clumps of small boulders with tufts of brush growing in them. Something about the formation drew Luke's attention, and as he looked at it, he realized that the skin on the back of his neck had drawn taut.

Mac had said that he had no reason not to trust Luke's instincts. Luke felt the same way about it.

He snatched his hat off, slapped it down hard on the rump of Clint Douglas's horse, and yelled, "Go! Ride hard!"

At the same time, he jammed his own boot heels into his horse's flanks and leaned forward in the saddle. The animal lunged forward, breaking into a run right behind Douglas's galloping mount.

As it did, a rifle shot cracked and a spurt of powder smoke jetted out on the rimrock Luke had been looking at. The bullet slapped through the air close enough to hear, but it missed both riders, who now pounded along the winding trail through the brush with as much speed as they could manage.

"Somebody's shootin' at us!" Douglas yelled unnecessarily over his shoulder.

"Keep going!" Luke shouted back at him. "Hunt cover!"

The problem was that no cover was to be found out here in the middle of the canyon. The brush wouldn't stop bullets, and the junipers weren't big enough to offer any protection. Their best bet, Luke realized, would be to get to the base of the canyon wall on the same side as the bushwhackers. The angle there would make it difficult for the riflemen to target them.

And there was more than one ambusher hidden up there, no doubt about that, because Luke saw several more spurts of powder smoke from the rocks. Bullets whipped through the brush and made the branches wave. Several shots kicked up dirt in the trail around the horses' flashing hooves.

It was only a matter of time until those would-be killers got the range.

"Clint!" Luke called. "Try to get to the canyon wall! I'll cover you!"

Douglas looked back over his shoulder. Luke waved to the right to reinforce his order. Douglas jerked his horse in that direction and plunged into the brush, but the obstacles the thick growth presented slowed him considerably.

Luke had to distract those ambushers if the young cowboy was going to have a chance to reach safety. He slowed, too, looped the reins around the saddle horn, and pulled both Remingtons from their cross-draw rigs.

The horse was well-trained and would continue running. With irons in both fists, Luke raised the Remingtons and began thumbing off shots, back and forth, one after the other. Gunthunder echoed from the canyon walls and filled the air as the .44s bucked and roared in Luke Jensen's skilled hands.

Firing on the run like this, it would be blind luck if he actually hit any of the bushwhackers, but the way he was filling the rocks with ricochets, anything was possible.

At the very least, he ought to be making the no-good sons duck for cover.

The left-hand Remington clicked empty first. Luke holstered it, grabbed the reins, and brought the horse to a sliding stop. Clint Douglas had made good progress through the brush, he saw, but the youngster wasn't safe yet. Luke fired the last round in the right-hand revolver and pouched that iron. He reached for the stock of the Winchester that jutted up from a saddle boot strapped under his right thigh.

At that moment, Douglas lurched on the back of his horse and had to grab the horn to keep from falling off. The boy might have slipped, but it looked to Luke as if he'd been hit. Luke bit back a curse as he slid the rifle free and brought it to his shoulder. In the same swift motion, he worked the Winchester's loading lever.

The repeater began to spit fire and lead as Luke blazed away at the rimrock, spraying the killers' hiding place with half a dozen bullets as fast as he could. A cloud of powder smoke wreathed man and horse.

Luke peered through the gray haze, and saw that Douglas was still mounted and had reached the base of the canyon wall. The young cowboy was slumped in the saddle, reinforcing Luke's hunch that he had been hit, but at least he hadn't collapsed. Luke jabbed his boot heels into his horse's flanks and sent the animal charging into the thick growth.

The horse was well-trained, but even so, it was reluctant to have those branches clawing at its hide. Luke had to prod it to keep moving. A slug sang past his head. He jerked the rifle up and snapped a shot at the boulders.

The next instant, a bullet burned across the horse's rump, causing it to squeal in pain.

That was too much for the animal to stand. Already spooked by the thunderous roar of gunfire and the sharp tang of burned powder, the sudden pain of the bullet graze made the horse rear up and paw at the air.

Luke, caught by surprise, tried to hang on, but he slipped out of the saddle and fell backward off the horse. He was able to kick his feet free of the stirrups, but that was all he managed to do before he was unhorsed.

He toppled onto a bush that broke his fall, but at the same time, branches scratched at him and whipped across his face. He hit the ground on his left shoulder with enough force to send a jolt of pain through him. He rolled onto his belly and started crawling instinctively toward the side of the canyon.

Instinct had also allowed him to keep his grip on the Winchester. He could fight back, but if he did so out here in the relative open, he wouldn't have a chance. The bushwhackers could just spray the brush until at least one of the bullets found him.

The heavy boom of shots from a handgun came to Luke's ears. He realized that Clint Douglas had to be firing the shots. The youngster was still alive and trying to give Luke some cover, just as Luke had done for him.

As the shots blasted out, Luke crawled as quickly as he could toward the canyon wall. When the shooting stopped, so did he. He pressed himself to the ground as closely as he could and lay completely still.

His hope was that Douglas's covering fire had forced the riflemen hidden in the boulders to duck long enough that they had lost sight of him. As long as he was motionless, the brush wouldn't move, either, so they wouldn't know exactly where he was. They wouldn't be able to see him through the dense growth.

He heard his horse crashing off through the brush, and then its hooves clattered on the trail. The horse was clear. Luke was glad of that.

But he was still in a mighty bad fix himself.

The men atop the canyon wall opened fire again. A volley of sharp cracks ripped through the air. Luke heard bullets rattling through the brush and thudding into the ground, but they were forty or fifty feet away from him.

The slim chance that they had lost sight of him appeared to have paid off—for the moment.

But they wouldn't continue concentrating their fire on the same area, Luke thought bleakly. In a minute or two, they would probably shift their aim and try some other spot. They might shift away from him—but it was just as likely they would shift toward him.

The shooting stopped. As the echoes rebounded from the canyon walls and gradually faded away, Luke heard men calling to each other, up there on the rimrock. He couldn't make out any of the words, but he assumed they were strategizing about what to do next.

They opened fire again, that was what they did next. Once more, rifle shots slammed out, blast after blast, and as he lay on the ground underneath the brush, Luke gritted his teeth together. The sound of bullets hitting the ground was closer to him, just as he had feared. The shots were still missing him, but only by half as much as they had a few minutes earlier.

When the bushwhackers reloaded and adjusted their aim, in all likelihood those bullets would be breathing right down his neck, Luke thought.

He had to move—*now!*

The shooting stopped, and Luke surged to his feet. Maybe they were trying to trick him into revealing his location. He had to take that chance. He couldn't just stay where he was and allow his enemies to riddle him with lead.

He hoped as he leaped up that Clint Douglas would provide more covering fire for him, but the young cowboy's gun remained silent. As Luke started to push through the brush as quickly as he could, he looked toward the canyon wall and saw Douglas's horse standing there with an empty saddle.

Douglas had either dismounted or fallen off his mount, and Luke had a bad feeling he knew which one it was.

The branches were like thousands of tiny hands clutching at him, trying to hold him back as he plowed through them. He ignored the pain as some of them scratched his face. He threw his left arm up to protect his eyes.

Up above, a man shouted. A heartbeat later, rifle shots smashed out. Luke had made it several strides before they reacted to his desperate attempt, but he still had what seemed like a long way to go before he reached safety. A terribly long way.

As he ran, he began firing the Winchester he still carried. On the move like this, he couldn't even try to aim his shots. He just angled the rifle up and flung lead in the general direction of the men trying to kill him. Maybe a few of the bullets would come close enough to spook them and disrupt their aim.

Slugs tore through the brush around him, plucked at his jacket. None of them found his flesh. He lunged ahead, and suddenly the sandstone and granite wall of the canyon loomed up in front of him. He put on one last burst of speed and reached the wall, turning to flatten his back against its rough surface.

When he turned his head and craned his neck to peer up at the rimrock, he couldn't see the boulders along the very edge. That meant the riflemen concealed there couldn't see him, either. The curves and bulges of the wall were just enough to shield him from view.

He looked in the other direction, saw Douglas's riderless horse again, and grimaced as he spotted the crumpled figure lying right next to the wall. Douglas wasn't moving.

Luke's first instinct was to hurry to the young cowboy's side, but shots still cracked and bullets sizzled through the air only a few feet in front of them. He saw them hitting the ground and kicking up dirt and gravel. It was unlikely any of them would ricochet up where he stood, but he couldn't rule out the possibility. However, for the moment he considered himself relatively safe—as long as he didn't move.

Which meant that he was trapped here.

CHAPTER 24

The bushwhackers kept up the deadly barrage for a couple of minutes, then the rifles fell silent again. Luke twisted his body and slithered out of his jacket. He hung the garment on the tip of his Winchester barrel and edged it out so that one sleeve and shoulder would be visible from the rimrock.

A shot cracked wickedly. The jacket jerked as the slug ripped through the sleeve. Luke tipped the Winchester down and let the jacket fall loosely to the ground.

That might or might not fool the bushwhackers into believing that he'd been hit, but at least the shot confirmed that they were watching and waiting for another opportunity to kill him.

Again he heard voices but couldn't distinguish what they were saying. He assumed they were debating whether he was dead.

He wasn't going to do anything to make them believe otherwise. Maybe some of them would come down here to check on him and make sure.

If they did, then he would have the chance to even the score for Clint Douglas, and right now, that was what Luke wanted. Just a chance to get some of the no-good skunks in his sights . . .

Hoofbeats drummed from back down the canyon.

Luke stiffened as he heard the unmistakable sound of a large group of riders approaching. Could it be more of the bunch that had opened fire on him and Douglas? That was a possibility.

But it was also possible the men might be some of the Triangle 7 hands. Luke and Douglas had ridden quite a ways up the canyon, but sound had a way of traveling pretty far. Someone riding on Ben Harmon's range might have heard all the gunfire and gone for help before coming to see what was going on.

With all that shooting, Luke mused, it must have sounded like a small-scale war up here.

He didn't have any choice except to stay where he was and wait. If the newcomers wanted him dead, like the men up on the rimrock, he wouldn't stand much of a chance, pinned against the canyon wall like this. There was no place for him to fort up. All he would be able to do was take one or two of the varmints with him when he crossed the divide.

As Luke peered down the canyon toward the approaching riders, he saw eight men round a bend and ride quickly up the trail toward him. A burst of relief went through him as he recognized the two hombres in the lead—Ben Harmon and Rich Coburn. The half-dozen men behind them were also members of the Triangle 7 crew.

The bushwhackers up on the rimrock might open fire on them, too, Luke realized, and he was about to shout a warning when he heard another swift rataplan of hoofbeats from above. It sounded like the men who had ambushed him and Douglas were lighting a shuck out of here, rather than hang around and pick a fight with Harmon and his men.

Hoping that was the case, Luke stepped out a little from the wall, waved the Winchester over his head, and shouted, "Over here! Be careful! Bushwhackers on the rim!"

Harmon turned in the saddle and barked orders at the men behind him. They all reined in hurriedly, dropped to the ground, and took cover behind their horses as they aimed rifles over the saddles. They were ready to return any fire that came from the rimrock.

No shots sounded. Harmon and Coburn dismounted as well and left their horses in the trail as they started pushing through the brush toward Luke.

"Jensen, are you hurt?" Harmon called

"I'm all right," Luke replied, "but Clint is hit."

He pointed toward the spot where Douglas lay and started in that direction, staying close to the canyon wall.

Harmon and Coburn altered their course to meet him there. Luke reached the young cowboy first and dropped to one knee beside him. Douglas's hat had fallen off. His red hair hung across his face as he lay curled on his left side. Luke leaned over and saw the large, dark bloodstain on the back of Douglas's shirt. Gently, he took hold of the youngster and rolled him onto his back, revealing a matching but somewhat smaller stain on the shirt front.

Douglas's blue eyes stared sightlessly at the sky above the canyon.

Rich Coburn cursed bitterly as he and Harmon came up and saw that Douglas was dead.

"Shot through the body, front to back," Harmon said grimly. "Poor kid. Probably never had a chance."

"No, but he stayed in the saddle and lived long enough to give me some covering fire," Luke said. He reached out and closed Douglas's eyes. "If he hadn't done that, I never would have made it. I'd be dead, too."

"Who did this?" Coburn asked. His voice shook a little from the depth of the emotion he felt. "Did you get a look at them?"

Luke stood up and shook his head. "No, they were hidden in the rocks up there at the top of this wall. I'd say there were three of them. Maybe four."

"Are they gone?" Harmon asked.

"I think so. I heard horses up there when you fellas showed

up. They sounded like they were moving away from here pretty fast."

Coburn said, "They didn't want to stay and fight," adding a few choice obscenities. "They didn't have any stomach for it when the odds were against them."

"Take four men, ride back down to the mouth of the canyon, and then follow the rim up here," Harmon ordered. "See if you can find anything that might tell us who they were."

"Do you want us to try to follow 'em, Boss?"

"The ground up there is so rocky, they probably didn't leave any trail for you to follow, but sure, look around and see what you can find. Just be careful. You don't want to ride smack-dab into a trap."

Luke's voice held a bitter note, too, as he said, "Like the kid and I did."

"Now, dang it, you were just followin' orders," Coburn protested. "Orders I gave you to look for those cows that had wandered up here. This is my fault, Luke."

"Nonsense," Ben Harmon said. "This is nobody's fault except for the murderin' snakes who pulled the triggers. Neither of you men had any reason to think you were going to run into trouble."

What the rancher said was true. They were still on Triangle 7 range. They shouldn't have run into an ambush here.

"Go on and see what you can find out about who did this," Harmon told his foreman. "The rest of us will take Clint back to the house."

Coburn nodded and moved off through the brush, headed back toward the trail.

"I'd like to go with Rich, if that's all right with you, Mr. Harmon," Luke said.

"Well, sure, if that's what you want. But after being bushwhacked and the kid being killed, aren't you pretty shaken up?"

"This is hardly the first time in my life I've been ambushed," Luke said, "and Clint getting killed just makes me want to find the men who did it all the more."

Harmon nodded and said, "I reckon that makes sense, all right. Go ahead."

Luke returned the curt nod and called after Coburn, "Hold on, Rich, I'm coming with you!"

He pushed into the brush and strode through the thicket, determined to catch up to the Triangle 7 foreman.

By the time Luke reached the trail, Coburn was not only mounted, he'd had one of the other men catch Luke's horse and bring it up. There were half a dozen men in the party that rode back down the canyon.

Luke was in the lead with Coburn. He said, "Clint and I hadn't found those strays yet when the shooting started."

"I don't care about the cattle," the foreman said. "I just want to find whoever did this. Those blasted cows can go hang, for all I care."

Luke let the subject drop. Suspicion had begun stirring around in his brain, though. He let those stray thoughts percolate rather than concentrating on them. As Coburn had said, they had more important business to tend to right now.

It took an hour to reach the mouth of the canyon, climb a steep, rocky trail, and then follow the rimrock to the cluster of boulders where the bushwhackers had hidden. Luke hadn't been up here before; everything looked different from this perspective, but he was experienced enough at such things to be able to tell where they were. When the brush-dotted rocks they were looking for came into view, he pointed them out to Coburn and said, "That's the place."

Coburn pulled his Winchester from its sheath and jacked a round into the chamber.

"Those varmints are long gone, not much doubt about that, but I reckon we ought to be ready for trouble anyway."

"That's always a good idea," Luke agreed as he took his own rifle from its saddle scabbard.

The other four cowboys drew and readied their Winchesters as well. Then the whole group rode forward slowly.

When they were about twenty yards from the rocks, Luke said, "You and I had better go ahead on foot to keep from disturbing any tracks the ambushers left."

"Good idea," Coburn said as he reined in. "Hold up right here, boys. Luke and I will check it out, but the rest of you stay mounted and keep your eyes open."

Luke and the foreman swung down from their saddles and moved ahead carefully on foot, rifles held at the ready. Luke's eyes moved constantly, studying the boulders and the ground around them. He spotted some dark piles of horse droppings off to the right, near a small clump of junipers, and pointed them out to Coburn.

"That's where they had their mounts tied," he said. "Far enough back from the edge that there was no chance of Clint and me spotting them as we rode through the canyon. You can see the tracks leading away from there. They left those when they took off."

Coburn growled in his throat. "I wish they'd stayed and fought it out. Nothin' I would've liked better than to drill a few holes in those murderin' skunks."

"Maybe you'll get your chance. Let's take a look at those hoofprints and see if there's anything distinctive about them."

Once again, Luke put his tracking skills to work as he peered closely at the marks left by the bushwhackers' horses. He noticed one thing right away: The horseshoe nails weren't bent over as far as the ones on the tracks left by the stagecoach robbers. Luke had been playing around with the idea that the same bunch was responsible for both outbreaks of violence, but based on this evidence, that didn't appear to be the case.

Of course, a gang could have extra mounts, he mused. They could have a whole blasted remuda. They didn't have to ride the same horses all the time. But without actual evidence, he couldn't make a definite connection between the crimes.

There was nothing much unusual otherwise about the hoofprints, just a few nicks and flaws that Luke mentally cataloged. If he saw the tracks again, there was at least a chance he would recognize them.

He and Coburn turned their attention to the boot prints left by the ambushers. The ground around the boulders was rocky and hard, so there weren't many places where the killers had left any tracks. Luke found a few good prints on a sandy spot between two of the boulders, however. He dropped to a knee beside them and studied them intently.

Coburn bent to peer over Luke's shoulder at the boot prints. "What do you think?" he asked. Before Luke could answer, the foreman went on, "There's somethin' funny about those tracks, ain't there?"

Luke pointed to numerous small indentations within the boot prints and around their edges.

"See those?" he asked.

"Yeah." Coburn sounded puzzled. "Those don't look like any boots I ever saw." He rested the rifle's butt on the ground to balance himself as he lifted his left leg and cocked it across his right leg. "The soles of my boots are smooth. So were the soles of every pair of ridin' boots I ever owned."

"That's because the boots that left these tracks weren't riding boots. Those marks were made by hobnailed boots." Luke turned his head to look up at Coburn. "The kind of boots that lumberjacks wear."

CHAPTER 25

By the time Luke, Rich Coburn, and the other men got back to Triangle 7 headquarters, Clint Douglas's body had been cleaned up, dressed in fresh clothes, and laid out in the bunkhouse, ready to load into the wagon to take into Pine Knob, where he would be turned over to John Endicott at the undertaking parlor.

Some ranches had their own small, private cemeteries, but the Triangle 7 wasn't one of them. The young cowboy would be laid to rest in the settlement's Boot Hill, which was actually on a hill, surrounded by nice rows of pine trees on three sides.

Ben Harmon came out onto the porch of the ranch house when Luke and the others rode up. The old Pony Express rider, Alamo Paige, followed him. Shorty and Kaintuck came from the barn, and the group of cowboys gathered outside the bunkhouse—no doubt made too uncomfortable by the presence of Clint Douglas's body to linger inside the building—stalked forward to greet the newcomers, too.

To a man, they were all solemn with grief over their murdered compadre, but anger and the desire for vengeance lurked in their expressions, too. Settling the score for Douglas would be uppermost in their minds, Luke knew.

That was one reason he hated to pass on the information he had, but there was no avoiding it. Even if he hadn't said anything to Coburn, the foreman had seen those distinctive boot prints and realized what they meant.

"Did you catch up with the sorry scoundrels who murdered that boy?" Harmon demanded as the riders reined in.

Coburn shook his head. "Sorry, Boss. There wasn't enough of a trail for us to follow. It petered out mighty quicklike in that rugged country."

"I was afraid of that," Harmon said with a disappointed scowl.

"But we did find somethin' mighty interestin'," Coburn went on. He nodded to Luke. "Tell him, Jensen, since it was you who noticed it first."

"We found boot prints left by the men who ambushed us from those rocks," Luke said. "They weren't regular boots. They were the hobnailed sort—"

"Like loggers wear!" Harmon interrupted as his eyes widened in surprise. "You mean it was timbermen who opened fire on you and killed poor Clint!"

That brought furious oaths from the other men. Shorty was particularly upset, bouncing up and down on his feet so vehemently that somebody could have described him honestly as hopping mad.

Kaintuck pounded his big right fist into his left palm and said, "I reckon we better saddle up and take a ride up to that loggin' camp."

Angry mutters of agreement came from the other men.

"Hold on a minute," Luke said. "Just because the bushwhackers wore the same kind of boots doesn't mean that Empire had anything to do with what happened."

"What else could it mean?" Paige asked. His face was bright red with rage. "They killed Clint, and they tried to kill you!"

A look of unease had come over Ben Harmon's face. He said,

"This doesn't sound like something Constance Elliott would do. I've had my disagreements with the woman, sure, but I don't think she'd stoop to bushwhacking and murder."

Coburn thumbed back his hat and sighed. "I had a hunch you'd feel that way, Boss. But I got to tell you, before we lost the trail, it was headin' in the general direction of Empire's camp."

"That's still not proof," Luke said. When several of the men looked at him angrily, he went on, "I'm not saying they didn't do it. I'm just pointing out that as far as the law is concerned, we don't have any evidence against them that would stand up in court. The stagecoach robbers' trail led toward this ranch, but that doesn't mean any of you are guilty of that."

"To blazes with court!" a cowboy yelled. "We're not talkin' about law, we're talkin' about justice!"

"Justice for that redheaded kid!" another man added. More angry comments piled on.

Harmon held up his hands to quiet the men down.

"Nobody's stampedin' over to that logging camp to raise a ruckus," he said. "I'm as mad as any of you boys, and if it comes time for a shooting war, then by grabs, we'll give it to 'em!" He pointed toward the bunkhouse. "But we've got a boy in there to take care of right now, and we're gonna tend to that chore before we do anything else. Let's get him loaded in the wagon."

"We'll throw our saddles on some fresh horses," Coburn said, "and then we'll ride into Pine Knob with you." His jaw tightened. "I reckon dealin' with those blasted tree-climbin' bushwhackers can wait—but not for too long!"

The fury over their payroll being stolen lingered among the Empire loggers for several days, but Constance Elliott assured them she was taking steps to make good the loss. If they would keep working and not go looking for any trouble with the Triangle 7 range riders, they would get paid in due course, and it would be pretty quickly, too, Constance pledged.

George Stanton supported her, of course, and since not many

of the men wanted to cross the burly superintendent, they went along with Constance's wishes, although grudgingly. A few, such as Alec Lafferty, still continued grousing loudly whenever they got the chance, but the complaints fell on mostly deaf ears.

Mac was glad of that. He took advantage of the lull to look into the near-fatal accident that had befallen Frank Rigoni.

Late in the afternoon on the day of the accident, Mac paid another visit to the rollway with Stanton. They examined the pieces of rope carefully, and Stanton agreed with Mac's suggestion that somebody had taken a knife to the restraint that was supposed to hold the logs in place.

"You can tell that whoever it was didn't just cut the rope clean through," Stanton said. "They worked on individual strands, fraying them to make it look like the damage was just natural wear and tear. A chore like that must have taken quite a while. They spent some time on it."

"Which means it's unlikely they carried out their sabotage during the day," Mac pointed out.

Stanton nodded. "Yeah, there would be way too many people around for that. Too big a chance they'd be seen. That means they came skulking around in the middle of the night to carry out their sabotage."

"So it could have been literally anybody."

"It had to be somebody from the Triangle 7," Stanton insisted. "Nobody else would have a grudge against us bad enough to do this."

Mac let that claim pass for the moment. Instead, he asked, "How do you get the logs stacked up like that, anyway? They're too heavy to lift without some sort of machinery, I'd think."

Stanton laughed. "We've got machinery, all right. Mule machinery! A team hauls the bottom layer in place with chains and ropes, then we have a ramp that can be adjusted. We position it at one end of the stack, and then more layers are hauled into place over it. Sometimes we don't bother building a pile. We just pull the logs into position and roll 'em on down to the creek right then. It's easier to let them stack up, though, until there's a good-sized bunch. Then we roll them down and have a creek drive to the sawmill in town."

Stanton grinned and continued, "It's kind of like rounding up a big enough herd of cattle to make taking them on a trail drive profitable."

Mac thought about it and shook his head. "I can see the logic in that approach," he admitted, "but it never would have occurred to me. So what you were doing here was gathering enough logs to make it worthwhile to take them to the sawmill."

"Yep, that's it, exactly."

Mac studied the ground around the end of the rollway. He saw a lot of footprints, of course. Men had swarmed around this spot when Rigoni was trapped underneath the log. Not surprisingly, most of the prints bore the marks left by the hobnails on the soles and heels of the boots.

But not all of them, Mac noted. There were a few prints unmistakably made by riding boots such as the ones he wore. Maybe he had left those tracks, he told himself.

But there were places he saw them where he didn't remember venturing during his only previous visit to the rollway.

That could mean the tracks were made by whoever sabotaged the rope.

An obvious answer sprang to mind. Tracks left by riding boots pointed to the men of Triangle 7.

Luke didn't believe that any of the men he had met on Ben Harmon's spread would be responsible for such a thing, but evidence was evidence. Those boot prints indicated that a range rider had been here, and the ones who had the biggest grudge against Empire rode for Triangle 7. It was difficult not to draw the conclusion.

Even so, Mac told himself to keep his mind open, and so for the next several days, he questioned the members of the logging crew when he could do so in a subtle manner. He wanted to know if any of them had seen strangers lurking around the camp or the logging lease, or if anyone not a stranger had been acting suspiciously.

He didn't turn up a thing.

Several days had passed when Carl Peters turned up at the camp on horseback. Mac was a little surprised to see the bookkeeper in a saddle instead of driving a buggy, and the man's garb was also unexpected. Peters wore canvas trousers, a flannel shirt, and a cloth cap. He could have passed for a logger except for his smooth, uncalloused hands.

It occurred to Mac that he didn't know anything about Peters's background. It was entirely possible the man had been a logger in his earlier days. In fact, that made sense. He certainly seemed to know the business.

Peters met with George Stanton in the main building. Mac brought coffee for them and heard Peters say, "Miss Elliott has been in touch with the stage line. They've agreed to make good the loss of the payroll, but they'll have to do it in installments. So while I can't promise the men their full wages immediately, I can tell you that by this weekend, they should be able to come into town and pick up some of their money."

Stanton, who sat in a chair turned away from his desk, clapped his hands on his knees and said, "That's good news, Carl. Mighty good news. I'm glad to hear it, and the men will be, too."

"They've kept up their work in a satisfactory fashion?" Peters asked with a frown. "No slowdowns because they're unhappy with the situation?"

Stanton shook his head. "No, they're working at a normal pace. Now, I won't deny that some of them were pretty unhappy about not getting paid, but they haven't stirred up any real trouble. As long as they know their money is on the way, I think they'll be all right." A worried look came over the superintendent's face. "Nothing better happen to that next shipment, though. I hate to say it, but Constance might have a mutiny on her hands if it does."

"Nothing's going to happen," Peters assured him. "Miss

Elliott's hired a couple of men to ride up to The Dalles and accompany the stagecoach as special guards for that run. It was my idea. Those blasted cowboys won't get this shipment."

He took a cigar from his shirt pocket, lit it with a lucifer he scratched to life on the sole of his boot, and puffed on the stogie, clearly satisfied with himself.

Mac wasn't sure two extra guards would be enough if a large, determined gang of outlaws wanted that payroll money, but it wasn't his decision to make.

If it had been him, he would have hired a couple more guards—then brought in the money some other way, letting the stagecoach run serve as a distraction. He kept that thought to himself, however, knowing that Peters probably wouldn't appreciate it.

"How are Walt and Frank getting along?" Stanton asked, changing the subject from the payroll.

"They're recovering nicely, according to the doctor, but they'll still be laid up for a while."

"What about that stagecoach guard who was wounded in the robbery?" Mac asked.

"The young Indian? He's still at the doctor's, as well. Abrams says that his broken leg will heal, but he may never walk exactly the same again. I gather it was worse than the injury to Walt Nichols."

Mac said, "That's a shame. The doc's had a real rash of broken bones to deal with lately."

Peters drank the last of the coffee in his cup and set the empty aside. As he stood up, he said, "I'm going to take a look around the operation."

"Checking on anything in particular?" Stanton asked. He pushed to his feet as well. "I'll come with you—"

Peters forestalled him with a gesture. "That's not necessary. I know my way around a logging camp, as I'm sure you're aware."

"Yeah, I know. But I don't mind coming with you, Carl."

"I'd rather you spend the time preparing a report on recent

production for Miss Elliott," Peters said in a firm tone that didn't allow for any argument. "She asked me to bring that back with me."

"Sure." Stanton didn't look happy about it, but he nodded and sat down again. "I'll have that ready for you in a half hour or so."

"Excellent. I'll pick it up when I get back."

Peters pulled on his cap, clenched his teeth on the cigar, and strode out of the house. Stanton watched him go. A look of disapproval settled over the superintendent's rugged face once Peters was gone.

"Sort of full of himself for a fella who sits in an office most of the time, isn't he?" Mac ventured.

"Carl was a good logger when he was young," Stanton said. "At least, that's what I've heard about him. That was before my time. According to the story, he was one of the best toppers in the woods until he had a bad fall. It was an accident that would have killed most men, but Carl survived. He was busted up bad enough that he never strapped on a pair of spikes again, though."

"I kind of thought something like that might be the case. Seems like he makes a good right-hand man for Miss Elliott."

Stanton nodded but looked somewhat dubious. "I hope that's right. Carl's opinions carry a lot of weight with her, that's for sure."

And Stanton looked like maybe he didn't always agree with those opinions, Mac mused. But Stanton wasn't the sort to try to interfere too much with Constance's business. He respected her too much for that.

"I think I might hitch up the wagon and drive into Pine Knob when Mr. Peters heads back that way."

Stanton grunted. "More supplies?"

"Well, we always need supplies," Mac replied with a grin. "I fix a pile of grub for you fellas, and then later the same day or the next, you just want to eat again!"

"Take Pete and Grady with you."

"I won't be buying so much that I'll need help with it," Mac pointed out.

"Maybe not, but I don't want you heading back out here by yourself. Things may have been quiet for the past few days, but I don't trust them to stay that way."

The order bothered Mac a little; he could take care of himself and didn't need bodyguards.

At the same time, he wouldn't mind the company, and if anything did happen, it might come in handy to have Pete Newton and Grady Dunn with him.

"Sure. While we're waiting for Mr. Peters to get back, I'll go through the larder and make sure exactly what we need."

"And I'll get that blasted report done," Stanton said, scowling at the desk. Like most men accustomed to working outside with their hands, sitting at a desk and scrawling words and numbers on paper rubbed George Stanton the wrong way.

Mac had the wagon ready to roll by the time Carl Peters returned to the main house a while later. The bookkeeper looked at the vehicle and frowned as he asked, "What's this?"

"I'm going into town with you," Mac replied from the porch, where he'd been waiting.

"I assure you, that's not necessary."

"It is if I'm going to make the bear sign I've been promising the boys."

Peters looked baffled. "What in the world is bear sign?"

"Doughnuts," Mac supplied with a grin. "They look like bear tracks. That's how they got the name. All due respect, sir, but if you'd been around as many cowboys as I have, you'd know that."

"I haven't been around that many cowboys," Peters responded as a sneer curled his lip, "and I'm quite grateful for that."

Mac held up some folded papers. "George told me to give you this. It's that report Miss Elliott wanted."

Peters took it from him and stuck it in a pouch strapped to his saddle. Then he put his foot in the stirrup and swung up onto the horse's back. Mac could tell that Peters wasn't going to wait for him, so he hurried down the steps and climbed onto the wagon seat as the bookkeeper rode away.

"Pete! Grady!" he called. "Let's go."

The two men were waiting near the bunkhouse. They trotted over and climbed into the back of the wagon. Mac took the reins and got the mules moving.

Peters was about a hundred yards ahead. Mac didn't bother trying to keep up; he just kept Peters in sight. He felt confident that Peters wasn't in the market for any conversation during the ride.

Pete and Grady did a good job of keeping Mac company. At Stanton's suggestion, each man had brought along a rifle. Mac was armed with his Smith & Wesson revolver. If they did happen to run into any trouble, they would be able to put up a fight.

Pete made a joke out of that, saying to his companion, "We're like shotgun guards, Grady. We're gonna be guardin' a valuable shipment."

"A valuable shipment of what?" Grady asked. "What are we gonna be carryin', Mac?"

"Flour and sugar, among a few other things," Mac said. "The makings for that bear sign I told you about."

Pete laughed. "Now that's what I like to hear! That's mighty precious cargo, and we'll guard it with our lives."

Mac sincerely hoped it wouldn't come to that.

CHAPTER 26

It was a grim procession that rode from the Triangle 7 into Pine Knob that afternoon. Ben Harmon had ordered four men to remain on the ranch so that it wouldn't be undefended if anybody tried to cause more trouble. He had left it up to Rich Coburn to decide on the men left behind, and the foreman had allowed the crew to draw lots for the task.

Luke was exempted from that drawing since he'd been with Clint Douglas when the youngster was killed. He had a right to stay with Douglas on this last ride, Coburn declared. None of the men argued with him about that.

More than a dozen riders flanked the wagon with its blanket-shrouded cargo. Alamo Paige was at the reins. Harmon, Coburn, and Luke rode a short distance ahead of the vehicle, leading the way.

They drew a great deal of attention as soon as they entered the settlement. The citizens of Pine Knob stopped whatever they were doing to stare at the grim-faced cowboys as their horses paced slowly along the main street. After a moment, some of the townspeople began moving along the boardwalks to keep pace, but they stayed back and didn't approach the wagon.

From the looks of the gun-hung men riding alongside the vehicle, it would be dangerous to treat this procession with anything less than the utmost respect.

Their destination was Endicott's Undertaking Parlor, but to get there, they had to pass Henry Throckmorton's general store. Luke noted the wagon parked beside the store's front porch He was fairly sure he recognized the vehicle.

Because of that, he wasn't surprised when he saw Mac step out of the building and come to an abrupt halt on the porch. Two other men emerged from the store right behind him and also stopped short.

Those two looked a little familiar. They were carrying rifles, and Luke saw how their hands tightened on the weapons. But neither man made a move to start trouble.

Luke was glad of that; those men worked for the Empire Logging Company, and it wouldn't take much to prompt a shoot-out between them and the Triangle 7 riders.

Luke met Mac's eyes for a second. Neither of them nodded or made any other sign that they knew each other. Mac looked puzzled, and Luke knew he had to be wondering what had happened.

Whatever it was, it had to be bad, Mac must have been thinking. He would be able to tell that by the expressions and the barely suppressed attitude of violence emanating from the Triangle 7 men. They were ready to start shooting if anyone gave them the least excuse, and everybody in Pine Knob could see that for themselves.

Luke wasn't worried about Mac, but he hoped the two loggers with him had the good sense not to start anything.

The townspeople may have kept their distance, but Marshal Abner Sundell didn't. He emerged from his office and stalked into the street, lifting a hand in a signal for Luke, Harmon, and Coburn to stop.

The three men reined in. Behind them, the wagon and the other riders halted as well.

"Ben, what in the world is this?" Sundell asked.

In a voice taut with anger, Harmon replied, "Marshal, I'll ask you kindly to move out of the way. We're here to see that one of our own is taken care of, proper-like."

"And that'll get done, of course," Sundell said as he jerked his head in a nod. "But it won't hurt anything for you to tell me what's going on."

"You can see for yourself. One of my men is dead." Harmon's voice softened slightly. "Young Clint Douglas."

"The redheaded kid?" Sundell looked down at the ground for a second and grimaced. He lifted his gaze back to Harmon and went on, "I'm sorry. Some kind of accident, I reckon?"

"Not a bit of it," Harmon snapped. "He was murdered. Gunned down by a bunch of bushwhackers."

"Tree-climbin' bushwhackers," Rich Coburn added.

The voice of the men in the street were loud enough for the townspeople on the boardwalks to hear what they were saying. At Coburn's accusation, several startled exclamations burst out from the bystanders, and excited murmurs could be heard as people asked questions or commented among themselves.

Sundell squinted at Coburn and asked, "Are you saying what I think you're saying, mister?"

Coburn opened his mouth to answer, but Harmon lifted a hand to forestall what was bound to have been an angry response.

"Let that go for now," the cattleman said. "We've got a more important chore to take care of."

Tightly, Coburn said, "There ain't no more important chore than settlin' up for Clint, Boss—but for right now, I'll go along with you."

"You sure will, since you ride for my brand." Harmon looked at Sundell again. "Are you gonna let us pass, Abner?"

"Of course," the marshal said as he stepped back. "Go ahead.

And for what it's worth, Ben—and all you other boys—I'm sorry about Douglas."

Harmon acknowledged that with a nod and nudged his mount into motion again.

As the men rode past, Sundell added, "But I expect you to tell me about that when you're finished with what you've got to do, Ben."

Harmon didn't look over at him, just kept riding.

John Endicott must have realized that something was going on, because he came out of his business to greet the men from Triangle 7, too. With a professionally solemn expression on his face, he nodded as the procession arrived in front of the undertaking parlor.

"Good day to you, Ben," he said. "I take it you've suffered a loss?"

"One of my riders," Harmon replied. "Young Clint Douglas."

"You have my condolences. The, ah, deceased is in the wagon, I assume?"

"That's right."

Endicott nodded and looked at Alamo Paige. "Drive on around to the rear of the building, Mr. Paige," he said. "My associates will meet you there and handle everything."

Paige got the team moving again. Luke, Harmon, and Coburn moved their horses aside to give the wagon room to roll into the alley beside the building.

Coburn said, "You do things up nice for the kid, Mr. Endicott. Whatever it costs, the boys and me will all pitch in to cover it."

"That's not necessary and you know it, Rich," Harmon said gruffly. "I'll take care of all the expenses. Clint rode for Triangle 7 and gave the spread everything he had. It's only fitting that I see this is handled properly."

"Don't worry about any of that," Endicott said. "We'll deal with such things later. For now, you can rest assured everything will be handled with dignity and respect."

Coburn grunted. "If you ask me, that *woman* ought to pay for it. It was some of those varmints who work for her that ventilated the kid." Contempt dripped from his voice at the reference to Constance Elliott.

Endicott looked a little alarmed. He said, "There's not going to be trouble, is there?"

"No trouble," Harmon told him.

Luke wasn't so sure about that. Rich Coburn seemed determined to start a fight with Empire, and judging by the anger on the faces of the other Triangle 7 hands, they shared that sentiment.

Luke hoped that Mac and the other two members of the Empire crew had taken advantage of the chance to get out of town while they could.

"The supplies are loaded, so we'd better get back to camp," Mac said as he looked down the street at the group of riders gathered in front of the undertaking parlor.

"Not just yet," Pete Newton said. He was gazing toward the Triangle 7 men, too, and his jaw was clenched in truculent, defiant lines.

"Did you hear what that big ape said?" Grady Dunn demanded. "He all but accused us of bushwhackin' and killin' that kid!"

Mac sighed and nodded. "I heard him. We all heard him. But we know it's not true, so what does it matter?"

"It matters because he believes it," Dunn said. "And we can't let that stand. It's a blasted lie!"

He moved toward the steps at the end of the porch, evidently intending to stomp down the street and confront the cowboys.

"Hold it!" Mac snapped.

Newton had started after Dunn. Both men stopped and swung around to glare at Mac. Their fists were clenched and they were ready to start swinging at somebody. Mac figured they didn't much care who.

"What did you say?" Newton asked.

"It sounded to me like you just gave us an order," Dunn added.

Mac said, "I did. The two of you aren't going to start a fight with those range riders."

"I don't know what you think gives you the right to boss us around, Mac," Newton said. "We take orders from Miss Elliott and George Stanton, and they're the only ones who can tell us what to do."

"I'm the camp cook," Mac said, "and you came into town on the camp wagon, and that means I'm in charge until we get back."

Dunn shook his head. "I don't know where in Hades you get reasonin' like that, but I don't have to go along with it." He gestured to Newton. "Come on, Pete. Let's show those varmints they can't talk like that about us."

"Hold on, Grady," Newton said, still scowling but starting to look a little less as if he were spoiling for a fight. "They've got us outnumbered five or six to one."

Dunn flung a hand dismissively toward Mac. "The odds wouldn't be that bad if McKenzie wasn't yellow!"

Mac felt anger well up inside him at that insult, but he controlled it.

"I'm going to let that foolish talk pass, Grady," he said. "But just so you know, even if I wanted to start a ruckus, too, the odds would still be four to one against us. That just doesn't make any sense."

Dunn reached over to the wagon, patted the smoothly polished stock of one of the rifles lying on the seat, and said, "We could whittle the odds down a mite before those horsebackers even know what's goin' on."

"You mean become murderers—just like what they've accused us of?"

Newton made a face and said, "Mac's got a point, Grady. We can't just blaze away at those boys. Besides, if bullets start flyin' around in the street, innocent folks are bound to get hurt."

Dunn looked like the calming words were finally starting to get through to him. He grimaced and said, "All right, but I want a drink before we head back to camp. The lies those cowboys are spreadin' around have left a bad taste in my mouth, and I need some whiskey to wash it out!"

Mac sensed that concession might be the best he would get. He said, "All right, but we'll leave the rifles here in the wagon."

Dunn was about to argue, Mac could tell, but Newton said, "All right, that's reasonable enough. We won't need 'em in the Lonesome Pine." He paused and added, "They ain't much use for close work, anyway, and that's what it'll be if it comes down to trouble in the saloon."

"There won't be any trouble," Mac said, hoping he was right about that.

Dunn pointed at the Smith & Wesson stuck in Mac's waistband.

"How about that gun of yours?" he asked. "Are you gonna leave it here, too, McKenzie?"

Newton laughed and said, "Mac's got a cooler head than you, Grady. Besides, that revolver is a whole lot more suited to a saloon shootout. That is, if he's any good with it. Are you any good, Mac?"

Mac remembered Patrick Flagg, the trail boss on his first cattle drive as a chuck-wagon cook. Flagg had been fast with a gun, and he had taught Mac everything he knew, molding a raw talent into a deadly skill. Mac wasn't a blindingly fast draw like Luke's brother Smoke was reputed to be, but he was quicker on the shoot than most men and had a deadly accurate eye.

He also believed that modesty often served a purpose, so he said, "I can handle a gun all right if I need to."

Newton left his rifle where it was lying on the wagon seat and said, "Come on, Grady. I want that drink, too."

Grudgingly, Dunn turned away from the wagon and the rifles. The two men fell in alongside Mac and started down the street toward the Lonesome Pine.

As they did so, Mac saw the wagon from the Triangle 7 roll into the alley beside the undertaking parlor. He hadn't been acquainted with the unfortunate cowboy laid out under the blanket in back. He'd heard Ben Harmon supply the name Clint Douglas to the marshal and that was all he knew about the dead man.

But he was sorry, anyway, and hoped Endicott did right by the poor young fellow.

Oren Butler, the proprietor of the Lonesome Pine, eyed the three men warily as they came into the saloon. He stood behind the bar and rested his hands on the hardwood as he frowned and said, "I don't want any trouble in here."

"Neither do we," Mac assured him. He and Newton and Dunn stepped up to the bar. Mac went on, "Whiskey for the three of us, and a mug of beer each. It's on me."

"Thanks, Mac," Newton said. Dunn just let out a still surly grunt of acknowledgment.

Butler got the drinks himself and set the shot glasses and mugs in front of Mac and his companions. Mac threw back the whiskey, then picked up the beer and turned halfway around to look over the room as he sipped the cool liquid.

Half a dozen customers were in the Lonesome Pine, all of them townsmen. Two stood further along the bar, nursing beers, and four sat a table enjoying what looked like a friendly, low-stakes poker game.

Newton and Dunn worked on their beers. Mac hoped it wouldn't take long to finish them, and then the three of them could get out of there before any trouble had a chance to develop.

Those hopes were dashed a moment later when heavy footsteps sounded outside the saloon and a tall figure appeared at the entrance, thrusting aside the batwing doors as he stalked into the Lonesome Pine. Rich Coburn led the way with all the other Triangle 7 riders trailing into the room behind him.

No, not quite all, Mac amended to himself as he realized he didn't see Luke or Ben Harmon. More than likely, the cattleman was over at the marshal's office. Sundell had stated plainly he wanted Harmon to come see him once the young cowboy's body was delivered to the undertaker. It was possible that Luke had accompanied Harmon.

That wasn't good. The Triangle 7 crew would have been less likely to stir up trouble if their boss was there with them.

The two townies drinking at the bar picked up their glasses and scooted along to the far end, leaving a big enough gap between them and the three Empire men for the cowboys to fill it up. The Triangle 7 riders did so, bellying up to the hardwood as they cast unfriendly looks toward Mac, Newton, and Dunn.

Dunn was the closest to them. That wasn't good, Mac thought. Dunn was the most hotheaded of the three of them.

In a loud voice, Coburn ordered whiskey for him and the other Triangle 7 cowboys. Oren Butler and his bartender both worked to fill those orders. When all the range riders had drinks in front of them, Coburn picked up his glass and said, "Here's to Clint Douglas, one of the finest young hombres who ever strapped on a pair of spurs!"

"To Clint!" several of the men echoed.

They all downed their drinks.

Coburn thumped his empty glass on the hardwood and leaned forward to look along the bar toward Mac, Newton, and Dunn. With a sneer on his face, he said, "I see you fellas didn't drink to our friend."

Quickly, Mac said, "We didn't know whether you'd take it kindly if we did that. But we're sorry for your loss, and we're sure he was a fine young man. Aren't we, boys?"

Newton and Dunn didn't respond to that prompt. Newton just scowled into his beer, but Dunn was more defiant and said, "I don't know anything about him, but if he was a cowboy—"

Butler planted himself on the other side of the bar and interrupted by saying, "Let's all just calm down and not say anything we'll regret later."

Coburn said, "I ain't in the habit of regrettin' anything I say.

Anything that comes outta my mouth, I mean it, and I don't care what anybody else thinks about it."

"Anything coming out of a cowboy's mouth is most likely the same thing that comes out the other end of the ugly critters he nurses," Dunn said.

Coburn drew in a sharp breath and stepped away from the bar.

Mac reached behind Newton, got hold of Dunn's shoulder, and hauled the logger back around on the other side of him. At the same time, he stepped around Newton so that he put himself between the Triangle 7 crew and his two Empire companions.

"Look, emotions are running pretty high right now," he said to Coburn. "I know you're mourning your friend, so my friends and I will get out of here and leave you alone. There's no need for any trouble."

Coburn gestured past Mac toward Dunn. "He needs to apologize for runnin' his mouth that way."

Dunn tried to crowd past Mac, who stood his ground as the logger said, "I'm not gonna apologize for anything I say to a blasted cow-nurse. You can all go to blazes!"

Butler yelled, "Now that's enough! I mean it!"

None of the men paid any attention to him. Dunn bumped heavily into Mac again, jolting him forward. At the same time, Rich Coburn stepped toward them and threw a punch. Whether he was aiming at Mac or Dunn was debatable.

But what was beyond any doubt was the way that bony-knuckled fist crashed into Mac's jaw with stunning force.

CHAPTER 27

Marshal Abner Sundell had a pot of coffee staying warm on the potbellied stove in the corner of his office. He poured cups for Luke and Ben Harmon and filled one for himself.

As he settled down in the old leather chair behind the desk, he looked across it at the two men seated on ladder-back chairs and said, "All right, Ben, tell me what happened."

Harmon nodded toward Luke. "Jensen can tell it better. He was with Clint when they were bushwhacked."

Luke sipped the coffee, which wasn't particularly good but had a bracing effect, then launched into the tale. It didn't take him long to give Sundell the facts of the ambush.

When Luke finished, Sundell asked, "You never saw the men who were shooting at you and Douglas?"

"Never even caught a glimpse of them."

"Then what makes you think it was some of the Empire logging crew?"

"I never said that was the case," Luke pointed out. "But when

Rich Coburn and I checked out those boulders where the ambushers were hidden, we found footprints left by hobnailed boots."

"You're sure about that?" Sundell asked sharply.

"Absolutely certain. There was no mistaking them."

The marshal frowned. "Just because a man wears hobnailed boots, that doesn't make him a logger."

Harmon said, "Nobody in these parts except loggers would be wearing boots like that, Abner, and you know it. None of my boys would be caught dead in anything but regular ridin' boots."

"No, probably not," Sundell allowed. He sat back in his chair and looked at Luke. "You weren't able to follow the trail they left when they rode off?"

Luke shook his head. "It's too rocky up there. Even if we'd been able to follow them, they had a big lead on us. They lit a shuck as fast as they could when the group from the Triangle 7 showed up."

"They didn't like the odds," Harmon said. "Yellow-bellied, bushwhackin' skunks."

Sundell thought for a moment and then said, "I can't just march over to Constance Elliott's office and accuse her of anything based on what you and Jensen have told me, Ben."

"I didn't ask you to accuse her. You wanted me to tell you what happened. You've been told."

Harmon scraped his chair back as if he were about to stand up.

"Hold on," the marshal said. "What do you figure on doing now?"

"I thought I'd go down to the undertaking parlor and finish making the arrangements for Clint with John Endicott, then I'll round up my men and head back to the ranch. I expect the funeral will be tomorrow and we'll ride in for that, of course, but between now and then, there's still work to be done on the spread."

Sundell nodded slowly and said, "I'm relieved to hear that. I was afraid you might try to push this into open warfare with Empire."

"There won't be any more trouble until we've laid young Clint to rest."

Sundell caught the implication in Harmon's words. "What about after that?"

"I'm not makin' any promises."

This time, the rancher got to his feet and turned toward the door.

Sundell came up out of his chair and said, "Blast it, Ben, you can't—"

Harmon wheeled back around to face him.

"I can—and will—do anything I have to in order to protect my men and my spread," he said. "If you want to help the situation, you might make that clear to Constance Elliott. I've tried to keep the peace, but no more. If Empire wants war, that's what they'll have!"

He stalked out of the office, ignoring Sundell when the marshal called after him.

Failing to stop Harmon, Sundell turned to Luke. "Can you talk some sense into his head, Jensen?"

"Harmon's not going to listen to me," Luke said. "I'm just a hired hand, and I'm an outsider, to boot. Not to mention a bounty hunter. My opinion doesn't mean a thing to him."

"Well, blast it, you can at least try. I like both Ben and Miss Constance. I don't want their men trying to kill one another, and I don't think they really do, either. Besides, trouble like that has a bad habit of spilling over into town!"

Luke stood up. "I'll try, but I can't make any promises," he said.

Sundell got a speculative look on his face. "Something just occurred to me," he said. "Maybe I ought to deputize you and give you the job of getting to the bottom of all this. That might be a way of heading off more trouble."

Luke held up his hands, palms out, and said, "Sorry, Marshal, but I don't have any interest in wearing a badge—"

The door opened abruptly and one of the townsmen stuck his head into the office.

"Better come quick, Marshal!" he said. "Somebody just came flyin' through the front window of the Lonesome Pine!"

Rich Coburn's punch drove Mac backward against Pete Newton, who tried to catch him. Mac bounced off Newton instead and reeled against the bar. His legs started to buckle underneath him, but he caught himself on the hardwood and pushed back up.

While Mac was doing that, Grady Dunn charged past him and let out a furious yell as he tackled Coburn. The Triangle 7 foreman was slightly off-balance from the effort he had put into that punch, so he wasn't able to brace himself for Dunn's attack.

The two men collided with enough force to knock both of them off their feet. They crashed to the sawdust-littered floor. Dunn was on top and started hammering blows at Coburn, who was too stunned for the moment to fight back.

One of the cowboys swung a kick at Dunn's head. Dunn saw the booted foot coming and jerked aside. The kick caught him on the shoulder and sent him sprawling. He rolled and came to a stop against the legs of the table where the four townies had been playing poker. That was enough of a jolt to scatter the cards, coins, and greenbacks on the table. The players yelled angrily as they leaped to their feet and made frantic grabs at the money.

Newton leaped over Coburn and hooked a fist into the belly of the man who had kicked Dunn. As that man doubled over from the blow, another cowboy punched Newton in the face. Newton's head rocked back, but he didn't go down. He slugged back and sent the cowboy staggering.

Oren Butler pounded both fists on the bar and shouted for the men to stop fighting, but nobody paid any attention to him as the melee continued.

Despite being heavily outnumbered, Mac knew he and his companions had to fight. The Triangle 7 men were ablaze with fury and grief, but they were outnumbered and would be beaten badly.

They might as well deal out as much damage as they could, Mac thought, as he pushed away from the bar and jabbed a straight right into the face of the closest cowboy. As the man stumbled backward, Mac hit him again, this time with a left cross that snapped his head to the side.

Mac didn't have a chance to throw a third punch because at that moment, one of the Triangle 7 riders grabbed him from behind and pinned his arms.

"I've got him, boys!" the man yelled as he stumbled around, trying to hold the wildly heaving Mac. "Give him what for!"

One of the cowboys charged and, judging by the bloodthirsty look on his face, he intended to beat Mac within an inch of his life. Mac jerked his right leg up in time for the attacker to run right into his foot. Mac planted his boot in the middle of the man's chest and shoved as hard as he could.

Fate had turned them so that the man Mac kicked flew backward, out of control, waving his arms and yelling as he barely managed to stay on his feet. His momentum carried him across the barroom and, by some fluke, he didn't hit any of the tables or chairs.

He did, however, hit the saloon's big front window, and he went through it with a crash that sent glass flying across the boardwalk outside. The cowboy fell across the sill and landed in the welter of glittering shards, crying out in pain as some of them cut him.

Mac had taken the first man to come at him by surprise with that tactic, but it didn't work again. Two cowboys angled in at him from the sides, positioned so that he couldn't fend them off by kicking. And no matter how hard he wrenched at the arms holding him from behind, he couldn't pull free from their grip.

Fists slammed into his face, rocking his head from side to side, and more blows pounded into his ribs and midsection. His head was swimming now, and a red haze dropped down over his eyes. He knew he couldn't withstand much more punishment like this without passing out.

If that happened, the Triangle 7 crew might put him on the floor and stomp the life out of him. Luke had said that these were good men, not outlaws or killers, but as furious as they were over the ambush murder of their friend, they might be capable of more violence than Luke believed.

Mac continued clinging to consciousness. He still threw his weight from side to side, trying to break free.

He had no idea how Pete Newton and Grady Dunn were doing in the fight. It was too bad he couldn't help them, but as far gone as he was, those boys were on their own.

The sudden roar of a gun was ear-achingly loud.

The man holding Mac jerked him up straighter, then planted a hand in the middle of his back and gave him a hard shove forward. Mac had no chance of staying on his feet. He fell to his knees and pitched to his belly. His head was turned to the side, and he could feel the sawdust on his left cheek.

"Get that man up, now," a harsh voice ordered. It sounded familiar to Mac, but he couldn't place it.

Strong hands took hold of his arms and lifted him to his feet. He blinked his eyes, shook his head, and his vision cleared. He saw Marshal Abner Sundell standing near the saloon's batwing entrance. A wisp of smoke curled from the muzzle of the revolver the marshal held. Sundell was the one who had given that order, Mac realized.

Luke Jensen and Ben Harmon were right behind Sundell. Neither of them had pulled iron, but their hands hung near the guns on their hips.

To Mac's left, Pete Newton was pinned with his back bent

unnaturally over the bar. One of the cowboys stood over him, left forearm pressed across his throat. The cowboy's right arm was raised and his fist was poised to fall.

"Step away from that man," Sundell snapped.

When the cowboy did so, Newton slid down the bar until he was sitting with his back against it and his legs stretched out in front of him. He shook his head groggily.

Lying atop the wreckage of a table that had collapsed was Grady Dunn, either unconscious—or dead. From the looks of it, the table's legs had broken when Dunn was thrown on top of it.

Some of the Triangle 7 hands bore the signs of battle, but the only one who had suffered any serious damage appeared to be the one Mac had kicked through the window. That man still lay there with his legs hooked over the sill.

Ben Harmon stepped up beside Sundell and said, "Rich, I thought I told you there wasn't gonna be any trouble while we were in town."

"We couldn't help it, Boss," Coburn said. "They were disrespectful to Clint's memory and to our ranch. We had to hand 'em their needin's!"

"Not today, you didn't." Harmon drew in a deep breath and blew it out in a disgusted sigh. He looked at Butler and went on, "Oren, it seems like I'm gonna be buyin' you a new window and at least one new table. You figure out what it all comes to and let me know. I'll take care of it right away."

"Thank you, Ben," Butler said stiffly. "I appreciate that. I hope you'll understand when I say that the Lonesome Pine is off-limits to your men from now on."

That brought exclamations of protest from some of the Triangle 7 crew. They abruptly fell silent when Harmon cast an angry glance in their direction.

"I understand," Harmon said, "but I hope you'll see your way clear not to make that permanent."

"I'll have to think about it," Butler said grudgingly. "But it holds for now."

Harmon nodded and addressed his men. "You heard the man. Any of you fellas get caught in here for the time being, you can draw whatever wages you've got comin' to you, because you won't be ridin' for the Triangle 7 anymore."

Coburn scowled and muttered, "It ain't fair."

"What was that, Rich?"

"Nothin', Boss, nothin'," Coburn said, shaking his head. "We'll do like you say, won't we, fellas?"

A few mumbled agreements came from the others.

Butler turned to Mac and went on, "Don't think Empire is getting off easy, McKenzie. The same is true for your bunch. Until I say different, you're not welcome in the Lonesome Pine, and neither are any of the rest of your bunch."

Mac's head had stopped spinning. He had recovered his wits enough to say, "I don't know why you're telling me. I'm just the cook, and a temporary one, at that."

"You can pass the word to George Stanton. And you're the only one who's awake enough to know what I'm saying." Butler leaned forward over the bar, peered at Dunn's recumbent form, and added, "Is that man dead?"

Luke went over to Dunn, reached down, and rolled him onto his back. Dunn's chest rose and fell.

"No, he's alive," Luke reported. "Just out cold."

The marshal holstered his gun now that the fight truly seemed to be over and ordered, "Get him out of here, McKenzie, and then I want all three of you Empire men out of town as quickly as possible."

Mac went over to Newton, took hold of his arm, and said, "Come on, Pete. It's time to get back to camp. I need your help with Grady."

Newton tried to stand, but then sagged back down and groaned.

Luke said, "He's in no shape to help you, McKenzie. I'll give you a hand."

Mac hesitated to make it look real, but after a moment he

nodded. "Thanks, Jensen," he said in a surly tone that didn't sound very sincere.

He and Luke each took an arm and lifted Dunn to his feet. Newton tried a second time to stand and managed to get up. He stumbled out of the saloon ahead of them. They carried Dunn along the street toward Empire's wagon parked in front of the general store. The toes of Dunn's work boots left ruts in the dust where they dragged.

Newton was far enough in front of them that he wasn't likely to overhear anything as Luke said, "I hoped you'd see this was a chance for us to talk."

"Yeah, but I'm not sure either of us know anything new. Did loggers really bushwhack you and that other cowboy?"

"Three men wearing hobnailed boots did," Luke replied. "And they killed the kid, no doubt about that. Almost sent me across the divide, too."

"You know, somebody wearing riding boots probably sabotaged the rollway out at Empire's camp and wound up nearly killing one of our men. You know what it's starting to sound like to me?"

"Like somebody's trying to keep the two sides at each other's throats and maybe stir up enough trouble to provoke a full-scale war?"

"I don't think we can rule that out," Mac said. "But who would profit from doing something like that?"

"That's what we need to figure out," Luke said, "if we're going to stop both sides from killing each other."

CHAPTER 28

Dunn was starting to come around as Luke and Mac lifted him into the back of the Empire wagon and stretched him out beside the supplies that had been loaded in there earlier. He was far from coherent, though, and just lay there groaning softly and occasionally shaking his head gingerly from side to side. Evidently, the cobwebs in his brain were being stubborn about clearing away.

Pete Newton leaned against one of the wheels. He was still shaking his head, too.

"Sorry, Mac," he said. "My brain's a little addled."

"Let me give you a hand," Mac said. He boosted Newton onto the driver's seat. Luke had to step up and grab Newton's arm when the man started to lose his balance and fall backward.

Between them, they got Newton settled. He stared down at the floorboards and groaned.

Mac and Luke walked up beside the mules' heads. Mac said quietly, "I hope neither of them is seriously hurt."

"The odds were stacked against you and your friends in that fight," Luke said.

Mac rolled his eyes. "I tried to tell them that, but they were too stubborn to listen. Plus, those cowboys came in there primed to explode."

"Not much doubt about that." Luke lowered his voice even more. "Keep your eyes open out there. If there's someone in that camp working against Empire, there's no telling what they might do next."

"The same goes for you on the Triangle 7." Mac paused, then added, "You might see if anybody out there is hiding some hobnailed boots."

A faint smile tugged at the corners of Luke's mouth. "Even if our idea is right, I doubt if any of them would be foolish enough to do that. I suppose it won't hurt to look around, though."

"And I'll see if anybody at the camp has some riding boots stashed." Mac raised his voice and went on, "Thanks for your help, Jensen."

Luke made a curt gesture and turned away sharply enough to convey the impression that he didn't care for Mac's thanks. The supposed enmity between them was clear to anyone who might be watching them.

At least, Mac hoped that was the case.

He climbed onto the seat, took the reins, and started the wagon out of town.

He had to pass the Empire Logging Company office on the way, though, and as he drew even with the building, the door opened and Constance Elliott stepped out onto the porch.

"Mr. McKenzie," she called. "A word with you."

Mac couldn't very well ignore that summons. He turned the wagon toward the office. Beside him, Pete Newton groaned again.

As Mac brought the wagon to a stop, Constance said, "I heard there was trouble earlier."

Mac nodded toward Grady Dunn in the back of the vehicle and then inclined his head toward Pete Newton.

"You can see for yourself, ma'am," he said.

"You appear to have some bumps and bruises, too. There was a fight?"

"Yes, ma'am."

"With Ben Harmon's men? In the saloon?"

"Seems like you already know all about it," Mac drawled.

Carl Peters had come out of the office behind Constance and stood nearby. At Mac's comment, he snapped, "Don't be insolent, McKenzie."

Looking at Constance instead of Peters, Mac said, "Begging your pardon, Miss Elliott. I meant no offense."

Constance's chin jutted out defiantly. "None taken, Mr. McKenzie. I'm sure those brutes who ride for Ben Harmon gave you no choice in the matter. They attacked you, didn't they?"

"Well, it was one of them who threw the first punch, I'll grant you that, but harsh words were flying back and forth from both sides before that."

At that moment, Pete Newton leaned the other way off the seat and was sick in the street. Carl Peters grimaced at the sight and sound. Constance looked concerned.

"Should that man see the doctor?" she asked. "And what about the one in the back?"

"I think they're both all right," Mac said. "They took some hard wallops to the head. They'll probably need to take it easy for a few days."

"Time lost from work, you mean," Peters complained.

"All right," Constance said, "but keep a close eye on them. Don't hesitate to send for the doctor if you think it's necessary. Be sure to pass that along to George, as well."

"I'll tell him, ma'am, you can count on that."

Constance's annoyed expression eased a bit. "I also heard that one of the Triangle 7 men was shot and killed." She sounded sympathetic.

"That's true. Somebody ambushed a couple of his riders, and one of them was wounded and didn't make it."

"Does anyone know who's responsible?"

Mac hesitated, unsure how much to tell her. But word of what had happened would get around town anyway, so he realized there was no point in holding back.

"Harmon blames Empire, ma'am," he said. "It seems that the bushwhackers left some boot prints behind. And they were wearing hobnailed boots, like loggers."

"That's outrageous!" Peters burst out. "How dare he make such a ridiculous accusation?"

Constance said, "Just because a man wears hobnailed boots doesn't make him a logger."

"No, ma'am," Mac agreed, "but those seem to be the only fellas around here who make a habit of wearing them."

Peters said, "I've got a good mind to find Ben Harmon and have a word with him."

"No, you're not, Carl," Constance said. "If anyone does that, it's going to be me. And I don't really have the stomach for talking to Ben Harmon right now."

She drew in a breath and went on. "Go on back to camp, Mr. McKenzie. Let George know what's happened. Tell him to keep the men close to camp for the time being. No trips into town until I let him know it's all right."

"What about the payroll that's coming in?"

"Let's allow things to cool down first. I'll send word to camp when it's all right for the men to visit Pine Knob again."

"All right," Mac allowed. "You're the boss. And since the crew has been banned from the Lonesome Pine, they wouldn't be able to spend their wages there, anyway."

"Banned?" Constance repeated.

"Until Mr. Butler changes his mind."

"Well, I can't say that I blame him," she said as she shook her head. "All right, Mr. McKenzie, drive on."

Mac nodded, lifted the reins, and got the mules going again. The wagon rolled on out of town.

"Sorry I got sick in front of the boss," Newton muttered as he lurched a little from side to side on the seat.

"She didn't seem bothered by it," Mac told him. "She just wants you and Grady to feel better."

"I don't reckon I'll feel better until I've evened the score with those blasted cowboys."

Unfortunately, the Triangle 7 cowboys undoubtedly felt the same way about the Empire crew. No matter how many orders were issued by Marshal Sundell, Constance Elliott, and Ben Harmon, the anger and resentment would still be there, festering until it was ready to form an open wound again.

On the way out of town, Mac glanced toward the Blue Top Café and saw Violet Channing looking out the window toward the wagon. He hadn't seen the attractive blonde since the first day he had arrived in Pine Knob. He had meant to pay another visit to the café, but things just hadn't worked out that way.

A war between Triangle 7 and Empire would spill over into the settlement, Mac thought, and endanger Violet and her grandfather and all the other innocent citizens. They might even be forced to take sides, and that would just make things worse.

The only way to prevent that trouble was to discover the truth about what was going on around here, to find out who was really responsible for the stagecoach holdup and the payroll robbery, the deaths of Fred Carter and Clint Douglas, and the injuries that had befallen several other men on both sides. It seemed to Mac as if he and Luke were the only ones really trying to get to the bottom of that. Everybody else was too busy getting mad and pointing fingers.

He and Luke needed some sort of break, he told himself—and they needed not to get killed in the process.

By the time they reached the Empire camp, Grady Dunn had recovered enough to sit up in the back of the wagon, although he still groaned every time the vehicle bounced over a rough spot in the trail.

Pete Newton's color was better, and he was more alert. Both men had the iron constitutions that years of hard, outdoor work had given them, and Mac was confident they would soon shake off the aftereffects of the battle in the Lonesome Pine.

George Stanton came out of the main house to greet them as Mac brought the wagon to a stop. He opened his mouth to say something, then stopped and frowned as he gazed intently at Newton and Dunn.

"You boys look a little green around the gills," he said. "Something happen in town?"

"They look a lot better now than they did when we started back here," Mac said. "There was a fight in the saloon."

Stanton scowled as his face darkened with anger. "With the crew from the Triangle 7, I'm guessing."

"That's right."

"Blast it!" Stanton said. "You fellows had your orders. You weren't supposed to start any trouble—"

"That Coburn skunk punched Mac, George," Newton said. "What were we supposed to do? We couldn't just stand by and not fight back."

Mac said, "Even if we hadn't fought, they would have jumped us. One of their men was killed in an ambush earlier today, and they were looking for a scrap."

"An ambush?" Stanton repeated. "I'm sorry to hear it, but what does that have to do with us?"

"They say we did it!" Newton yelped. "They claim it was some loggers that bushwhacked 'em."

Mac explained about the prints of hobnailed boots that Luke and Rich Coburn had found. Stanton waved a hand and made a disgusted sound. "That doesn't prove a thing," he said.

"Maybe not in a court of law, but in the minds of those cowboys, we're guilty."

Stanton blew out a breath and shook his head. "Well, they've got rocks for brains and there's nothing we can do to change that. Let's go ahead and get these supplies unloaded and carried in."

"You ain't heard the rest of it, George," Newton said. "We're banned from the Lonesome Pine!"

Stanton grunted in surprise but said, "Good! Maybe some time without pickling your brains in that Who-Hit-John will be good for you."

Mac said, "Harmon's men are banned, too. I don't expect that situation will last too long, though. Oren Butler relies on both bunches for a significant percentage of his trade. Give things a week or so to cool off and I'm sure he'll welcome everyone back. In the meantime, Miss Elliott also said to keep the men here in camp for a while."

"What about payday?" Stanton asked.

"It's postponed for the time being."

Stanton shook his head again and said, "That won't go over very well, but what the boss says, goes." He looked at Newton and Dunn. "Pete, Grady, you boys go lie down. You still look pretty sick. Mac, you got knocked around some yourself, so you can just supervise while I get some of the other men to unload those supplies and carry them in."

"I'm all right, George," Mac insisted. "If you don't mind giving me a hand with it, I'm sure we can get everything squared away pretty quickly."

"All right, if you think you're up to it."

Newton and Dunn climbed down from the wagon and shuffled off toward the bunkhouse, their movements still a little shaky. Mac didn't feel quite as chipper as he'd made out, but he and Stanton made short work of the unloading chore and then Stanton led the mules off toward the stock barn to unhitch them from the wagon and put them back in their stalls.

Mac stayed in the kitchen. He poured himself a cup of coffee from the pot on the stove, and the strong black brew made him feel a little better. The men would be coming in from their day's work in a few hours and he needed to get started on supper.

He had just gotten out a bowl to start mixing up some biscuit dough when he caught a glimpse of movement through the window over the counter. This was at the back of the building that looked toward a stand of scrubby pines that were too small to bother with cutting down. They would still have to grow for a number of years before they would be ready.

But the trees grew thickly enough that they provided cover for anyone who wanted to lurk in them. That thought had just gone through Mac's mind after he spotted somebody moving around out there and set alarm bells to clanging inside his head when the window shattered, spraying glass at him as something deadly whipped past his head.

CHAPTER 29

Several of the glass shards stung Mac's face and hands as he fell backward out of the line of fire. The bullet that had broken the window had come much too close for comfort as it whined past his ear, but other than the small cuts, he wasn't hurt.

He wasn't going to stand up and let the bushwhacker take another shot at him, though. He crouched below the window level as he pulled the Smith & Wesson from the waistband of his denim trousers.

Rising quickly, he thrust the revolver at the hole in the window and thumbed off two swift shots in the direction of the trees. He didn't like not being able to see what he was shooting at, but considering how close he had just come to getting his brains blown out, he wasn't going to worry too much about that.

Whoever was out there was an enemy and could take his chances.

Mac ducked back down after firing the two shots. He heard heavy, rapid footsteps nearby and swung toward the door into the kitchen. He had the gun up and ready in case he was also being attacked from this direction.

Instead, it was George Stanton who burst through the doorway, and as he spotted the Smith & Wesson pointing at him, he skidded to a fast stop and thrust out his hands, palms toward Mac.

"Hold your fire, Mac!" he said. "It's me!"

A rifle cracked again, somewhere outside. More glass shattered as the bullet came through an unbroken part of the window and slammed into the wall beside the door. Stanton yelled and dived to the floor.

"Are you hit?" Mac asked the superintendent.

"No, but that slug came too blasted close!"

"I know the feeling," Mac said. He pushed the release latch, tilted the revolver's barrel down to open the cylinder, ejected the spent cartridges, and replaced them with two fresh rounds he took from his pocket. He also slid a cartridge into the chamber he usually kept empty so the hammer could rest on it.

Any time somebody was shooting at him, he wanted a full wheel if possible.

As he closed the revolver, he said, "There's a Winchester in that cabinet over there, George. If you'll get it and keep that fella occupied for a few minutes, I'll go out the front and try to circle around on him."

Stanton stared at him. "Are you loco? You'll get killed. The boys will hear those shots and come a-runnin' to see what's going on."

"I know they will," Mac said. "That's what I'm worried about. They're liable to charge right into the line of fire. We don't know that varmint is after just me. He could be trying to kill any of us he can get a shot at."

Stanton thought about it for a second and then nodded. "You're right. We ought to try to deal with him before the others get here. But be careful, Mac."

"Sure, I always am," Mac said. It wasn't exactly a lie—but it did stretch the truth a mite.

Stanton crawled over to the cabinet Mac had indicated and opened it to take out the Winchester.

"It's loaded," Mac told him.

Stanton nodded and scooted over to the counter, avoiding the broken glass that littered the floor. Mac crawled the other way, toward the door. Stanton pushed himself up into a crouch and waited, watching Mac.

When Mac was ready, he nodded to Stanton, who stood up, thrust the Winchester's barrel through the broken window, and blazed away, firing several rounds as fast as he could work the rifle's loading lever.

Mac sprang to his feet and lunged through the doorway in the same rapid motion. With the revolver in his right fist, he ran through the house and burst out onto the porch.

Instantly, he dropped to one knee and tracked the Smith & Wesson from side to side, just in case another bushwhacker was waiting for him on this side of the house.

No shots came toward him, and he didn't see anybody moving around.

That surprised him a little, because Pete Newton and Grady Dunn had gone into the bunkhouse and he thought the gunfire might have drawn them out. But considering the shape they'd been in when they returned from Pine Knob, it was possible both men were sleeping so deeply that the shots hadn't roused them.

With no threat around here that he could see, Mac went hurriedly down the steps and around the house. He could still hear the sharp cracks of two rifles—one inside and one out—as he worked his way along the side wall of the building.

When he reached the rear corner, he edged one eye past it to risk a look toward the trees. He saw a spurt of muzzle flame in the shadows underneath the pines and knew that was where the ambusher was hidden. If he opened up on the rifleman from this angle and emptied the revolver, the odds were high that he would kill the man, or at least run him off.

Mac didn't want to do either of those things.

He wanted to capture this varmint who had come mighty close to killing him. If he did that, he could find out who the man was and question him about who he was working for. Mac's instincts told him there was a hidden hand behind all the trouble that had plagued both Empire and the Triangle 7 in recent days.

That mastermind was the man Mac truly wanted to get in his gunsights.

He retreated to the front of the house and ran toward the stock barn. He darted across an open area and hoped he did so fast enough that the bushwhacker didn't spot him. He had to run that risk, though, if he hoped to circle around and take the hidden rifleman by surprise.

The wagon was parked on the other side of the stock barn and provided even more cover for Mac as he moved closer to the trees. The pines grew all the way to the edge of the path leading through the woods to the rollway. When he came to the last open stretch, Mac paused, drew in a couple of deep breaths, and then sprinted toward the trees, halfway expecting to hear a shot and feel the stunning impact of a bullet.

Nothing of the sort happened. The back-and-forth gunfire from the house and the woods continued as he reached the trees. As soon as the growth and the thick shadows shielded him, he leaned a shoulder against the rough bark of a pine trunk and caught his breath.

He was still a relatively young man, he told himself. He shouldn't be getting too old for this sort of thing already.

Maybe he just wasn't cut out to be a bounty hunter and adventurer. At this moment, he sort of missed his café back in Wyoming. . . .

Maybe he would go back to that life someday, he thought as he squared his shoulders. But he wasn't done with *this* life yet, and he had a would-be killer to corral. Summoning up all the stealth he could manage, he began cat-footing through the woods as he took a roundabout path toward the hidden gunman.

He followed the sound of the gunshots and steadily closed in on his quarry. After a few minutes, he was getting close enough that he started to worry that an errant bullet from George Stanton's rifle might hit him instead.

Then, with a sudden crackling of brush, the ambusher gave up and fled. Mac clearly heard him pushing through the branches of the undergrowth only a few yards away.

Biting back a curse, Mac abandoned stealth and charged through the woods, too, as he tried to intercept the bolting bushwhacker. Branches clawed at him and tried to hold him back. He spotted an indistinct shape plunging through the shadows ahead of him. Somehow, it didn't look like a man, but it had to be.

Mac burst into a narrow opening in the brush at the same instant as the man he was after. He left his feet in a diving tackle, still holding the revolver in his right hand.

In the brief moment as he threw himself at the bushwhacker, he realized why the man had looked odd during that fleeting glimpse through the brush. He was wearing a long gray duster and had a wide-brimmed hat crammed down on his head, held in place by a taut chinstrap. A bandanna was tied around the lower half of his face.

Mac barely had time to see all that before he crashed into the man and they both went sprawling.

Mac had caught the man around the waist from the right side, and he landed on top. His weight coming down on the other man made the hombre grunt and gasp. He lost his grip on the rifle he was carrying in his left hand. It slid away across the ground.

Unfortunately, the fall jolted the Smith & Wesson out of Mac's grip, too. He made a grab for it, but as he did, the man he had tackled rammed an elbow back into his ribs. That knocked him to the side.

The bushwhacker tried to buck up from the ground and throw Mac off. Mac hung on with his left hand and hammered a punch to the back of the man's neck with his right. That forced the man's face into the carpet of pine needles and detritus underneath them. The bandanna must have protected him to a certain extent, but he still sputtered and spat from the mouthful of dry pine needles he got.

Mac raised his fist and was about to hit the man again when he heard someone push through the brush behind him. Thinking it was probably George Stanton or one of the other loggers, he said, "I've got him! Give me a hand!"

No one said anything, which puzzled him enough to make him throw a glance back over his shoulder.

He looked around just in time to see the broken branch sweeping toward his head. He didn't get more than a fragmentary look at the man swinging it before the makeshift club smashed into his skull just above his right ear. The brutal blow pitched him to the side, off the man he had tackled.

Mac hit the ground on his left shoulder as blackness welled up around him to swallow him like the maw of a starving beast. The last thing he thought before he passed out was that there had been two enemies after all.

The Triangle 7 cowboys were a sullen bunch as they rode back toward the ranch.

Some of them had picked up a few bumps and bruises in the fight. The one hurt the most was Chet Moran, the man Mac had kicked through the front window of the Lonesome Pine. Moran had sore ribs that made him mutter and curse every time he took too big a breath, and the broken glass had cut him in numerous places. Dr. Abrams had cleaned the wounds and bandaged the worst gashes.

The thing that bothered them more than anything else, though, was being banned from the saloon. They didn't go into town to drink and gamble all that often, but like most cowboys, they didn't cotton to being told they couldn't do something. They were a breed who would charge Hades with a bucket of water if the man they rode for ordered it, but having to take orders from anybody else put burrs under their saddles.

Luke had been around enough range riders to be aware of

exactly how they felt, even though he didn't share their resentment.

He rode on Ben Harmon's left; Rich Coburn was to the cattleman's right. The other cowboys and the wagon with Alamo Paige at the reins followed behind them.

Coburn said, "How long do you think Butler's gonna stick to that decision he made, Boss?"

"He'd be well within his rights to ban you idiots for life," Harmon said. "Oren's an easygoing sort, though. He'll probably cool off and get over being mad in a week or so. I'll give him that long and then ride in and see him. Once I've settled up with him, he'll probably tell me to pass the word to you boys that you can come back."

"I sure hope so," Coburn said. He rode along in silence for a minute before saying, "You're gonna make sure that Elliott woman pays Empire's share of the damages, ain't you, Ben?"

Harmon's voice was sharp as he replied, "You let me worry about that."

Coburn leaned back in the saddle and frowned. "You're gonna pay all of it, ain't you?" he said in an accusatory tone. "You ain't even gonna ask her to throw in her share. That ain't right, Boss. Those blasted loggers were as much to blame as we were. Shoot, they were more to blame, because it ain't natural for fellas to clamber around in trees like they do."

That didn't quite make sense to Luke, but he didn't ask Coburn to explain it. He doubted if the foreman could. Coburn's dislike of the loggers took precedence over any sort of logic.

Coburn went on, "But you're gonna let her get away with it because you're still sweet on—"

Harmon's voice lashed out like a whip. "You better think about what you're fixin' to say next, Rich. You're about to wander into the weeds where you don't want to be." The rancher blew out a disgusted breath. "You've been riding for me for a long time, but that doesn't give you license to go pokin' your nose into my private business."

Coburn didn't respond immediately. He looked a little like a kicked dog as he rode along in silence.

Finally, he said, "Sorry, Ben. I didn't mean to go gettin' above myself. You're right, of course. It ain't none o' my business."

"Well, don't sull up like a possum," Harmon snapped. "It's over and done with. For now."

"Yeah. For now."

Coburn's tone of voice made it clear that he fully expected trouble to break out again.

For that matter, so did Luke. They would be fools not to, he mused.

When they reached the ranch, Harmon said, "Luke, you've already been through plenty today. The rest of the fellas still have chores to do, but I want you to take it easy the rest of the day, and tomorrow, too, except for going into town for Clint's funeral."

"There's no need to take it easy on me, Mr. Harmon," Luke said. "I wasn't hurt during that ambush." He looked up at the sky. "There are still a couple of hours of daylight left. Clint and I never did find those cattle that strayed up the canyon."

Harmon looked surprised. "You're not thinkin' about going back up there to look for them again, are you?"

"I don't like leaving a job unfinished. I'll throw my saddle on a fresh horse and take another look around."

Coburn said, "Not by yourself you won't, blast it. That'd just be temptin' fate. Those scalawags who bushwhacked you earlier might've come back and be ready to try again." He nodded decisively. "I'm comin' with you, if you're bound and determined to go."

"I think the odds of those ambushers making another try in the same place are pretty slim," Luke said. "I won't mind having the company, though." He rubbed his chin in thought and went on, "Maybe the two men who spotted those cattle to start with could come along, too, and show us just where they were."

"That's a good idea," Harmon said, "if, like Rich said, you're determined to go ahead." He turned to look at the other men, who were all still mounted where they had come to a stop in the ranch hard. "Ham, Merrill, get yourself some fresh mounts. You're going up to that canyon with Rich and Jensen."

"Sure, Boss," Hamlin Daly said as he nudged his horse toward the corral where the ranch's remuda was kept. Merrill Lewis followed him.

"All of you keep a mighty close eye out for trouble," Harmon said to Luke, who nodded.

"With four of us, two men can watch the rimrock while the other two look for those cows," he said.

Within a quarter of an hour, they rode away from ranch headquarters mounted on fresh horses and headed for the higher range where the canyon was located.

Luke asked the two punchers, "How many head did you see up there the other day?"

"Well, it's hard to say," Daly replied. "Some of 'em could've been deeper in the brush where we couldn't see them."

"Or around a bend," Lewis added. "But I'd say, just the ones we saw, about a dozen."

"Maybe fifteen," Daly said.

"Not a whole bunch," Coburn said, "but enough to go after. The boss wouldn't want to lose even that many. And honestly, if you saw a dozen cows up there, there could be three or four times that many of the cantankerous critters hidin' out that you didn't see."

Lewis nodded. "That's what we thought, Rich, and that's why we made sure to report it."

"When was that?" Luke asked.

"Three days ago?" Lewis looked over at Daly. "Or was it four, Ham?"

"Four days ago, countin' today," Daly replied. He shook his head. "You know, this could be a wild-goose chase, boys. Those cattle could have wandered back out onto the range. We may not find a thing in that canyon."

"Except bad memories," Luke pointed out.

"Well, yeah, no doubt about that." Daly sighed. "Poor Clint."

"It's a puredee shame, what happened to him," Lewis added.

The conversation cast a gloomy pall over the four men. They rode on in silence for a while until the canyon mouth came into view. Despite his normally icy nerves, Luke cast glances at the rimrock on both sides as they entered the canyon. Nothing out of the ordinary met his gaze, though.

As they moved deeper into the canyon, the gloom thickened and it wasn't just because of their mood. The sun was lowering toward the peaks to the west. There really hadn't been time today to tackle this chore. If they located the missing cattle, they would be doing good to round them up and chouse them out of the canyon by nightfall, and it would be long after dark before they reached the ranch headquarters again.

But that didn't really matter, Luke reminded himself, because he knew good and well that they wouldn't find those cows.

He didn't say anything about that until they reached the spot where he and Clint Douglas had been ambushed that morning. He reined in, and the others, although visibly surprised, followed suit.

"What is it?" Rich Coburn asked. "Did you see something, Luke?"

"Yeah, I see something," Luke said as he moved his horse around so that he was facing toward Hamlin Daly and Merrill Lewis. With the slick speed that had saved his life on many occasions, he drew one of the Remingtons with his right hand and eared back the hammer as he leveled the revolver at the two shocked cowboys. "I see a couple of traitors, and I want to know why they sent that kid and me into a death trap."

Chapter 30

Daly and Lewis froze as they stared down the barrel of Luke's gun, but he could tell that both men had been reaching for their Colts before he drew down on them. He had a hunch that the speed and unexpectedness of his action was all that had saved him and Coburn from being blown out of their saddles.

Coburn's surprise exploded out of him in words. "What in the blue blazes are you doin', Luke?" he demanded. "Stop pointin' that iron at Ham and Merrill and put it away."

"I don't think so," Luke said. "Take a good look at them, Rich. They were behind us, and they were about to draw. Why do you think that is?"

"Well, shoot, I don't know."

"You've gone loco, Jensen," Daly said. "I wasn't reaching for my gun."

"Neither was I," Lewis said. "My hand, uh, just happened to be close to it."

"Yeah," Daly agreed. "Just a coincidence."

Luke said, "They're lying. They never saw any stray cattle up here. That was just a ruse to lure some of the hands into a trap. The trick wasn't aimed at me and Douglas, specifically. They just wanted to get a few Triangle 7 riders in the gunsights of their friends."

Lewis shook his head stubbornly. "Why would we do a thing like that?"

"You tell me," Luke said, "but I suspect it's because you two are part of the bunch that's trying to stir up trouble between Triangle 7 and Empire. You wanted Harmon's men to find some dead bodies and hobnailed boot tracks and assume the loggers were responsible for the killings. Like I said, you didn't care who the dead men were, as long as they rode for Ben Harmon. The idea was to send the whole crew stampeding over to the logging camp with guns blazing."

Coburn said, "Luke, that don't make a lick of sense."

"Doesn't it? One of Empire's men was almost killed by an act of sabotage carried out by someone wearing riding boots. They jumped to the conclusion that Triangle 7 was responsible. But George Stanton managed to keep them from going wild and starting a shooting war over it. So the gang that stole the payroll had to try again. That ambush this morning was the next move."

"The next move in *what*?"

"A campaign to destroy both outfits by pitting them against each other," Luke said. By answering Coburn's questions, he was talking out the rough theory that had formed in his own mind, and as he did, he was more convinced than ever that he was on the right track. "Why they're trying to do that, I don't know, unless they figure they can do enough damage that they'll be able to take over both operations cheaply. I've seen schemes like that tried before, many times."

Daly looked at Coburn and said, "Are you gonna let him get away with this, Rich? He's gone crazy and started makin' up a bunch of lies." He glared at Luke and went on, "You can't prove any of that bull, Jensen!"

"Actually, I believe I can," Luke said. "You didn't expect

anybody who rode up here looking for those cows to ever come back alive, so it didn't matter if there were no tracks to indicate that cattle were up here in this canyon recently."

Daly and Lewis both stiffened in their saddles, their reactions confirming for Luke that his thrust had gone home.

"I don't know if you've been keeping an eye on the ground, Rich," Luke continued, "but I have, and I haven't spotted any tracks other than the ones Clint and I left when we rode up here this morning."

Coburn frowned and said slowly, "Well, now that you mention it—"

"It's been a few days since we saw those cows," Lewis interrupted. "The weather's done away with the tracks."

"What weather?" Luke wanted to know. "It hasn't rained, and there hasn't even been much wind. If a dozen or more cattle have been wandering around up here, we would have seen their tracks."

Coburn's eyes widened as that soaked into him. He said, "Good gravy, you're right, Luke! The mouth of the canyon is narrow enough that they couldn't have come through there without us noticin'. I never thought to look, I just took the word of—"

He stopped short and twisted in the saddle to look at Daly and Lewis. His face darkened with fury, and his hand made an instinctive motion toward the butt of his gun.

That movement caught Luke's eye just enough to divert his attention for a split second.

And in that fraction of time, the other two men, figuring their string had played out, made desperate moves of their own.

They clawed revolvers from holsters and raked spurs against their horses' flanks. Lewis yanked his reins to the left, Daly to the right.

It was a move probably made instinctively, but a good tactic nonetheless. That split up the two men and made them harder targets.

Both of them were dangerously fast on the draw, too. Their guns flashed out of leather and the barrels rose with blinding speed.

But Luke was faster, and his Remington was already in his hand. The long-barreled revolver belched flame and lead in the instant it took Merrill Lewis to raise his own gun. The .44 slug punched into Lewis's chest and rocked him back in the saddle. That caused his arm to keep rising, so when his finger jerked the Colt's trigger and the gun blasted, the bullet sailed harmlessly into the sky above the canyon.

Because of the way the horses had leaped away from each other, shooting Lewis meant that Luke had to take his attention away from Daly for a heartbeat. Coburn had pulled his iron, too, and in that brief span, the guns of both men roared their deadly challenge.

Coburn cried out as the slug from Daly's jolted him around in the saddle. He made a grab for the saddle horn as his spooked horse reared up. Coburn's fingers slipped off the horn and he fell, crashing perilously close to the hooves of his mount as the horse continued dancing around skittishly.

Luke snapped a shot at Daly, but the man ducked low, and Luke was pretty sure his bullet went over his head. Daly fired at Luke but missed as well, the hurried shot going wide. Daly hauled his horse's head around and kicked the animal into a hard run up the canyon toward some distant trees.

Luke sent a bullet after him, but Daly's horse didn't break stride and he continued riding, bent low over his mount's neck. Luke debated for a second whether to holster the Remington and pull his Winchester from its sheath. Daly was already almost out of effective handgun range.

Then Luke glanced toward Coburn and saw that the Triangle 7 foreman was still sprawled unmoving on the ground. His horse hadn't stepped on him yet but might at any moment as it continued dancing around.

A quick look after Daly told Luke that the man was still fleeing as fast as he could. At least for the time being, Daly wasn't a threat.

Neither was Merrill Lewis. The man had tumbled off his horse and lay on his back, arms outstretched to the sides. His eyes were open and he was staring up at the fading light in the sky, but Luke could tell he wasn't seeing anything.

Those two glances took only a heartbeat. In the next second, Luke was off his horse. He holstered the Remington and grabbed the reins of Coburn's horse. He led the animal far enough away that it wasn't likely to step on Coburn and then ran back to the foreman and dropped to one knee beside him.

Coburn lay on his left side. Luke took hold of him and rolled him onto his back. The left side of Coburn's shirt was soaked with blood. Luke saw the hole where Daly's bullet had ripped through the shirt and lifted Coburn enough to spot a similar hole on the back.

So the slug had gone straight through, which was probably good. Judging by the location of the holes, Luke figured the bullet might have broken a rib but had missed the heart and hadn't glanced off enough to do a lot of other damage. It was a messy wound but likely not a fatal one.

At least not if Luke could stop the bleeding and then get Coburn back to ranch headquarters so he could be patched up better before being taken to Pine Knob for some actual medical care.

He was about to pull Coburn's bandanna off the foreman's neck and use it as a makeshift dressing for one of the bullet holes when something kicked up dirt a couple of yards to the right.

At the same time, Luke heard a rifle crack and the high-pitched whine of a bullet.

Daly had stopped and was shooting at them.

Luke jerked up his head and looked along the canyon. A spurt of muzzle flame told him that Daly had reined in at the edge of some trees, dismounted, and opened fire on them. The second shot plowed into the ground to their left. Daly had overcorrected a little on his aim.

But it wouldn't take him more than another shot or two to find the range. Searching for some cover, Luke spotted a small mound of dirt and rocks about twenty feet away. It wasn't much, but it was the only place he had a chance of reaching that might shield them from Daly's rifle fire.

Luke grabbed Coburn under the arms and grunted with effort as he hauled the unconscious man upright. Bending at the waist, Luke let Coburn fall forward over his left shoulder and then straightened. Another bullet sizzled past them as Luke turned toward the mound.

Luke broke into a lurching run with Coburn draped over his shoulder. His heart slugged heavily in his chest as he stumbled forward. A slug kicked up dirt at his feet. He had been lucky none of Daly's shots had found him so far, but he knew such luck couldn't last.

He was already stumbling, so he allowed his momentum to carry him and Coburn toward the rocks. Two more lunging steps and his balance deserted him. He threw himself forward and practically tossed Coburn through the air.

Coburn landed behind the mound, but Luke came up a few feet short. He crawled frantically, driving his elbows and knees against the ground. Another bullet struck the ground close enough to spray dirt in his eyes. He squeezed them shut and kept going.

When he judged he had crawled far enough, he stopped and blinked rapidly until his vision cleared. He was behind the mound, lying next to Coburn.

For a second, Luke thought the foreman was dead, but then he saw Coburn's chest rising and falling raggedly.

Luke's pulse was a crazy concerto inside his skull. Every beat of his heart felt like it was going to burst right out of his chest. He lay there on his belly, sucking down air, until the wild hammering inside his head and chest slowed and settled down to a steady rhythm.

A couple of shots thudded into the mound, throwing dirt and rocks into the air, but then Daly's rifle fell silent. He must have realized that he couldn't hit Luke and Coburn from where he was. He might be able to shift around enough to have an angle at them, but doing so would mean he had to come out in the open.

Which he could do without risking anything, Luke thought grimly, because he couldn't reach Daly with the Remington, and his Winchester was still in the saddle boot on his horse. The mount had wandered off, taking Coburn's horse with it, and now both animals were a hundred feet away.

Might as well have been a hundred miles for all the good they would do for the two men pinned down behind the shallow mound.

Coburn groaned suddenly and tried to sit up. Luke threw out an arm and pressed it across the foreman's chest.

"Stay down," Luke told him. "You're hurt, and Daly's just waiting for us to show ourselves."

Coburn sagged back down on the ground. "Wha . . . wha . . . happened?" His eyes were wide with pain and confusion, and he looked totally disoriented.

Luke maintained his grip on Coburn. "You've been shot, Rich," he said, putting urgency in his voice to get through to the wounded man. "Ham Daly shot you, and he's still trying to kill us."

"Daly . . . why . . . he's one of us."

"No, he's not. He and Lewis are traitors. They sold out the Triangle 7." Luke thought back to what Clint Douglas had told him about when Daly and Lewis had signed on with Ben Harmon's crew. Another nebulous idea began to form in his mind. "It's possible they've been working against the ranch right from the start."

"That's . . . loco. Where's . . . Lewis?"

"Dead," Luke said. "I drilled him when they pulled iron on us. Do you understand what I'm telling you, Rich?"

Coburn sighed and then made a face, evidently from a fresh twinge of pain. "I reckon . . . I do. I hate to think . . . I've been ridin' with fellas . . . who would do that."

"Some men will do almost anything if there's a big enough payday at the end."

"How bad . . . am I hurt?"

"You'll live," Luke said, hoping he was right about that. "The bullet went straight through, or almost, anyway. Might've nicked a rib. You've lost quite a bit of blood, but if those bullet holes don't get infected, you'll recover."

"As long as . . . I don't pick up any more . . . right?"

"Right," Luke agreed. "Which means we've got to figure out a way to get back to headquarters without Daly ventilating either of us."

"If we don't get back . . . Ben and the boys will come lookin' . . . for us."

That was true, Luke thought. Harmon and the rest of the crew would want to know what had happened if he and Coburn didn't return. But their curiosity probably wouldn't prompt them to form a search party until after dark—which wouldn't be that much longer, he realized as he looked up at the sky. A few golden rays remained, but the sun was almost down and the black curtain of night would fall quickly once it was.

That would allow Ham Daly to sneak up on them. He would have to make a move. He couldn't afford to wait around for Harmon and the other men to show up.

To be sure of that, Luke asked Coburn, "Rich, is there another way out of this canyon besides the way we came in?"

"Not that I know of. If there is, I ain't ever heard tell of it." He paused and then went on. "Luke, I'm startin' to hurt pretty bad, and I feel weak as a newborn kitten. Has the sun already gone down?"

"No, it's still up, barely."

"That's mighty strange . . . 'cause it's gettin' dark as midnight around me. . . ."

Luke cursed under his breath. "Blast it, don't you die on me, Rich," he said.

"I dunno . . . if I can help it—"

Coburn's head fell back. Luke thought he was gone, but after a moment, he heard the faint rasp of breath in the foreman's throat. Coburn was alive, but there was no telling how much longer he would be able to hold out.

When night fell, he would have to risk leaving Coburn behind the mound and trying to catch the horses. If he could manage to get Coburn in the saddle and mount up himself without too much racket, they might be able to make a run for the canyon mouth before Daly knew what was going on.

The last rays of sunlight disappeared from the sky, which quickly turned a darker blue. The shadows inside the canyon thickened. Luke began to wonder if visibility was getting poor enough that he could risk trying to catch the horses without waiting for full darkness.

But he wasn't the only one worried about waiting too long, because at that moment he heard hoofbeats charging toward them. He risked a look and spotted Daly galloping down the canyon in their direction. The treacherous cowboy guided his horse with his knees, raised the rifle to his shoulder, and started cranking off rounds aimed at the mound so fast that it sounded almost like a Gatling gun.

CHAPTER 31

Daly must have realized that as long as he stayed in the canyon, he was trapped just as much as Luke and Coburn were. So he was trying to bust out with this fierce burst of rifle fire, forcing Luke and Coburn to keep their heads down while he galloped past them.

It didn't work. Luke drew his second Remington and rose up behind the mound. Daly had made a big mistake—he was in handgun range again. Luke had been in dozens of showdowns like this. He clenched his teeth and kept a tight rein on his nerves as he leveled the big revolvers and returned Daly's fire.

The back of a racing horse was no place for accuracy. The bullets from Daly's Winchester tore through the air around Luke but didn't find him.

At the same time, the guns bucking and roaring in Luke's fists threw out a storm of lead that was much more accurate. As muzzle flashes ripped apart the shadows in the canyon, bullets smashed into Hamlin Daly and swept him backward out of the saddle. The rifle flew from his hands and sailed off into the air as Daly landed hard on his back.

The horse never slowed, pounding on past the mound where Luke and Coburn had taken cover and disappearing into the gathering gloom.

Luke leaped to his feet and ran to the spot where Daly had fallen, keeping both guns trained on the man as he approached. Daly had pulled one knee up and was jerking it back and forth. Luke knew that probably wasn't a conscious motion. It was just a spasm as nerves and muscles began to surrender to death.

Daly's Colt had slid out of its holster as he fell and now lay beside him. Luke kicked it away, well out of reach. He pointed the Remingtons down at Daly, but the man was too far gone to be any threat. The front of his shirt was sodden with blood. Luke figured at least three or four of his bullets had caught Daly in the chest.

Daly's eyes were open. His back arched a little as he gasped for air. His pain-dimmed vision finally focused on Luke standing over him, and curses rasped from his lips as they drew back in an agonized grimace.

"You . . . you killed me!" he managed to say.

"You didn't leave me much choice," Luke told him. "Anyway, you signed your own death warrant when you threw in with Asa Dunnigan."

It was a shot in the dark, no doubt about that. But the shocked surprise on Daly's face, overwhelming even the pain of his wounds, told Luke that he had guessed correctly.

"You and Lewis were part of Dunnigan's gang before you ever came to Oregon, weren't you?" Luke pressed on relentlessly. "Maybe he sent you here, maybe you just joined forces with him again when he showed up in these parts. I don't know, and it doesn't matter. But he's the one who's been working against Empire and Triangle 7, isn't he?"

"Asa . . . He'll kill . . ."

An even stronger spasm shook Daly. He jerked up off the ground as blood flooded darkly from his mouth. When he fell back, his eyes were still wide, but Luke knew he wasn't seeing anything anymore.

The threat Daly had voiced as he died was pretty plain, though. He was saying that Asa Dunnigan was going to kill Luke.

But not if Luke could figure out who Dunnigan was masquerading as first.

Luke left Daly's body where it was and hurried back over to Coburn. He knelt beside the foreman, holstered one gun, and rested a hand on Coburn's chest. When he was satisfied that Coburn was still breathing, he quickly filled the cylinders of both Remingtons. It was unlikely any other enemies were around, but Luke knew better than to risk getting caught without fully loaded guns.

He took Coburn's bandanna and his own, folded them into thick pads, and bound them tightly in place over the bullet holes with Coburn's belt. Then he went after the horses. It took a few minutes to catch both mounts because the animals were still rather spooked from the gunfire and the smell of blood, but Luke managed to do so.

With Coburn unconscious, Luke had to lift his dead weight into the saddle and tie him in place. By the time he finished that, his shirt was soaked with sweat and his heart slugged heavily in his chest.

The sun was down, night was falling rapidly, and a breeze kicked up, making a chill go through Luke as it hit his wet shirt. He found his hat, which had flown off when he was diving toward the mound. Then he swung up onto his horse and rode down the canyon leading the horse that carried Rich Coburn.

During the trip back to the Triangle 7 from Pine Knob, after delivering Clint Douglas's body to the undertaker, Luke had been able to put together the pieces of the puzzle enough to realize that Daly and Lewis had been lying about seeing stray cattle in the canyon.

Given what had happened, the only reason he could see for the lie was that the two men wanted some of the Triangle 7 hands to ride into a death trap. He had hoped to prove that by decoying them into the canyon and then confronting them with the lack of tracks, and the plan had worked. Getting confirmation that the campaign of sabotage against Empire and Triangle 7 was tied in with the reason he and Mac had come to this area in the first place—Asa Dunnigan—was an added bonus.

He hadn't planned on Coburn getting shot, of course, but that risk had always been there. Luke would do whatever he could to save the foreman's life.

And then he would figure out his next move. He was pretty sure that Dunnigan wasn't to be found on Ben Harmon's ranch . . .

Which made his hunch that the outlaw boss was secretly part of the Empire crew even stronger.

Mac had been knocked out several times in his life. Regaining consciousness was never a pleasant process—but it sure as blazes beat the alternative.

That was what he told himself as pain seeped back into his brain along with awareness. The inside of his skull felt like an angry giant with a club trying to pound his way out. After a while, Mac realized that was just the beat of his pulse he felt and heard. He forced himself to lie still and keep breathing as he willed the misery to go away.

Blackness still surrounded him, even after his eyelids fluttered open. He didn't know if he was blind or just stuck somewhere that no light penetrated. More time passed—he had no idea how much—before he became aware of a faint gray glow in front of him.

An area of darkness moved across that glow, blotting it out for a moment. Then it came back, and Mac realized he was looking through an open doorway. What he saw was the glimmering of starlight, and someone had just walked across it.

His brain was beginning to function again. He remembered chasing the ambusher in the woods, tackling him, and then getting knocked out by someone—probably the bushwhacker's accomplice—who bludgeoned him with a broken branch.

What had happened after that, though? And where was he now?

Judging by the darkness surrounding him, quite a bit of time had passed. Night had fallen.

Another question occurred to him. Was he a prisoner? It seemed possible, even likely, so he tried to move his hands and feet.

His feet and legs moved; they weren't tied. But someone had pulled his arms behind his back and lashed his wrists together. They hadn't been gentle about it, either. His shoulder sockets ached from the roughness with which his arms had been handled. His hands weren't completely numb, but the bonds around his wrists were tight enough that they made the fingers feel big and clumsy.

Definitely a prisoner, he told himself.

Now he could start trying to figure out *where* he was being held.

He was convinced the rectangular shape of the light he could make out was a door, and where there was a door, there had to be a building. He was lying on his left side, so he rolled onto his back and tried to sit up. That was difficult with his hands tied behind his back. The fresh explosions of pain that moving around detonated inside his head didn't help matters.

Finally, he made it into a sitting position with his legs stuck out in front of him. Using his heels and rear end to propel him, he scooted toward the deeper darkness to the left of the door. He moved slowly and carefully and made as little noise as possible. Whoever was outside, he didn't want to alert them that he was awake again.

After a few moments, his left shoulder bumped against something substantial. He leaned against it and could tell it was a wall made of logs. So, a cabin of some sort, he thought. At the logging camp?

That seemed impossible. All the buildings in the Empire camp were constructed with logs, but nobody could have tied him up and dragged him into one of them with the crew around. George Stanton had been in the main house, trading shots with the bushwhacker, and Mac was confident that when he hadn't come back, Stanton would have come looking for him. Also, the men working at the rollway would have heard the shots and come running to see what was happening.

No, whoever knocked him out had dragged him deeper into the woods, away from the camp. He might have even been draped over a saddle and carried a good distance away. Mac had a hunch he was being held at the hideout of the gang that had stolen the payroll and tried to stir up a war between Empire and Triangle 7.

The location of that hideout would be a good thing to know—but he'd have to escape from it to make that discovery.

He leaned against the wall and took deep breaths. The pain in his head subsided to a dull ache. He kept wiggling his fingers in an effort to maintain some feeling in them. Twisting his wrists, he tested the bonds and found them too strong and well-tied to work his way free from them any time soon.

A match rasped somewhere outside but still close by. Mac smelled the lucifer igniting. A moment later, a tendril of tobacco smoke curled into the dark chamber. A guard was posted right outside the door, and the man had just set fire to a quirley.

Mac figured he could stand up, but that wouldn't do him any good. If he stepped outside and tried to make a run for freedom, the guard would be aware of it and probably clout him with a rifle butt or just shoot him.

Even so, he thought he would feel better on his feet. Bracing his shoulder against the rough logs, he struggled upright. When he had both legs under him, he leaned back against the wall again and listened.

He could make out voices in the distance but not what they were saying. Then he smelled smoke again, but it wasn't burning tobacco this time. It was woodsmoke, and soon after, it was joined by the smell of roasting meat. That was a cooking fire he smelled.

That convinced him more than ever that he had been brought to the gang's hideout.

A little while later, footsteps approached Mac's makeshift prison. A man said, "I got a plate of grub and a cup of coffee for you, Dave."

"Much obliged." That was the guard posted right outside the door.

"Any trouble from the prisoner?"

The guard made a scoffing sound. "Not a peep out of him. I don't reckon he's awake yet. I don't understand why his throat ain't been cut yet."

Mac didn't understand that, either, but he wasn't going to look the gift horse in its proverbial mouth.

"I think the boss wants to talk to him before we get rid of him," said the man who had delivered supper to the guard. "Find out just how much he knows."

"If he's dead, it don't matter how much he knows, does it?"

That brought a chuckle from the other man. "Well, that'd sure simplify matters, wouldn't it?" Mac could almost see the man shrug. "But I don't give the orders around here, do I? Asa does, and everybody better do what he says if they know what's good for 'em."

Mac stiffened and caught his breath. *Asa.* That could only be Asa Dunnigan, the man he and Luke had ridden into these parts hoping to find.

It made sense. Dunnigan had a reputation as a cunning leader who could put together a band of owlhoots and pull off daring plans. Infiltrating both the Empire loggers and the cowboys from the Triangle 7 and then pitting the outfits against each other could result in a big haul if Dunnigan was able to move in and take over both operations.

Luke was convinced Dunnigan wasn't working on Ben Harmon's ranch. More than likely, that meant he was part of Empire's crew. There were several possibilities who he might be . . .

Dunnigan probably wanted to know if Mac had figured out his true identity. But either way, Mac had to end up dead. It was just a matter of time.

And maybe not much time, at that, because the guard went on, "I thought I saw the boss ride in a little while ago."

"Yeah, he's here. His partner rode out from town and brought some news." The second man sounded pleased that he knew something the guard didn't. "The stagecoach line is replacing that whole payroll for Empire. It's coming in tomorrow."

Mac's brain began to spin. Dunnigan had a partner in town? Mac hadn't considered that possibility, and Luke hadn't said anything about it.

"We already knew the payroll was going to be on the stage."

"No, the word was that part of it would be, that the stage line was going to pay off in installments. But that's not true. That was just a story to keep the real word from getting out. They're bringing in the whole thing in a wagon. The stagecoach is just a decoy."

Well, that wasn't a bad plan on the part of the stage line, Mac mused. He had had the same idea when Constance Elliott and Carl Peters had brought word to the Empire camp about the payroll delivery. It seemed that the thought had occurred to someone else, too, and he wondered if Constance or Peters had suggested it or if that had been the plan all along.

Didn't matter, he thought again. Dunnigan's gang knew about it now, so they would be able to stop the wagon and double their loot by stealing the payroll a second time.

He needed to get out of here and reach Luke with what he'd learned. They could head for Pine Knob, alert Constance to the danger, maybe bring in Marshal Sundell and set a trap for the outlaws.

Unless Sundell was in on it and *he* was Asa Dunnigan's mysterious partner. That was possible, Mac knew. Plenty of lawmen had gone bad when the temptation was enough.

That was pure speculation on his part, though, and it could all be hashed out later. He had to escape before Dunnigan got around to questioning—and then killing—him.

"I'd better get back," the second man said. "Enjoy your supper."

"Thanks again, Chuck."

Mac heard the man walking away. The guard slurped coffee, and then a spoon clattered against a tin plate.

That meant he had both hands full. If he had a rifle or a shotgun, he had set it aside.

Mac knew he might not get a better chance than this in the time he had left.

He edged toward the doorway until he could see outside. The noise the guard was making as he ate would be enough to cover up any slight sounds he made, Mac hoped.

The cabin was in a clearing with enough starlight shining down for Mac to be able to make out a few details. The guard stood to the right of the doorway, his head bent forward as he shoveled beans into his mouth. On the other side of him was a tree stump with a rifle leaning against it.

Mac had only one weapon—himself. He had to turn his body into a battering ram, knock the guard out of the way and off his feet if possible, and then dash into the woods to elude the pursuit that was bound to follow him. It was the longest of long shots, but his only alternative was to wait for Asa Dunnigan to kill him.

He couldn't afford to wait, either. Dunnigan was in the outlaw camp and might come over here any time. Also, the guard was wolfing down his food and would be finished with his supper soon, which meant he wouldn't be as distracted. Mac eased closer to the opening.

The guard set his spoon in the plate and held it in his left hand while he turned away and reached down with his right toward the coffee cup he had placed on the stump.

Mac sprang into action.

As he charged out the door, he turned slightly and rammed his right shoulder into the guard's back. The man was taken completely by surprise and let out an incoherent exclamation as the impact drove him off his feet. Cup, plate, and spoon went flying. As the guard fell, his head slammed against the stump and his body knocked the rifle down with a clatter.

Mac stumbled and fell, too, but he missed the stump and used his momentum to roll right back up onto his feet. He was about to dash toward the trees when he saw, about twenty feet away, that the guard wasn't moving. The man just lay there, silent and still.

Mac hesitated. The guard must have knocked himself out when his head struck the stump. This was Mac's chance to get away without any of his other captors being aware of it. He glanced toward the campfire burning a good fifty yards away. Several men were moving around it, but none of them seemed to be looking in this direction.

Mac leaned over the guard. He stiffened as he spotted a dark stain on the ground, spreading around the man's head.

The guard wasn't just knocked out. He had busted his head open on the stump's edge, Mac realized. He was either dead or probably soon would be.

Mac glanced toward the fire again. Nobody headed this way. He used a foot to roll the guard's limp body onto its back. The man's forehead was dark with blood.

The bone handle of a knife stuck up from a sheath attached to his belt on the left hip.

Keeping a close watch from the corner of his eye on the men around the fire, Mac twisted around and lowered himself onto his knees. He felt behind him with his bound hands. His fingers brushed against the knife's handle and then closed around it. He drew the blade from leather and turned it so he could work its keen edge against the rope around his wrists.

The next few minutes were mighty hard on Mac's nerves. He had to be careful not to slash his wrists and open a vein, and he had to watch the other outlaws in case any of them headed in this direction.

Neither of those things happened, and after a short span of time that seemed much longer, the rope parted and fell away. Mac fumbled with the knife, his fingers suddenly clumsy, but he let it go and concentrated on rubbing and shaking feeling back into his hands.

After a moment, he reached down and snagged the guard's revolver from its holster. It was a Colt, not the Smith & Wesson Mac was used to, but at the moment, he didn't care a bit. He'd have taken an old-fashioned blunderbuss if that was all he could get, as long as he was armed.

He shoved the gun in his waistband, punched half a dozen cartridges from the loops on the guard's shell belt, and put them in his pocket. He knew he needed to get out of there, but he cast one more look at the campfire.

Asa Dunnigan was right over there, he thought. The man he and Luke had come here to capture. Having their quarry this close was maddening.

But there were also at least a dozen other outlaws in the camp; Mac could see that many in the light from the flames. No telling how many more might be around. He would stand no chance against those odds. The smart thing to do was to light a shuck out of there as fast as he could, no matter how frustrating it might be.

Then another man stepped up into the reddish glare of the

fire, and Mac recognized him with a feeling like a punch in the gut.

Now he knew for sure that the most important thing was to find Luke so they could bring Asa Dunnigan to justice and destroy the schemes aimed at Empire and the Triangle 7.

Mac eased around the cabin, cat-footed toward the woods, and broke into a run as the thick shadows enfolded him and swallowed him up in darkness.

CHAPTER 32

It was well after dark by the time Luke reached the Triangle 7 headquarters, leading Rich Coburn's horse. Coburn was slumped forward in the saddle, held on the mount only by the ropes Luke had used to bind him in place.

But he was alive and had even roused a couple of times during the ride, coherent enough to ask Luke where they were and what was happening, even though he had lapsed back into a stupor again now. Luke knew that was a good sign. Coburn's robust constitution was trying to fight off the effects of being shot and losing quite a bit of blood.

"Hello, the house!" Luke shouted as he rode in. Lamplight glowed in a couple of the main house's windows and spilled through the open door of the bunkhouse, as well.

Several men emerged from there first and hurried across the ranch yard toward the two horses. The front door of the main house swung open and Ben Harmon stepped out onto the porch, followed by Alamo Paige.

"Who's there?" Harmon called. "Jensen, is that you?"

"It is," Luke replied, "and I need a hand. Rich is hurt."

The cowboys gathered around the horses. Luke swung down from the saddle and pulled loose the knots in the ropes holding Coburn on his horse. Strong, eager hands took hold of the foreman and lowered him from the animal's back.

"Bring him in the house," Harmon ordered. "How bad is he hurt?"

"Shot once clean through the body," Luke said.

Harmon nodded and said, with the emphatic confidence of a man who had patched up bullet wounds before, "Put him on the dining-room table, boys. Kaintuck, Shorty, you go clean it off and put a blanket on it. Alamo, get some clean rags and a basin of hot water."

The two wranglers and the cook hurried to carry out those tasks. When the table was ready, the men holding Coburn carefully stretched him out on it, positioning him on his right side along one edge so that Harmon could reach the wounds easily.

The rancher sent Shorty to his office to fetch a bottle of whiskey that was in the desk drawer.

"And don't take any swigs from it on the way back!" Harmon added. "It's for medicinal purposes only."

"Whiskey's good medicine for lotsa ailments," Shorty muttered as he left the room.

"I'd better go with the old pelican and see that he don't get lost on the way," Kaintuck said as he hurried after his fellow wrangler.

While they were gone, Harmon used a knife to finish cutting away Coburn's shirt. Alamo Paige brought the rags and basin of water from the kitchen, and Harmon began cleaning away the dried blood around the wounds. He wouldn't remove the makeshift dressings Luke had tied onto Coburn's body until the two old-timers returned with the bottle of whiskey.

"Where are Ham and Merrill?" one of the cowboys asked.

"Yeah, we haven't lost two more hands, have we?" another man added.

Harmon looked at Luke and said, "Yeah, I was wondering a mite about that myself."

"I'm sorry," Luke said. "They're both dead."

"I was afraid of that when you came back without 'em. Another ambush?"

Luke shook his head. "No. I had to kill both of them. And that was after Daly shot Rich."

That declaration brought wide-eyed stares and angry exclamations from the crew.

He forged ahead. "I had to shoot them to keep them from killing Rich and me. They were responsible for the trap that was waiting for me and Clint Douglas this morning. They never saw any stray cattle in that canyon. They were just trying to lure some of us in there so we could be ambushed and killed."

Harmon gave him a gaze of intense skepticism. "That's loco," the cattleman said. "Those two fellas have been ridin' for Triangle 7 for months and have been good hands."

"They've been biding their time, that's what they've been doing. Waiting for orders from their real boss."

"What boss?"

"The man in charge of the gang that stole the Empire payroll. They've been trying to start a shooting war between you and Miss Elliott's outfit, too." Luke gave voice to the theory that had begun to form in his head. "I think they work for a man named Asa Dunnigan."

A cowboy said, "Hey, I think I've heard of him. A wanted outlaw, ain't he?"

"Wanted in quite a few places," Luke replied with a nod. "But I think he's been lying low in these parts for a while, sizing up the situation and figuring out a plan so that he can make a good cleanup. Stirring up trouble between you fellows and Empire is all part of that plan."

Harmon still looked doubtful, but less so than he had a few moments earlier. Evidently, Luke's ideas had taken root in his mind, and he must have decided that he couldn't dismiss them outright.

"I want to hear more about this," he said as Shorty and Kaintuck came back with the whiskey. "But right now I need to finish tending to Rich. Jensen, you stay right here. Kaintuck, Shorty, Alamo, you, too. The rest of you boys go on back to the bunkhouse. I don't need your help with this."

The men didn't care for that order, but despite a few muttered complaints, they left the house and went back to their quarters.

Moving with sure, steady hands, Harmon uncovered the bullet holes, cleaned the blood away from them, and washed them out thoroughly with whiskey. The fiery bite of the liquor made Coburn stir and groan, although he didn't fully regain consciousness. Then Harmon covered the wounds with fresh bandages and tied them in place.

"We'll put him to bed in the spare room and take him to Doc Abrams in town first thing in the morning," Harmon said. "As late as it is and as much as he's been through, I reckon the best thing for Rich right now is to just let him rest for a spell. It looks to me like he ought to pull through."

"I think the same thing," Luke agreed. "He won't be on his feet for a while, but I believe he'll make a full recovery."

Harmon, Paige, and the two wranglers carried Coburn to the spare room and got him settled comfortably in the bed there. Luke would have helped, but Harmon waved him away.

"You did plenty keeping him alive and bringing him back here," the rancher said. "We'll take care of this."

When they were finished with that chore, Harmon and Paige returned to the dining room. Kaintuck and Shorty headed for the bunkhouse.

"Now, I want to hear more about this idea of yours," Harmon said to Luke.

"Want me to put on a pot of coffee, Boss?" Paige asked.

"I reckon that would be a mighty good idea." Harmon looked at Luke. "I think we've got a lot of talking to do."

Harmon folded the blanket stained with Coburn's blood and tossed it in a corner to be dealt with later. He and Luke sat at the dining-room table and sipped coffee as Luke explained his theory and everything that had happened in the canyon.

Harmon listened solemnly, nodding every now and then. He still looked skeptical when Luke started, but by the time Luke was finished, he appeared to be convinced.

"I reckon Rich can back up everything you've told me?" he asked.

"When he wakes up and has his wits about him, he can," Luke said. "He took part in the gunfight, too, so he knows what happened."

Harmon shook his head. "I sure hate to believe it of two fellas I thought were loyal hands, but if everything you told me is true, I don't reckon I have any choice. The whole thing hangs together." He frowned. "But who's this Dunnigan fella? You say you think he's around these parts pretending to be somebody else?"

"That's the logical answer. It's possible he sent some of his gang, including Daly and Lewis, into the area first to establish themselves, then he showed up later under a false name and began putting his plan into motion."

Harmon leaned forward in his chair and wrapped his hands around his cup.

"That's what's really got me buffaloed," he said. "I never heard tell of an outlaw who'd take so much time and care in planning his jobs. Most of the time, don't they act more on the spur-of-the-moment, as the sayin' goes?"

"They do," Luke agreed, "but that's what sets Dunnigan apart and has made him so hard for the law to catch up to. He's a smart man, no doubt about that. Probably could have been successful in an honest line of work if he'd chosen to live his life that way. But he'd rather be an outlaw."

"There must be something broken in the head of a fella like that."

"That's as good a way as any to describe it, I suppose."

Harmon scraped a thumbnail along his jawline. "What are you gonna do now?"

Luke finished his coffee and set the empty cup on the table. "I'm convinced that Dunnigan himself isn't here on your ranch, pretending to be one of your crew," he said.

"Well, I'm glad of that," Harmon said dryly.

"Some of the men come close enough to matching the description I have of Dunnigan, but none of them signed on at the right time to be him. That means it's likely he's working on the logging lease as one of Constance Elliott's men."

Harmon sat up straighter and frowned. "You're not sayin' you think Constance knows who he is, are you?"

He looked and sounded angry, which made Luke wonder why Harmon would take offense at the idea of suspicion being cast on the woman who had broken their engagement at the altar.

The most likely explanation was that Harmon still had feelings for her, no matter what had happened between them.

"I think that's very unlikely," Luke said. "She's had sabotage at her camp, too, so I believe he's probably fooled her the same way he's fooled everyone else around here."

Harmon jerked his head in a curt nod. "Well, good. Constance and I have had our disagreements, but I don't believe she'd ever be a party to anything dishonest."

"That's my impression, as well." Luke paused, then said, "As for my next move, I'm going to see to it that Rich makes it to town in the morning so that Dr. Abrams can take care of him, and then I'm going to take a ride out to Empire's camp and have a talk with my partner."

Harmon's eyebrows rose. "Your partner?"

"That's right. Mac McKenzie."

"McKenzie? The fella who took Empire's side in that saloon brawl and then signed on with 'em as the camp cook?"

"That's right. Mac and I work together as bounty hunters. We came to this part of the country looking for Dunnigan. It was just luck that we rode into Pine Knob at different times and then got mixed up in the same ruckus. But we realized right away it was a chance for us to take a long look around without arousing any suspicions."

Luke smiled and went on, "Mac was sort of a secret weapon, I suppose you could say. Dunnigan might hear that I was a bounty hunter and be careful around me not to give himself away, but he wouldn't have any idea that Mac was after him, too."

"Yeah, I reckon. We all thought McKenzie was dead set against us, like the rest of that bunch."

"I'm not sure I'd say that Miss Elliott is dead set against you," Luke said.

Harmon glared. "Never you mind about that. If you're right about this hombre Dunnigan, then whatever's between me and Constance doesn't have anything to do with the trouble that's been going on."

"That's the way it seems to me. Mac and I need to put our heads together and see if we can figure out who Dunnigan is and what his next move is going to be. I think it's time we flushed him out and made him reveal himself."

"And if you can do that, what then?"

"We take him into custody, of course—if he'll allow that. If he won't . . ."

"There's liable to be more gunplay."

"We'll be ready for it if there is," Luke said.

The two of them looked in on Coburn a short time later and found the foreman sleeping peacefully and naturally. As Harmon had said, the rest would do him good.

After that, Luke went to the bunkhouse, which was dark and

quiet now. He undressed and turned in, stretching out on his bunk and quickly falling into a deep sleep.

He was at an age when sleep didn't always come easily to him, and when it did, it wasn't always restful because of the various aches and pains of the years that had accumulated. However, this had been a long, violent, and bloody day, and he was happy to let exhaustion claim him.

Even though he was slumbering soundly, the instincts ingrained by long years of surviving a dangerous life allowed him to wake up quickly and completely when he needed to. He didn't know how long he had been asleep when he came awake suddenly.

The bunkhouse was still dark. Dawn had to be a ways off. Luke didn't know what had disturbed him, but it had to be something.

Luke's gunbelt hung on the chair beside the bed. Without him even being aware of it, he had reached out in the darkness and closed his hand around the butt of one of the Remingtons, drawing it smoothly from the holster. He sat up and raised the revolver in front of him.

"Luke."

The soft call came from the door, which was open again. Luke recognized the voice as Ben Harmon's and saw the silhouette of the rancher's burly form filling up the doorway. He swung his bare feet to the floor and, wearing only his long underwear and carrying the .44, went to the door to find out why Harmon had summoned him.

"Something wrong, Ben?" he asked. "Rich hasn't taken a turn for the worse, has he?"

"No, he's fine," Harmon said. "But you got company."

He stepped aside to reveal another man standing there, and Luke stiffened and drew in a sharp breath as he recognized the newcomer.

Even in the feeble starlight, he knew he was looking at Mac McKenzie.

CHAPTER 33

Five minutes later, Luke sat at the table in the house with Mac, Harmon, and Alamo Paige. He was fully dressed now.

Mac, with his clothes disheveled, beard stubble covering his cheeks and jaw, and weariness and strain making his face drawn and haggard, looked like he had been through a wringer.

But his eyes were still bright with anger and determination as he filled in the other three men on everything that had happened to him in the past twelve or so hours.

"Do you think that bushwhacker was aiming at you in particular," Luke asked, "or just shooting at the house to cause trouble and hit anybody he could?"

"Everybody in camp knows that window is in the kitchen and that I stand there to work," Mac replied. "I think he was waiting for me and tried to put a bullet through my head. There's only one reason I can think of that somebody would want to do that."

"They figured out you were working with me."

Mac nodded. "That's the way I see it." His face grew even more serious. "I thought our little conversation at the wagon in town this afternoon went unheard, but Pete Newton or

Grady Dunn must not have been in quite as bad a shape as they were acting like. Or maybe even both of them could be part of Dunnigan's bunch. They haven't worked for Empire long enough to be free from suspicion."

"If that's what happened," Luke said, "more than likely they would have come gunning for me pretty soon, too. But they didn't have to, because I played right into their hands by traipsing up to that canyon and insisted that Daly and Lewis come along. They wouldn't have wasted any time getting rid of me, either, if I hadn't sprung a trap right back on them."

Harmon shook his head and said, "It makes my head hurt just trying to keep up with all the thinking you boys must do. Here I figured bounty hunting was just trackin' down owlhoots and shooting them."

"Sometimes it's that simple," Luke said, "but Asa Dunnigan's not a typical owlhoot."

Mac nodded. "That's right. I haven't told you the whole thing yet. Constance Elliott is bringing in a whole new payroll tomorrow—later today, I should say—to replace the one the gang stole last week. We were told the stage line was going to make the loss good, but in installments, and the first one was supposed to come in on the stage. But that's just a diversion. The whole thing is coming in on a wagon. Dunnigan knows about it and has his sights set on grabbing the whole thing again."

"You heard them talking about that?" Luke asked sharply.

"That's right."

"How did Dunnigan even find out about it?"

"Because Carl Peters told him," Mac said.

Luke and Harmon both stared at him in surprise. After a moment, Harmon exclaimed, "Peters! You're saying he's working with Dunnigan?"

"I saw him at the hideout, and he sure wasn't a prisoner," Mac said. "He was walking around bold as brass, and I can't think of any other reason he'd be there."

Harmon shook his head. "I can't believe it. Peters has worked for Empire for years. He worked for Constance's father before the old man passed on. Peters is devoted to the company, and to her."

"Maybe he feels like he hasn't been shown the proper appreciation for being devoted to the company for that long," Luke said. "And it's possible he may be so devoted to Miss Elliott that he didn't like it when she almost got married to you instead of him."

"Peters? In love with Constance?" Harmon scrubbed a hand over his face and then sighed. "I reckon it could be true. He's always followin' her around and looking out for her. It might've put his nose out of joint when he thought I was gonna take over running things—"

"Is that what caused you to call off the wedding?" Mac broke in. Then he held up his hands, palms out. "Not that it's any of my business. But I know George Stanton and the rest of the Empire crew—the ones who aren't actually outlaws—hold a grudge against you because of what happened at the church that day, Mr. Harmon."

Harmon blew out a breath and said, "That's not exactly the way it was. I was never gonna replace Peters in the company. Shoot, I don't know anything about logging, and I don't want to know! I'm a cattleman. But I figured that when Constance and I got hitched, she'd step back and let Peters run things whole hog, maybe consultin' with me now and then if he needed to. I told Constance how happy I was that she wouldn't have to have anything to do with the business anymore and could concentrate on just being my wife. I didn't, uh, I hadn't completely ruled out the idea of maybe having a young'un or two. . . ."

"You told her this just before the ceremony?" Luke asked.

"Well, yeah. Was that a bad idea?"

"I don't know Miss Elliott all that well," Mac said, "but I'm surprised all she did was call off the wedding."

With a rueful expression on his weathered face, Harmon said,

"Yeah, if she could've got her hands on a shotgun, she might've dusted my britches with buckshot, the way she looked."

"So Peters thought he was going to take over and run things," Luke mused. "Maybe he planned to start skimming some of the profits to pay him back for his years of hard work."

"Not to mention the injury he suffered while working for Miss Elliott's father that kept him from being a logger anymore," Mac put in.

Luke nodded. "It's possible he's already been helping himself to some of the money. But when the wedding was called off and he knew things were going to continue as they were before, he could have decided to square things some other way. Dunnigan could have seen that and approached him with an offer. From what I know of him, Dunnigan is good at finding a weakness and exploiting it."

"I reckon that all makes sense," Harmon said, "but it leaves the same question: What are you fellas gonna do now?"

Luke glanced at a window and saw the gray light of dawn spreading outside.

"We need to get to town and find Miss Elliott so we can tell her what's going on," he said, "and then we'll see if we can meet that payroll wagon before Dunnigan's gang hijacks it. If we can get our hands on some of those outlaws, maybe we can force them to tell us who Dunnigan is pretending to be."

"Sounds to me like a roundup," Harmon said. "Reckon you could use some help?"

"We'd be glad to get it," Luke told him.

Alamo Paige, the cook and former Pony Express rider, stepped into the dining room from the hallway, where he'd obviously been eavesdropping on the discussion.

"I'm comin' along," he declared. "It's danged well about time we had some real excitement around here!"

The sun was peeking over the horizon by the time Luke, Mac, Ben Harmon, Alamo Paige, and half a dozen other hands from the Triangle 7 rode into Pine Knob. But the hour was still early, and it appeared that the town was just starting to come awake.

A few business owners stood on the boardwalk, sweeping the areas in front of their stores. Several horses were hitched here and there along the street, but no riders were moving. No tinny strains of piano music floated over the batwings at the entrance to the Lonesome Pine Saloon.

After leaving Rich Coburn at Doc Abrams's house, the group rode directly to the office of the Empire Logging Company. Harmon had told Luke and Mac that Constance was an early riser and often was in the office by this time.

When the rancher dismounted and tried the door, though, he found it locked.

"What about her house?" Luke asked. "Maybe she's still there?"

"Could be," Harmon agreed. "Won't take long to find out."

There was no answer when he knocked on the front door of Constance's house, a whitewashed frame two-story structure on a side street. Harmon opened the door and called to her, but he got no response.

"I don't understand," he said as he came back to the horses. "With that payroll coming in, she really ought to be around today."

"What about the café?" Mac suggested. "She might have stopped for some coffee or something to eat, rather than having breakfast at home."

"Wouldn't be like her," Harmon said, shaking his head, "but I reckon we can't rule it out."

He, Luke, and Mac headed for the Blue Top Café. Harmon told Paige and the other men to return to the logging company office and wait there.

The café was open for business and had several customers. Violet Channing smiled a greeting directed mostly at Mac when he and Luke and Harmon came in. She seemed a little surprised to see Mac with the cattleman. He supposed most folks in Pine Knob, including Violet, knew he was working for Empire.

"Good morning, Mr. McKenzie," she said. "It's good to see you again."

She looked pretty and fresh as the proverbial daisy this morning, Mac thought, and he was sincere when he said, "I'm sorry I haven't been back in, Miss Channing. I've been meaning to stop by and have another fine meal."

"I'm sure you've been busy."

"You could say that," Mac replied dryly.

They had already looked around the room when they came in, and it was obvious that neither Constance Elliott nor Carl Peters was here. Mac went on, "Has Miss Elliott been in this morning?"

"Constance? No, she hasn't been here." Violet paused for a second and then went on, "But I did see her go by earlier, while I was sweeping the porch just before we opened up. She drove past in her buggy with Mr. Peters."

"Peters," Harmon said sharply. "Was Constance all right?"

Violet looked confused by the question. She frowned slightly and said, "She seemed fine. She waved at me as they drove by."

"She wasn't being forced to do anything?"

"Goodness, not that I could tell." Violet's forehead creased even more. "Is something wrong?"

Before any of the men could answer, the tinkling of the bell over the door prompted them to turn their heads and look in that direction. They all saw Marshal Abner Sundell come into the café. The lawman stopped short just inside the door and peered curiously at the three grim-faced men standing at the counter talking to Violet.

Sundell paused only for a couple of heartbeats and then came on in with a new determination in his step. "Ben," he said, with a nod to Harmon. "I get the feeling something's going on here, and I want to know what it is."

"You know anything about where Constance has gone with Carl Peters?" Harmon asked.

"I'm not at liberty to talk about that—"

"We know about the payroll, Marshal," Luke interrupted him. "We know the whole thing is coming in today on a hired wagon, not the stagecoach."

Sundell made a face. "Blast it, Jensen, keep your voice down. Constance told me about that but asked me to keep it under my hat. She was worried those outlaws might make another try for it if they knew what she was planning."

"She was worried about the wrong person," Mac said. "She already had a traitor a lot closer to her."

"What are you talking about?"

"Carl Peters has been working with the outlaws," Luke told Sundell.

The marshal looked as taken aback by that revelation as Harmon had been at first. He sounded just as disbelieving, too, as he asked, "Are you sure about that?"

"I saw him with my own eyes talking to the outlaws when I was a prisoner at their hideout," Mac said. "There was plenty of light from the campfire. I didn't have any trouble recognizing him."

"But that's loco!" Sundell objected. "I've never been particularly friendly with Peters, but I've known him for a long time."

"What kind of man is he?" Luke asked. "The sort to nurse a grudge?"

"Well . . ."

Sundell's hesitation was all the answer they needed.

Harmon asked, "Do you know where they were goin' when they left town in Constance's buggy this morning?"

Sundell drew in a deep breath. The information he had just

received was forcing him to rethink a number of things; that much was obvious on his face.

When he nodded abruptly, it was equally obvious that he had come to the same conclusion the other men had reached.

"Constance said they were going to meet that payroll and accompany the wagon on into town. She wanted to be sure the money got here all right."

Harmon grated a curse and then said, "That means they're liable to run smack-dab into the middle of that holdup. Peters will be all right because he's working with those owlhoots, but there's no telling what'll happen to Constance."

"I'll put together a posse and go after them," Sundell said.

"No need, Abner. Seven of my men rode into town with us this mornin'. That makes ten for your posse, counting us three, and they're already mounted and ready to go!"

"Let me grab my horse and a rifle," Sundell said grimly.

Luke asked, "Do you know the route the wagon will be following?"

"It's coming through the pass just like the stagecoach does. The coach won't be along until this afternoon, though. That wagon was supposed to come through before midday. Constance figured the gang would be watching for the stage and wouldn't pay any attention to a plain wagon."

"How many guards are with it?" Mac asked.

"Four. Two with the wagon and two men on horseback trailing a ways behind, but close enough to get there in a hurry in case of trouble. Constance didn't want to make a big show and draw attention to any of it."

Actually, that wasn't a bad plan, and Luke and Mac both knew it. It might have even worked if Constance hadn't unknowingly had a viper at her bosom in the person of Carl Peters.

Ten minutes later, the group rode out of town, following the trail that led to the pass and ultimately over the mountains to The Dalles. The buggy carrying Constance and Peters had a big lead on them, but she had been handling the reins and hadn't seemed like she was in any hurry when they left Pine Knob, according to Violet Channing. It was possible the posse might catch up by midmorning or a little later.

But they didn't know for sure when the wagon would roll through the pass or where Asa Dunnigan's gang would hold it up. The robbery—and whatever went with it—might be over by the time Luke, Mac, and the others could arrive at the scene.

They pushed their horses as hard as they dared and hoped they wouldn't get there too late.

CHAPTER 34

The pass was in sight ahead of them but still several miles away when they heard gunfire from that direction. Harmon cursed again, and the words had a frantic sound to them.

"Let's go!" he called as he leaned forward in the saddle, jabbed his boot heels into his horse's flanks, and sent the animal leaping ahead at a gallop.

Luke and Mac followed and quickly pulled alongside the cattleman. Marshal Sundell and the Triangle 7 cowboys followed just behind. They had made good time on the trip out here, stopping only occasionally to let the horses rest when they absolutely had to, but from the sound of it, they might be too late anyway.

But it was too soon to be giving up, so they pounded ahead, following the trail as it wound through the foothills between thick stands of trees on both sides.

They rounded a bend and caught sight of the wagon up ahead, stopped at an angle across the trail. One of the horses in the team was down, probably shot to make the vehicle stop.

The buggy was nearby, lying on its side where it had overturned.

Both horses hitched to it were dead. The buggy was pointed in the same direction as the wagon, toward Pine Knob.

Luke knew what had happened as soon as he saw that. Constance and Peters had met the wagon carrying the payroll and turned around to accompany it to the settlement. Then the outlaws had struck, either calling on Constance and the wagon driver to stop or possibly just opening fire on them.

Neither had stopped, though. They had fled along the trail, only to pass right between the guns of owlhoots who were hidden in the trees on both sides.

Those same outlaws were now raking the wagon with lead. Shots came from underneath the vehicle where the guards had taken cover. Luke didn't see Constance. He hoped she was under there, too, keeping her head down.

But the wagon didn't provide enough cover to protect the defenders for very long. Luke glanced over at Mac and called, "You go left, I'll go right!"

Mac jerked his head in a nod of understanding. He hauled out the Colt he had taken from the dead guard at the hideout. Luke drew both Remingtons. They split up, and so did the posse, a group following each of them as they charged toward the trees where the outlaws were hidden and opened fire.

The members of the gang had good cover, but the sudden attack took them by surprise. Luke, Mac, and the others had an angle on them, too, and as they swept in, their bullets whipped through the brush and downed several men who were hidden behind the pines.

The outlaws, swinging around to meet this new threat, inadvertently exposed themselves to the guards holed up underneath the wagon. The guards redoubled their efforts with their Winchesters and rifle slugs ripped through two or three more ambushers.

Luke leaped from his horse with the agility of a much younger man and landed with the Remingtons spouting fire and lead from both hands. One of the outlaws rocked back as bullets punched into his chest.

As that man collapsed, Luke swung the revolvers and drilled another owlhoot, who was drawing a bead on him. That man spun around and pitched lifelessly to the ground.

On the other side of the trail, Mac had just about emptied the Colt. He had one round left, he figured, and he sent it smashing through the head of an outlaw who burst out of the brush and came at him with guns blazing. The man stumbled, dropped his guns, and fell on his face.

Mac took advantage of the opportunity to scramble behind one of the wheels and underneath the wagon. Three men glanced at him but kept shooting toward the trees. He didn't recognize any of them but knew they had to be some of the guards Constance had hired.

The fact that the fourth guard wasn't here probably meant that the outlaws had gotten him.

Constance wasn't here, either, and that fact sent alarm jolting through Mac.

A moment later, the shooting began to die away. Mac peered through the wagon spokes and saw a few men emerging from the woods, their hands empty and held high over their heads. The surviving outlaws had had enough and were surrendering.

Luke poked his head under the wagon and called, "Mac, are you there?"

Mac crawled hurriedly from under the vehicle and stood up. He reached for the extra cartridges in his pocket and began poking them into the Colt's cylinder as he asked, "Are you all right, Luke?"

"Yeah, how about you?"

"They threw a lot of lead my way, but none of it found the target." Mac snapped the revolver's loading gate closed. "Have you seen Constance?"

"I was just about to ask you the same thing," Luke replied with a grim look on his rugged face.

The guards were crawling out from under the wagon now, too. One of them heard the exchange between Luke and Mac and said, "That older fella who was with her took her."

Ben Harmon rode up in time to hear that. "You mean Carl Peters?"

"I don't know his name," the guard said. "All I know is that he was in the buggy with her, but when it wrecked, he grabbed her and dragged her into the woods."

"Did it look like she was hurt?"

The guard shook his head in response to Harmon's urgent question. "I couldn't tell you, mister. It didn't look like it, what little I saw, but we already kind of had our hands full trying not to get killed."

Marshal Sundell told several of the Triangle 7 men to keep the prisoners covered. The rest of the group spread out and searched the woods where the guard had last seen Constance.

There was no sign of her, or of Carl Peters.

"He must have carried her off with him, the no-good skunk!" Harmon said. "When we rode up and he saw that the robbery had gone bad, he must've dragged her onto one of the gang's horses and rode off."

That explanation made sense to Luke and Mac, both of whom nodded.

"But where did he take her?" Mac asked.

"Only one place I can think of," Luke said. "Back to Empire's camp so he could confront Dunnigan and demand his share of the loot they've gotten so far."

Harmon said, "Why would he do that? He doesn't know we're on to him."

"He must have said or done something that gave him away to Constance," Mac said as he thought furiously. "Otherwise he would have waited here and pretended to be an innocent victim, never knowing that we were about to expose him."

Luke nodded. "That has to be it."

"Well, then, what are we waitin' for?" Harmon demanded.

"Let's get to that logging camp before he has a chance to get away!"

Marshal Sundell quickly deputized one of the Triangle 7 hands to take charge of getting the prisoners, the wagon, and the guards and payroll on to Pine Knob safely. One of the outlaws' mounts could be hitched to the wagon to replace the horse that had been slain.

Meanwhile, Luke, Mac, Sundell, Ben Harmon, and Alamo Paige headed for the logging camp. They knew Peters and Constance couldn't be far ahead of them.

Harmon and Sundell were familiar with shortcuts that would get them to the camp quickly, but it was likely that Peters knew the same shortcuts and would use them.

By the time they approached the Empire camp, they hadn't seen any sign of the two people they were looking for. As they rode in, the place looked quiet. Deserted, almost.

"Maybe we beat Peters and Constance here after all," Mac said as they reined up in front of the big main building.

The sudden blast of a gunshot from inside the house shattered that hope.

Sundell grunted and rocked back in his saddle. He clutched at his left arm with his right hand. Glass shattered, and more shots roared as men opened fire from two windows.

Luke, Mac, Harmon, and Paige returned those shots with blistering speed and devastating accuracy. A man crashed through one of the windows to land in a bloody heap on the porch. Mac recognized Pete Newton in the split second he had before a bullet whining past his ear forced him to dive off his horse.

A man with a shotgun charged out the door and blasted one barrel toward the newcomers, but Luke and Harmon had hauled their horses away from each other and the buckshot passed between them.

Before Grady Dunn could adjust his aim and fire the shotgun's second barrel, Alamo Paige drilled him cleanly through the chest.

As Dunn staggered back toward the wall, Harmon shot him in the head.

"Hold your fire! Hold your fire!"

The strident yell came from inside the house. Carl Peters rushed out onto the porch with his hands up and a frantic look on his face.

"Don't shoot!" he cried as he ran toward the steps. "I'll confess! I'll tell you the whole—"

A shot crashed behind him, and his eyes bugged out as a bullet slammed into his back and knocked him forward. He fell down the steps and wound up with his torso on the ground in front of them while his legs were still angled up. A dark stain appeared on the back of his coat, directly between his shoulder blades.

Alec Lafferty appeared in the doorway, his left arm looped tightly around Constance's waist while his right hand held a gun muzzle pressed against the side of her head.

"Constance!" Harmon shouted.

"I—I'm all right, Ben," she managed to say, although she looked anything but all right.

"Let her go, Lafferty," Mac said as he leveled the Colt at the two people on the porch. "Or maybe I ought to call you Dunnigan."

"I had a hunch you might have figured it out when that business with the payroll went wrong," Dunnigan said. "Peters told me about it when he came rushing in here with Miss Elliott. The fool tried to demand his share from me. Said he'd see to it that I hang if I didn't give him what he wanted." The outlaw chuckled. "He got what he had coming to him, all right."

Constance said, "Someone's got to help George. This man shot him. I . . . I think he's badly hurt."

"No, he's dead," Dunnigan said, "and that's what the woman will be in less than a minute if you men don't all throw down your guns and get out of here. Miss Elliott and I are leaving, and you're going to give us an hour's start before anybody comes after us."

"You're loco, mister," Harmon said. "You're not goin' anywhere."

"Better give it up, Dunnigan," Mac said. "You can see for

yourself how outnumbered you are. And if you hurt Miss Elliott, you'll be dead a second later."

"Maybe—but so will she." Dunnigan frowned at him. "Just who in blazes *are* you, McKenzie? Why have you caused me so much trouble?"

"He's my partner, Dunnigan," Luke rasped. "And you're the man we came to these parts to find."

Dunnigan looked at Mac. "You're a stinking bounty hunter, too?"

Mac sighed. "Yeah, but I'm not going to collect on you."

He had just caught sight of movement in the doorway behind Dunnigan and Constance. Dunnigan was unaware of it, though, since all his attention was focused on the half circle of gun-toting men in front of him.

"Nobody's going to collect blood money on Asa Dunnigan," he said with a sneer.

"That's right," George Stanton said from behind him. The left side of the superintendent's face was covered with blood, but he stood tall, holding an axe.

Dunnigan hissed in surprise and tried to turn. That loosened his grip on Constance. She writhed suddenly and tore free from his grip, throwing herself to the side.

Dunnigan twisted around toward Stanton, but he couldn't bring his gun into line before the head of the axe Stanton swung with both hands slammed into his forehead and cleaved deep into his brain. The gun went off as Dunnigan reflexively jerked the trigger. Stanton staggered but didn't go down. He stayed on his feet as he wrenched the bloody axe blade from Dunnigan's shattered skull. Dunnigan's knees buckled and dropped him into a gruesome heap on the porch.

Constance scrambled to her feet and threw her arms around Stanton. "George! George!" she cried.

Stanton let the axe dangle from his right hand as he put his left arm around Constance's shoulders and held her against him.

Luke heard Ben Harmon say softly, "Well, shoot."

But the rancher was smiling faintly, and he didn't seem too upset about what he was seeing.

Maybe he had realized that some matches were just better than others.

Dunnigan had grazed Stanton's right side with that second shot, to go with the wound he had suffered earlier, a furrow on the side of his head above his left ear, which had bled a lot and made him look like he was dead or dying. He would be laid up for a while, but Constance assured him that she would take care of him—and that Empire could get along without him for the time being.

Marshal Abner Sundell was wounded, too. The bullet that had gone through his left upper arm had broken a bone, but Doc Abrams thought it would heal cleanly.

"All right, no one else is allowed to get shot or break any bones," the doctor declared after his finished setting Sundell's arm. "I don't have room for any more patients!"

Grudgingly, Luke agreed to serve as unofficial deputy and keep the peace in Pine Knob until Sundell could handle the job again. He could afford to do so, because George Stanton insisted that he and Mac take the reward for Dunnigan and the other outlaws who had been captured or killed.

"I don't want it," Stanton maintained from his bed in one of Doc Abrams' rooms, with Constance sitting beside him holding his hand. "I was just taking care of a varmint when I went after Lafferty—I mean, Dunnigan. I don't want any pay for that." He smiled. "Besides, it's nice to know I can still swing an axe after working mostly at a desk the past few years."

Mac had a feeling Stanton would continue riding that desk and would have even more responsibility, now that the treacherous Carl Peters was dead. And there would be another wedding, too, Mac suspected, only this one would take place as planned.

By evening, everything was sorted out. Mac and Luke found themselves on the boardwalk just outside the marshal's office, where Luke would be holding down the fort for the next few weeks.

"What are you going to do in the meantime?" Luke asked his partner.

"Well, Walt Nichols still isn't recuperated enough to take over the cooking job out at the Empire camp," Mac said. "I figured I'd stay on there for a while."

Luke leaned a hip on the railing along the edge of the boardwalk. "You miss cooking, don't you?"

"Yeah, I reckon I do. It's something I'm good at."

"So's bounty hunting."

"Maybe. And I'm not ready to give it up just yet, either. But one of these days . . ."

"One of these days comes for all of us," Luke said as twilight deepened around them. "Sometimes sooner than we expected, and sometimes we hang on longer than we ever figured we would. But if a man lives long enough, a day comes when he knows he can't keep doing what he's been doing."

"That's kind of sad, isn't it?"

Luke shrugged. "Sad's just part of it. Might be something better waiting, too. A man never knows."

"Well, I know what I'm going to do right now," Mac said. "I'm going to walk down to the Blue Top and have some supper."

"And visit with that sweet little blonde who runs the place?"

"Maybe," Mac replied with a laugh.

"You know, her grandpa's not going to be there forever. She might need to hire a new cook one of these days."

"I suppose that could happen," Mac said, "but I'll be long gone before then."

"We'll see," Luke said. "We'll see."

He leaned on the railing, looked around the town—his town, for the time being—and watched his friend and partner walk off into the dusk, whistling a little tune.

TURN THE PAGE FOR AN EXCITING PREVIEW!

JOHNSTONE COUNTRY.
WHERE THERE'S ALWAYS ROOM
FOR ONE LAST HEIST.

In this explosive new story from the bestselling Johnstones, a once-notorious gang of retired bank robbers reunite for one last ride—and one last shot at glory. . . .

Clay Carson thought his outlaw days were behind him. Years ago, he rode with the fearsome Dirty Creek Gang—and robbed half the banks in Texas. But then a fatally bungled heist in Fort Worth brought it all crashing down. The gang broke up, went their separate ways, and that was the end of that.

But today the past came calling for Carson in the form of a telegram. It's from Lemuel Jones—his old gang leader—who asks him to do something reckless, stupid, and downright crazy: round up the old gang for one last ride.

Jones says he hid away the gang's biggest payday from their boldest bank job, and he just needs Carson and the gang to help him get it. Carson assumed his old boss gambled it away—and has doubts about his old gang members, too. All but one of them has gone straight, with respectable jobs like store clerk, ranch hand, and even bank teller. The only outlaw left has been captured and sentenced to hang. Which means the crew would have to bust him out of jail and ride off with a posse on their tail.

It's crazy, all right. But the Dirty Creek Gang is just crazy enough to give it a shot—even if it's their last. . . .

CHAPTER 1

Clay Carson thought he'd gotten over being jumpy.

As the buckboard rattled along the dusty Texas road, he kept glancing over his shoulder. Worse, he slid his foot over to rest against the stock of his rifle. A deft kick could lift it for a quick grab. He knew from experience he could lever in a round, aim, and fire in the blink of an eye. Too many varmints had doubted that and now lay dead, scattered across Texas and Indian Territory.

A few of the varmints had been men who were inclined to put an ounce or two of lead into his hide. So far, he had always beaten them to the draw. But those were the old days. At least a year in the past. Carson had no reason now to suspect every stranger he saw or worry about a lone rider on the road behind him. He had no reason—but old habits died hard, especially when they had kept him alive.

He wished he had his trusty six-gun slung at his hip, but the rifle would do, provided he kept trouble at a distance.

What's got into me today?

The mule pulling the buckboard ignored him. It kept its flop-eared head down, straining to pull its load. While out plowing and tending the fields, the mule, named Solomon for his stubborn wisdom, had been his only company on the lonely farm for most of the past year. Carson had come to trust the animal more than he did most men. Solomon didn't ask questions, didn't pry into the past, and never judged.

Maybe it's been too quiet. Maybe I can't help but think it's time for the other boot to drop.

Even his own reassuring words did nothing to prevent him from looking behind him again.

Nothing.

He rode along the empty road, the vast, flat prairie land stretching as far as the eye could see—miles of open space without a living soul in sight. The mesquite and live oaks stood like lonely sentinels scattered here and there, while wind devils spun dust into the air and vanished just as quick. Overhead, the sun hung low and hot, turning sweat stains into permanent tattoos on his shirt.

He snapped the reins, urging Solomon to move along a little faster. The sooner he got to town, loaded supplies for the farm, and returned to his cozy niche that had been his home for nigh on a year, the easier he'd breathe.

The town appeared first as a shimmery mirage, then hardened into real buildings with a few people moving around between them. Several old men, propped up in chairs under shady awnings, waved to him as he drove past. He returned their greeting.

He might be the only thing out of the ordinary for them all day.

Ferguson wasn't the crossroads of anywhere.

Since the railroad had bypassed the town a couple years back, it had hung on by the skin of its teeth. Many businesses had pulled up stakes, moving closer to the steel rails to chase prosperity, while others simply shuttered their doors for good.

That was one reason he'd decided to stay here.

The nearsighted, overweight town marshal hadn't so much as looked at a wanted poster in years. Carson had once heard him bragging about using them to start fires in his potbellied stove, to keep warm in the winter and to brew his vile coffee year-round. With a sleepy marshal like that, and a town that saw few travelers, Ferguson was the perfect place for a man hankering to stay lost.

Clay Carson smiled crookedly at the thought. The law from half a dozen other towns had probably given up hunting for him. Other crimes must occupy their interest by now.

He still looked around, taking special care to check his back trail. Old habits died hard.

He climbed down and stretched his cramped limbs. He was lean and still mean—he hoped—but Father Time was beginning to take his due. Working on the cotton farm was still easy enough for him, though some nights required a liberal application of horse liniment to ease his aching muscles. Other mornings not even the potent liniment worked out the kinks in his back for him to face another day toiling in the field.

A quick look in the window of Ferguson's only general store showed the reflection of a man edging into his middle years. He tugged his straw hat down to hide the retreating hairline of what had once been a full head of brown hair. He was beginning to look too much like all the old-timers in town, which bothered him.

"You need to grow back that big, bushy beard, Mr. Carson. I thought it looked real fine when you first came to Ferguson."

The woman speaking stood in the doorway, leaning on a broom. The pile of dust around her feet showed that she would never win against the persistent grit but was too stubborn to admit defeat. Even a touch of breeze caused swirls to form faster than anyone, even dedicated to the pursuit, could sweep it all back into the street, where it belonged.

"Miz Cline." He touched the brim of his straw hat. "You're looking mighty fine today."

"You're such a liar," she said, gracing him with a bright grin. "But don't you stop now, you hear?"

She pushed a stray wisp of graying hair back toward the bun perched on her head.

"You're not buttering me up to give you more credit, now are you?"

"That's between Mr. Cline and my boss."

"You're more pleasant to talk to than Frank Bellamy," she said. "And to look at. If you're doing the asking, I'll be doing the agreeing."

She flirted with him because they both knew it passed the time and wouldn't amount to anything. Dottie Cline was firmly married to Ezra. Even if she hadn't been so devoted to the crusty owner of the store, Carson wasn't inclined to make a play for her. As affable as she was, she reminded him too much of his third-grade teacher in Arkansas, who had made life miserable, if not downright intolerable, because of her hectoring.

That had been the same year when his ma died of tetanus. He'd never been happier to move on with his itinerant snake-oil-selling pa and his endless parade of ladies. The education he got was more about people than book learning, but along the way he had developed a taste for dime novels. The more lurid, the better. He took special interest in yarns about the outlaws. Wild imaginations fueled those stories, which he knew firsthand. Someday, he'd try his hand at writing one with real characters and situations.

Most likely, editors would reject those stories because they would seem too wild, if not downright loco.

"Mr. Bellamy needs fifty pounds of flour, what sugar you can spare, and his missus wants a dozen spools of thread she saw in your window last time she was in town."

"You get Ezra to help you load the flour. I've got a five-pound bag of sugar set aside, but the thread?" Dottie Cline pursed her lips. "Don't rightly know if I have that many spools anymore. I'll check in the back room."

"Will that take long?"

"Not if you help me," she teased.

"If I did that, we'd spend the rest of the day hunting."

"Then why don't you go on over to the Horny Toad and wet your whistle? I won't be too long, I don't think." She frowned, pushing the broom ahead of her as she vanished into the store.

Carson heard Ezra Cline growling like a hungry bobcat as she dragged him into the storeroom.

Knowing the search for the elusive thread would take a spell, Carson turned toward the town's only saloon.

At this time of day, it was as deserted as a ghost town. He poked his head in and looked around. The barkeep sat on a stool at the end of the bar, head on his crossed arms and snoring up a storm.

Carson wasn't particularly thirsty. Certainly not enough to risk waking the barkeep. The man had a temper. Disturbing his hibernation brought out the grizzly in him. Besides, two half-drunk customers ran bugs up the barkeep's arm, racing for some finish line under his collar. Whichever bug won would awake a sleeping behemoth.

That was more excitement than Carson wanted.

Carson backed out and looked around town. Over the past year, he'd been here on errands dozens of times. Sometimes he brought in bales of cotton to ship over to San Angelo when the mule skinners drove their wagons in. Other times, like today, he hauled supplies for the farm. Keeping two sections of farmland under cultivation took considerable effort—and not a little backbreaking work. At least he didn't have to do it alone. The Bellamy sons were good workers, but they were close to the age of wanting to spread their wings and fly away from home and hearth.

He could tell them about the world away from their farm. It might curl their hair. Or it might intrigue them so much they'd leave right away. With things the way they were in the Bellamy family, Frank wouldn't take kindly to anything that drove his two boys away.

Carson settled into a chair by the two swinging batwing doors and rocked back like the old men he'd seen on his way to the general store.

It felt wrong doing nothing. It made him anxious when he wasn't on his feet, doing and fetching and losing himself in work.

What it really meant was his guilt hadn't faded one whit over the past year, and he jumped at shadows. That made him wonder if it wasn't time to ride on. If he made an effort, he could reach Montana in a month or so. Or California. He'd never seen the Pacific Ocean, nor had anyone he'd ever ridden with. The descriptions in books he read made it sound odd and dangerously wonderful, especially for the men in ships crossing to China or curling around the Horn to reach far-off Boston.

As exciting as that sounded, he'd never want to go that far across endless stretches of water. He could barely swim, not that a sailor had much need for such skills. If a ship went down a hundred miles offshore, none of the crew could swim to safety on dry land unless they grew gills and tail fins.

"Stay astride a good horse with solid ground under my hooves," he said. Sailing off to the Orient was daring and worth reading about. He'd have to content himself with something less adventurous—and with the chance of walking to the next town if his horse pulled up lame.

"Carson! Clay Carson!"

At the sound of his name, he rocked forward and tensed. His hand pressed hard into his right hip. All he felt was the rough expanse of his jeans. His six-gun hung in its holster from a peg in the barn back at the farm. And his rifle was still in the buckboard.

"Didn't mean to startle you."

The smallish man ran up to him, waving a dingy white envelope.

"It's just that I was glad to see you, so I didn't have to ride all the way out to Frank's place to give you this."

He thrust out an acid-stained hand holding the envelope. Dark brown spots marred his fingers where sulfuric acid had eaten away the skin. When the man moved just right, so he turned upwind, the stench of lead and acid was enough to churn Carson's stomach.

Carson wondered how the telegrapher endured his life cooped up in the Texas and Pacific Telegraph office. Fumes rose from the lead-acid batteries and made anyone used to being outdoors choke and cough. Carson felt his nose stopping up and his eyes watering as he thought about the last time he'd gone to the office to send a telegraph for Mr. Bellamy.

"I just lost my balance in the chair," Carson lied. "You have a 'gram for Mr. Bellamy?"

The telegrapher's woolly-worm eyebrows wiggled about. He shook his head, checked the name on the envelope, and then thrust it out.

"No, sir, it's for you."

Carson froze. Nobody knew he was in Ferguson.

"You mean you want me to take it to Mr. Bellamy?"

"Nope, not a lick of it, Mr. Carson. This here's for you. It came over the wires in the middle of last night."

Carson stared at the man.

"I know what you're thinking. How's he record a 'gram that comes in at three in the morning? Well, sir, I work long hours and just happened to be behind the bug—that's what we professionals call that telegraph key—when the clacking started. Here." He stepped forward and shoved the envelope within inches of Carson's grasp, as if afraid he'd get his hand bit by a rabid dog.

Carson stared at the paper.

"You take care now, Mr. Carson, sir. And don't you go killing anybody." The telegrapher backed away, wiped his sweaty palms on his pants legs, and almost ran off.

Carson looked up and down Ferguson's main street. These days it was about the town's only street, unless alleys and rutted paths counted as streets. He saw nothing unusual.

Hands quaking, he tore open the envelope. A quick scan did nothing to stop the shakes. It was worse than he'd feared.

He understood why the telegrapher had hightailed it like he had the pox. The man had written every letter as it came from Hidetown, at the far northwest corner of the Panhandle. He had received a wire from the most infamous outlaw in Texas who wasn't John Wesley Hardin. Carson forced himself to read the telegram three times, to be sure it said what he feared:

COME PRONTO STOP
NEED TO DIG UP FORT WORTH LOOT BEFORE I DIE STOP
/S/ LEMUEL JONES